A ROYAL MISTAKE

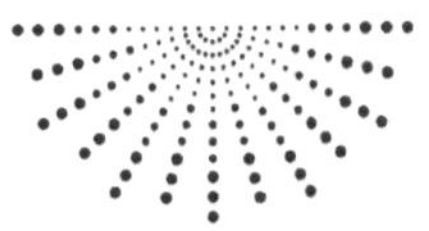

PIPER RAYNE

Cover Photo: Wander Aguiar Photography

Cover Design: By Hang Le

1st Line Editor: Joy Editing

2nd Line Editor: My Brother's Editor

Proofreader: Shawna Gavas, Behind The Writer

A Royal Mistake

He's not your average Joe from the corner bar.
He's the heir to the crown.

I should know, I've followed him for years.
Not in a stalkerish way. Magazines and online gossip blogs
are fair game when you're royalty.
But I do know every detail about him, down to the brand of
boxer briefs he wears.

All my *studying* of the man who plays a starring role in my
dreams pays off when I win a dinner with him. As if that
wasn't enough, he barters a deal with me that has him
moving into my spare guest room.

I forgot that fairy tales don't exist though because just as I'm
about to get everything I want, including the prince, I find
out there's someone in Prince Adrian Marx's life I don't
know—*his fiancée.*

A ROYAL MISTAKE

CHAPTER ONE

Sierra

You'd think the reason I'm sitting on a small charcoal sofa in this tiny room with no windows is because I have some fascination with fairy tales. But that theory would have been proven wrong the minute I came out of my mom's womb with fire-engine-red hair because hello, how many princesses with red hair had their own movie when I was growing up? Yep, one. And she's a mermaid. Mermaids are about as real as a red-haired princess would be. That and the actual natural blondes in this world.

Now that I'm older, my crazy red hair has toned down to a more auburn color, and I'm proud to be in the one-percent minority of red-haired people in the world. It makes me unique.

But as with most things, when people are different, there

are stereotypes. I can't deny that I can be fiery at times and my temper can get the best of me. But I'm not loose like the high school football team believed. I had four years of "does the carpet match the drapes" jokes to contend with while their gazes zeroed in between my thighs.

That experience, along with a lot of others, made me tough.

But before I head off on some tangent and raise my "I'm a carrot-top and proud" flag, let's get back to where I am and how I got here.

Win a date with Prince Adrian Marx

That was all I read on the charity website, and I knew I'd do whatever I had to in order to make it happen. Even pay the high entry fee to enter the contest.

Do I love the prince *because* he's a prince? Not exactly, though I've always been into keeping tabs on the monarchy. From the first magazine cover I saw him on, I was enthralled.

The guy is gorgeous. Which is why he's in so many magazines. And why every time he steps out of his sprawling mansion into his grand courtyard in Sandsal, photographers snap a picture. Needless to say, thanks to their hard work, I already know what the prince looks like under his clothes—except for whatever he's hiding in his boxer briefs.

Based on what I've seen on social media and in the press, he seems like he doesn't quite fit the mold as far as how one might think a member of the royal family would behave, which is what makes him so intriguing. I want to know more about him.

A short knock sounds on the same door I used to come into this room a half hour ago, then it opens. A tall man with a brown flat-top pokes his head in but doesn't release the knob. "The prince will be ready for you in five minutes. The cameras are setting up now. Have you already signed the release so we can get some pictures?"

I nod.

He nods, snorts, and shuts the door.

Nice guy. Not.

You'd think sparing a bottle of water wouldn't be a big deal for the royal family, but there's nothing in this room except me, a loveseat, a coffee table, some old magazines, and a potted plant that's seen better days. I'm in a fancy hotel in Manhattan, and though I'm not sure exactly what this room is for, I think maybe at one point it was an employee break room.

I stand from the couch, antsy now that the time to meet the prince is almost here. I'm rarely ever nervous—except for when I walk into my dad's house, and that's mostly because the silence inside makes me crazy with anxiety.

My phone dings in my purse, so I pull it out, happy for the distraction from my nerves.

Mick: *You're never going to believe this!*

Mick is my work BFF at the TV station, but he's always dramatic, so I don't get too excited over his text.

Me: *What's up?*
Mick: *I just overheard Georgia in Jack's office saying she's going to be retiring.*

Holy shit! For once in his life, Mick wasn't being overly dramatic.

Me: *No way!*
Mick: *This is your chance to move into the anchor position. You got this!*
Me: *Let's not get ahead of ourselves. I'm sure it won't just be me who wants that job.*

Mick: *Yeah but you'd be the best at it. Where you at, girl? Let's go celebrate.*

Guilt floods me. I didn't tell him I'd won a date with Prince Adrian. I will, but Mick's as into Adrian as I am, and all his questions and predictions of how the night would go would have made me more nervous than I already am. I'll tell him after it's all said and done.

Me: *Sorry, I'm just in the city visiting my dad. He needed me for something.*
Mick: *Yuck. Well I'd say have fun, but I know you won't.*
Me: *You can fill me in on the details on Monday.*
Mick: *You know it. I got your back.*
Me: *Thanks, Mick! Chat soon!*

The John Cena lookalike opens the door without a knock.

"Ever heard of knocking?" I snipe, pushing my phone into my purse.

He narrows his eyes as though we speak two different languages and he doesn't get my point. Technically his accent suggests that maybe English isn't his first language, but he doesn't stumble over his words. "The prince is ready."

My stomach knots and I grab my purse off the couch. "Do you have to call him the prince? Is that an official thing you have to do?"

He glances over his broad shoulder without amusement. Nor does he answer me.

Silent treatment. Cool. Mature. Not.

We walk out of the room and down the hallway of the boutique hotel, then up in a private elevator that requires a key and a password. JC, as I think of him since he reminds me of John Cena, looks over his shoulder while he punches in the code as if I'm trying to spy on him.

"You can relax. I'm not one of those crazy girls who stalk the prince."

He grunts.

If he saw the stack of magazines featuring the prince in the corner of my room, I'm not sure he'd believe me.

The elevator doors open, and I move to step out first, but his arm lands across my stomach like a steel rod and I rear back, almost falling to the floor of the elevator.

"Hold up." He looks to the right then to the left then back to the right.

He releases his mom-style seatbelt and I step out into a part of the hotel the average person can't get a room in. Elaborate doesn't describe it. There's nothing modern about this space—it's stately and worldly, very European. Intricately designed carpets lay below my feet while dark wood frames the doors and ceiling. Splotches of dark green paint can be seen behind the framed artwork that looks as if I stepped into a Catholic church.

We're halfway down the hall when JC says something, so I turn back, but he's talking into his jacket.

Security mic. Of course.

"The door is straight ahead. You may enter."

My final footsteps take me to a set of double wooden doors with luxury fixtures.

He's behind there.

Prince Adrian Marx.

JC clears his throat like I'm taking too long after I've waited for what feels like forever.

I glare back at him. "I'm just making sure I'm presentable."

Running my hands down my conservative dress, I wish I had worn what I really wanted to, something that made me more comfortable. That ship has sailed though, so my hand twists the doorknob and I open the door.

I hold the door open for JC, but he shakes his head and turns his back so he faces the hallway.

I step into what appears to be the foyer of the suite. Marble floors gleam, the beautiful gold-and-white stone feeling more modern than the path to get here.

"WHAT THE HELL? DON'T MOVE!"

I freeze where I am.

"Hi." A man in beige slacks, a button-up shirt, and a sweater vest comes rushing into the foyer and holds out his hand. "I'm Jean."

I shake his hand. He's quick to let mine go as though we're in the middle of a receiving line at a wedding and people are waiting behind me.

"Sorry, the prince is playing Xbox."

"Xbox?" I clarify.

Jean sighs with an expression to say he doesn't understand it either.

I'm not against grown men playing video games. Most of my guy friends do, but doesn't the prince have more important stuff to do? I mean, he's a prince.

"Afraid so." Jean signals for me to follow him. "Sir. Your date is here."

"Aw, buddy, I gotta go. Duty calls."

I hear a loud thud and assume it's the controller. Doesn't seem like he's doing much prep work for our date. A bit of my excitement over the evening dies.

Jean finally allows me to enter the room. This is it. The moment I first set my eyes on the prince. I'm fully ready and anticipate being mesmerized by his blue eyes... but all I see are sweatpants and a T-shirt with a stain streaked down the front.

"Sir, you said you were getting changed," Jean says, sounding embarrassed.

Instead, the prince wipes his cheese-covered hand down

his shirt and holds it between us. I stare at it. He quickly figures out that I'm not going to shake his hand. Rude or not, he laughs to himself and puts it in his pocket.

"Sorry, I was online with my brother. With the time difference, we rarely get to speak. Wanted to get in a game with him. Do you play?"

His accent throws me at first, although I knew he had one. People in Sandsal use a mix of different languages, but his accent comes off as more French than anything. It's not a thick accent, but it's there.

"Not really."

He nods then looks at Jean. "What's the plan?"

How much more unromantic can you get? After waiting forever for him to finish playing with his toy and his brother, he's now asking this Jean guy what's planned for our date. I inwardly roll my eyes.

"Dinner." Jean smiles at me. "On the terrace."

I glance around, looking for the photographer and his crew since JC warned me they'd be here.

"The prince has decided not to have pictures." Jean answers the question I never asked.

"Too nosy." Adrian picks up his drink and downs the rest of it. "I'll be right back." He saunters out of the room without any urgency in his step.

Jean shoots me his overly polite smile once more. "I'll check on the dinner."

"Excuse me," I say.

He turns around with a look of concern. Maybe he thinks I'm going to bail.

"Do you mind if I make a phone call while I wait?"

He releases a breath and his smile loses the tension it was laced with. "Oh, certainly." He gestures behind me. "You'll find some privacy on the south terrace."

I follow the direction of his hand and see a large formal

dining room I suspect Mr. Sloppy Prince won't be using unless he has a buffet for his gaming buddies. Once I'm through the double doors and on the terrace overlooking Central Park, I pull out my phone to call Blanca.

"Something's wrong if you have time to call me," she says. The easy lilt in her voice is ever-present. She's too nice for her own good.

"He's—"

"Hold on, putting you on speaker."

"Is he dreamy?" Rian asks.

My friends think my crush on the prince is humorous, but they were speechless when I said I'd scored a date with him.

"Definitely not."

"Uh oh, what's wrong?" Blanca asks.

I wish I had it in me to lie, but I'm so frustrated that I spent all day at a spa, had someone come in to do my makeup, and bought a new dress just for this douche to wipe his dirty hands down his shirt before trying to shake mine. "If I wasn't in the penthouse suite on a terrace overlooking Central Park and hadn't been patted down by a bodyguard who'd give Dwayne 'The Rock' Johnson a challenge, I'd think I've been duped."

"Why?" Bianca asks.

"He wasn't even ready when I got here. He was playing Xbox with his brother. And his shirt was dirty, and his hand was covered in fake cheese."

"Okay…" Blanca says.

"Nothing wrong with some Xbox," Dylan chimes in.

"I didn't know the guys are there." I'm sure they can all hear the annoyance in my tone.

"Yeah, sorry. Do you want me to take you off speaker?" Blanca asks.

I lean on the railing and stare into the darkness of Central

Park, thankful the prince wasn't polite enough to take my coat when he greeted me. "No. I'm just annoyed."

"Ditch the prince. We're about to play a game of Exploding Kittens," Rian says.

"While eating chocolate cake." Dylan's voice sounds muffled as if he has half the cake in his mouth already.

I think about my options. Heading home to Cliffton Heights means a night spent with Blanca and Ethan. That uncomfortable feeling settles in my gut. It's getting easier to be around them, and I couldn't be happier that my best friend has fallen in love. Okay, I could be happier if it weren't with my ex, but I'm not bitter about it either. It's just weird to be around them still. Hopefully that will change when Blanca moves in with Ethan tomorrow. She's only moving to an apartment at the end of the hall, but hey, a little distance will be a good thing for all of us, I suspect.

Yeah, forget about going back home. Whether this date is going to suck or not, at least it won't include watching Blanca and Ethan flirt with each other.

"Nah, I'm going to stay."

Just then, the door behind me creaks open and I glance over my shoulder. My phone almost slips out of my hand.

The man cleans up well.

His longer-than-average dark hair is slicked back, and his clean-shaven face makes it easy to see how beautiful this man really is.

"Sorry," he says with no edge of lying in his tone.

"I gotta go." I hang up on my friends, sliding my phone into my purse.

"Sierra, right?" He walks across the patio with his now clean hand held out for me.

"Are you a twin?" I ask, shaking his warm, strong, callus-free hand.

He chuckles and his gaze dips over my body, igniting a wave of heat straight between my thighs. "No."

Guess my first impression was wrong. The prince really is a heartthrob.

CHAPTER TWO

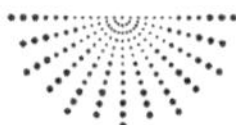

Adrian

surprise her by stepping out on the terrace. She's probably gushing to her friends about being in my penthouse.

She circles around at my entrance and stills, the phone dipping down her cheek until she tells the person on the other end that she has to go.

And there's the look. The one I was expecting.

I'm now clearly the version of Prince Adrian Marx she was looking for earlier. Was the cheese-covered hand down my shirt taking it a tad too far? Maybe. But I'm sure her expectations were sky-high before she walked in. Now let's see what she has to say when there are no cameras around to prove she sat down to dinner with royalty.

She steps toward me and I meet her in the middle of the terrace, holding out my hand for hers. Like the princess I'm sure she wants to be, she lays her hand in my palm. I raise it to my lips, kissing the top while bowing slightly. A giddy laugh falls from her lips.

"Pleased to make your acquaintance," I say.

"Yes. You as well."

She doesn't curtsey, but I've had other dates who have.

Standing straight, I offer her my arm. "Are you done with your phone call?"

Her arm easily slides through mine and I hold her hand with my free one, the way my mom taught me from the age of five. The same way my manners classes reinforced through young adolescence.

We walk off the terrace and through the expansive penthouse toward the terrace on the other side, where Jean has set up twinkle lights, candles, and soft music. But before I can open the patio doors, Jean clears his throat behind us.

"Please head out and make yourself comfortable. I'll only be a moment." I escort her out of the door and head back in, finding Jean with my cell phone in his hand. "What is it?"

"The queen would like a word."

"And who will woo my date?"

Jean looks around me. "I'll handle her. The queen is more important."

I take the phone from his hands and head into my bedroom so no one can overhear this conversation. Plus, I'm not a big fan of getting reamed out in front of other people.

"Mommy dearest," I say.

"Don't, Adrian. The cameras were sent for a reason. They're proof that you fulfilled the duty of the date. It's another spotlight moment for the charity."

"This whole thing is a waste of time. I should be with my friends in the Bahamas. Not here, having dinner with some wannabe princess."

"When will you ever grow up? There are expectations

that are going to press down on you soon. At some point, you need to step up and accept what you were born into."

"And what if I don't want what I was born into? Felicia is more than capable of handling responsibilities there."

My older sister kicks ass and should be the next in line to the throne, but because she wasn't born with a cock and balls between her legs, all she can hope for is to marry well and push out a few kids.

My mom blows out a breath, annoyed that we're having this conversation again. "You know the rules of succession. You are next in line to rule, so I suggest you get used to the idea. Nothing is going to change this."

I have no rebuttal that I haven't already tried.

"I think we've been more than accommodating in indulging your *finding yourself* phase. You run around the world like you own it, which means you enjoy the money with none of the responsibility that goes along with the title of prince."

She's right. My life is a permanent vacation. I only show up to functions when she twists my arm, or they freeze my bank account. And I have been known to whine about how I don't want to do anything that my role in our family dictates.

As usual, my mother doesn't allow me to get a word in edgewise. "Now, Jean is going to allow the photographer to come in. They're going to snap pictures of the two of you together, posed and candid shots. You will smile and behave like the prince I know you are. Is that clear, Adrian?"

She's using the stern voice she usually reserves for when I do really stupid shit, like the time I took the private plane to Australia to surf when my dad was due to travel the next morning to help a town that had been struck by a tsunami.

"Fine," I mutter.

There's a long pause. This is where her mom guilt soaks

in. The guilt that her dear children have to grow up with the whole world watching.

"I don't think we ask much of you," she says. "We allow you to travel and see the world. But we are your family, and you need to accept the fact there are responsibilities here at home." She waits for my response, but how many times can we go through this? "I know you're struggling with what's happening in a few months, but it will be fine. You'll adjust. She's a wonderful girl. Give me some credit." I can tell from her tone that she's smiling.

I know the woman I'm arranged to marry. At least I know *of* her. I've stalked her on Instagram just to see who I'll be spending the rest of my life with. The problem is, she doesn't seem to love to do anything fun—she visits museums and bookstores. There's not one picture of her wearing a bikini on the beach.

"Now, please just handle this tonight like you were told. It's one night and then your obligation is over."

"Is that him?" Felicia screams from somewhere behind my mother. "*Adrian!*" She must've torn the phone from my mom's hands. "What the hell? Why did you throw the cameras out?"

"They're intrusive and annoying. Plus, don't you think it'll be uncomfortable for her?"

"Listen—" Felicia lowers her voice. I'm assuming she's removed herself from our mother's presence. "I handpicked this woman. She works as a reporter for a small news channel. It's kind of weird that any woman knows so many facts about you, but whatever, I'm not judging what she's into. If you mess this up, she'll probably do a piece on our entire family. Do you think that's wise right now? With everything else going on?"

Her implication is clear, and I hate the reminder. Two weeks ago, Felicia found my father in a compromising situation with a woman who isn't our mother. He's living in another wing of the house now and the woman is threatening to leak the story. We're in deep distress, which was why I went through with this date—it got me out of Sandsal.

"This is your time to help this family."

I nod although I don't answer.

"Please, Adrian."

I sit on the bed and stare at the floor. "Fine. I'll allow them in. After this date, I'm coming home and I'm going to have a conversation with Dad."

"I thought you were going to the Bahamas. Last time you had a conversation with Dad regarding this, you broke his nose."

"Still bruised?"

She laughs. "Yeah."

"Okay, well, I better get to the date."

"Thanks," she says.

"Did you really handpick her? I thought this was supposed to be a random selection."

"I wasn't going to let you spend the night with one of those gushy girls who want you to ride in on a white horse. I'm a cool sister like that. She seems halfway normal, although I'm not sure why she thinks you're so fascinating."

"Because I'm a cool guy."

She laughs. "Keep telling yourself that."

"Talk to you later."

"Love you," she says.

"Love you." I hang up and head to the door.

Jean is waiting patiently outside.

"Go ahead and allow them up."

He smiles and nods, heading to the door to alert Declan of the change of plans.

I head to the terrace and step outside. Sierra is looking up at the night sky. She's gorgeous, and I wonder if that's why

Felicia picked her. My sister knows I love redheads. But I doubt Felicia would tempt me unless she's thinking this is my last chance to enjoy myself before my engagement. She's always been a helluva lot wiser than me.

"I'm sorry. That was my mother. A change of plans. The cameras will be arriving to take some pictures of us for the charity."

She nods. "Okay."

"They'll want posed as well as candid ones. It's annoying but good for the charity."

"Yeah, for sure."

She stares at the sky again, and I take her in. Her pale skin appears more golden in the light from the moon and the candles casting their glow on her. Why is she here on a date with me? Doesn't she know I'm not much without my title?

"What are we looking at?"

Here in the city, there aren't a lot of stars to be seen, and I hear the traffic noise of Manhattan below us. It's nothing like back home, but something about the noise of the city keeps me distracted.

"Nothing really. I was just thinking about how small I feel sometimes."

"Care to elaborate?"

She glances at me before shifting her gaze back to the dark sky above us. "The world is so big, but sometimes we get so caught up in our own little bubble, you know? I think of all the homeless people in the park right now, probably worried about the impending winter. How will they keep warm? Or the panhandlers who have a family to support. Or the orphaned children who have no idea if Santa's real and if they'll get a gift this Christmas."

I nod, not sure why we have to talk about such a deep subject. We barely know one another.

She swivels around and stares at me for an uncomfortable

moment. "It must feel good being able to help all those people. I mean, I get to go on a date with you, and in exchange, the food pantry gets all the sweepstakes money."

"I guess we're fortunate to be able to pimp ourselves out."

She tilts her head, trying to understand what I'm saying.

"I mean I should be happy that people want to pay to go on a date with me."

She nods, more appeased by that answer. "I have a feeling you're not a typical prince."

Give the girl a prize. "Does that intrigue you?"

A true smile creases her lips. "It does. I'd rather not have the fake prince, but actually get to know you as a person."

"Then you should know something about me." I glance at Jean at the door, waiting patiently with the cameramen behind him. "I hate getting my picture taken."

"Good thing I love it." Her hand slides into mine, and she leads us to the door. "I'll get you through this."

And she does exactly that. The photographer directs us, and we pose like two teenagers going to prom. Except I'm not some pimple-faced adolescent boy. My hand is firm on her hip, and I can't help but notice the way her body fits perfectly into mine. She encourages the photographer to continue out on the patio as we clink champagne flutes.

Once the photographer leaves and we're seated for dinner, I find that I'm actually looking forward to having dinner with her. As she's talking with Jean, I sneak a text to my sister.

Me: *Thanks Felicia. She's pretty great.*
Felicia: *I know. Enjoy your night.*

I flip my phone to silent and shove it into my pocket, fully intending on finding out exactly what makes Sierra tick.

CHAPTER THREE

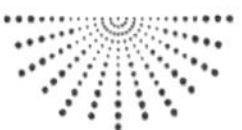

Sierra

Prince Adrian isn't the asshole I thought he was. In fact, he can be charming when he puts forth an effort.

"Tell me why on earth you wanted a date with me?" He pours more champagne into my glass. "Be truthful."

I feel my cheeks heat. Might as well tell the truth since I'll be walking out of here in a few hours, never to cross paths with him again. "Well, you're hot. And you look like you know how to enjoy life, from the articles I've read and your Instagram feed. As embarrassing as it sounds, I've always had a fascination with royal families. It all looks so perfect."

His face distorts and he straightens the napkin in his lap. "You do know that perception isn't necessarily reality, right?"

I laugh. Try growing up in my family. I was supposed to be the perfect military daughter. Even while mourning my mother's death, my father told me to hold my head up high, that I should be proud that my mom had died for her country. Ironic coming from him. No one ever knew how depressed he became. How many times I pretended he was working so I could eat at a friend's house, or the times I borrowed Blanca's clothes because my dad had to work so much he couldn't get to my laundry. The excuses for rides home from volleyball practice. And I think people felt they were doing good by helping me so much. They helped the poor girl who had lost her mother. It made people feel good about themselves.

"I do. So tell me some inside secrets." I lean forward.

Again his face distorts, and he adjusts the napkin in his lap, but he recovers quickly as though it never happened. "I'm allergic to peanuts."

"Oh, they published that last year when you had that reaction while at the movie premiere in London."

His eyebrows raise.

Maybe I should keep my mouth shut about how much I've read about him. "I only know that because I was dying to see that movie and it was research. Did I tell you I'm a reporter?"

He chuckles. Luckily, a server comes out with two silver dome-covered plates. Saved by dinner.

"Filet and chicken with shrimp," the server says with a flourish as if he's revealing the Hope Diamond.

The plate is filled with a small piece of filet with a béarnaise sauce, chicken with what appear to be piccata, and grilled shrimp that looks like it has a glaze on it. The server disappears and reappears again with several trays of side dishes.

"This is your potato. Mashed, baked, and scalloped." He disappears again and returns seconds later. "Vegetables. Green beans, asparagus, and glazed carrots."

Each side dish has its own tray. How much did they think two people could eat?

"Thank you." Prince Adrian bows his head.

"Please let us know if you're missing anything."

"Will do," Prince Adrian responds.

The server leaves as I stare at the array of dishes laid out in front of us. "This is a lot of food."

He lifts his glass. "Welcome to a royal's secret life. Where you don't have to make choices because you get one of everything."

I lift my glass. "A girl could get used to this."

He smiles and our glasses clink.

"So, since you clearly know everything about me, tell me about yourself." He uses his utensils perfectly—the fork hold, the cutting off one piece and eating it before cutting any more. He doesn't touch the potato plate, which I seem to gravitate toward.

"Not much. I grew up in Carroll Gardens, which is a borough of New York City. Went to college for journalism. Worked my way up to finally becoming a street reporter for a small channel in Cliffton Heights, which is about an hour-and-a-half train ride from here." I shrug and cut off a piece of chicken.

"You live alone?"

"I live with two… actually tomorrow, I'll only live with one girlfriend."

"Oh." He places his silverware down and wipes his mouth. "So you're a lesbian?"

I laugh. "No. I live with a girl who is a friend. Do you think a lesbian would want to win a date with you?"

He shrugs. "I have a charismatic personality. Am I not a good date?"

"Yeah, that cheesy handshake request almost made my knees weak."

His laugh is contagious. The way his face lights up... I'd love to see him in a casual environment. "Sorry about that. I tend to act like a toddler who isn't getting his way when it comes to things like this." He motions with his fork, which I'm guessing means the elaborate set up wasn't done by him.

Not that I thought it would be. Why would he plan a date for a stranger who won it through a contest?

"It's okay. You threw me and I almost left, but you're lucky I don't love being in my apartment lately."

His focus shifts from his steak to his chicken. It's intriguing that he starts and finishes one food item before moving on to the next. "Why is that?"

I shrug.

"Come on. It's just us and the night sky. I told you the royals' secret." I quirk my eyebrow and he chuckles, knowing that wasn't a secret. "Okay. Let's see... how about... my mom locked me in the car when I was two."

"Really? Aren't you guys with security all the time?"

He shakes his head. "A lot, but my mom said it was going to be just me and her that day. It's this thing she has where she takes one day every month and spends it with one of us. Either me, my sister Felicia, or my brother Rowan."

A pang of jealousy jolts me like the prongs from a Taser. Memories of visits to the zoo, park, and shopping with my mom flood my mind.

"You okay?" he asks, and I snap back to the present.

I smack on my fake smile. "Yeah. So what happened? Was it kept out of the press?"

He stares at his plate. "My dad came to our rescue without security. I have no idea how he did it, but my mom used to say he really was the prince she married because there he was on Felicia's white horse, Twinkle, with a coat hanger in hand. Unlocked the door and no one ever knew it happened. The press would've ridiculed her." His small smile says it's a fond memory. Like one of those stories the Biancos recite over and over every Christmas. But still, there's some kind of pain in his eyes.

"That's very heroic."

He sips his champagne. "See? There's a secret only the insiders of the Marx family know. So tell me now why you don't want to be at your apartment."

"Really?"

"Why don't you want to be at your apartment?"

I place my silverware down. I want to exchange my plate full of meat for the potato one. "My best friend recently started dating my ex."

He cringes as I assumed he would. That sentence gains the same reaction from most people. "That sucks."

I nod, picking my silverware back up. Screw it, I'm having mashed potatoes. I take the large spoon that's shoved in the middle of the mashed potatoes and heap some on my plate.

"You're still hung up on him?"

My head shoots up. "*No.*"

"Sorry. I assumed."

"Ethan and I were all wrong for each other. He's a bit of a control freak and so am I. We were like two rams headbutting one another with every decision that had to be made."

"And your friend. Do you not like her?"

"No, I like her."

"Then why can't you be around them if you don't have feelings for him and you like her?"

I allow myself a minute to think it through. "They're in that touchy stage. That one where they can't keep their hands off one another. They keep kissing and saying nice things to one another. It's only been months and they're already moving in together. Down the hall from me, no less."

He concentrates on me, not offering any advice, which I love. I hate when people try to fix my problems. Sometimes you just need someone to listen, that's all. Ethan's constant need to bandage up my problems always got us into fights, whether my problem had to do with him or not.

"You're just lonely then?"

My fork slips out of my grasp and hits the china plate before cascading to the ground. "No, I'm not lonely. I'm fine. I have a dream job, great friends. I might not be royalty or have a bank account with a lot of zeros, but I'm comfortable and happy."

"Okay." He raises his brows and looks back at his plate to concentrate on his meal.

"What?"

He glances up for a moment but moves back to perfectly cutting his chicken. "I said okay."

"No. You said *okay*." I mimic his tone. The one that suggests I'm full of shit. That I'm *not* happy. Who does he think he is? I could point out that he's not happy. There's a reason he tried to dress like a slob to put me off and then sent the cameras away. But I'll be polite.

"Yes, and I meant okay. If you think you're happy, then who am I to say different? We just met."

"Exactly."

The server comes out and hands me a fork, which reminds me there are eyes on us. Of course there are.

"Do you ever grow sick of living in a fishbowl?" I ask.

He looks at me and tilts his head. "What do you mean?"

"The fact someone is watching us right now. That they were able to see I dropped my fork and brought one to me without me having to ask. You want to question my happiness? Maybe you should examine your own."

There's that spiteful side of me roaring like a damn tiger again. Shit, I promised I'd keep her quiet tonight. Then again, I didn't think the prince would be pointing fingers at me.

"Truth?"

"Yeah."

"Of course I get sick of it. I hate it." He looks at the stars, and it's clear his mind is working.

I study him for a moment. I'm not sure I've ever seen a more beautiful man. He has a raw edge mixed with sophisticated elegance. His manners are polished and flawless, but there's a more rugged man clawing to get out. That's about all I've been able to decipher about him so far.

He turns to me. "Want to get out of here?"

My eyes widen. "What?" Our plates are still half full and I'm sure there's a great dessert coming.

He pushes away his plate, slides out his chair. "They've got their pictures. Come on."

"Where are we going?"

The most wicked smile crosses his face. My assumption is right. There's a wicked man who's dying to get out of the straitjacket of his royal blood. "Wherever we want."

"What if someone recognizes you?"

He takes my hand and warmth spreads up my arm. "What did that contest promise?"

"A date with Prince Adrian Marx," I say, still confused as to what's going on. Surely he already had plans with his buddies to go to some hot new club after we finish dinner.

He eyes the table covered with a bunch of dishes and glasses of champagne. "This isn't a date with Prince Adrian Marx. Would you like to really experience a date with him?"

Our eyes meet and a pull I didn't feel until now tugs at me. I'm usually the first person to try something out of my comfort zone, but for some reason, I don't think I'm prepared for whatever he has in mind. Still, a night out with a prince whose eyes are pleading with me to experience one night with him… I'd be crazy to say no.

I nod, and the smile that lights up his face makes my stomach flip-flop like there's a little gymnast in there.

"Let's go then."

"Where do you want to go?"

"That's the best part—I want to go wherever the night takes us. No plans."

He couldn't have said anything more perfect.

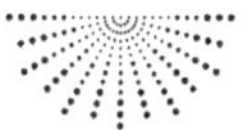

CHAPTER FOUR

Adrian

*D*eclan drives us through the busy streets of Manhattan while my mind is busy thinking of how we can ditch him. He's not going to let me pay him off this time. I'm sure my mom has him on strict orders after I left Sandsal after breaking my dad's nose.

"Club?" Sierra asks from next to me.

I shake my head. "How about Times Square?"

She hems and haws but finally nods. Finding her hand in the back of the black SUV, I squeeze it, hoping it will let her in on the fact that there's more to my plan.

"Hey, Dec, we're going to Times Square."

"Sir, I'm not sure that's a great idea."

"No one will recognize me."

Which is true. I might be a prince, but few people actually recognize me. Felicia is unfortunately right when she says that it's the younger girls who seem to spot me. The ones who follow me on social media because I'm a prince and do crazy things like climb a cliff just to jump into the ocean. They think I'm the crazy bad boy prince, but I do listen to my mother—sometimes.

"Do you have a hat back there?" Declan asks.

Sierra smiles and her perfume wafts around the small interior. I love that it's not overpowering.

"No," I say. "We'll be fine. We're just going to walk down and back."

Once we get closer, I figure I might as well try paying Declan off before I outright ditch him.

Leaning forward, I hand him a one hundred. "How about you drop us off up ahead and I'll call you when we're ready?"

He looks at me through the rearview mirror as if I've lost my mind. I stuff the hundred dollar bill back in my wallet. I lean back and squeeze Sierra's hand one more time in a warning. Although she has no idea what I'm doing, I hope she goes with what I'm about to do.

Sliding my hand up her neck, I tilt her head toward me and lean in so we're cheek to cheek. For all Declan knows, we could be kissing. It wouldn't be the first time I've put him in that position.

A soft purr murmurs out of her and my dick perks up. "We're going to have to make a run for it. As soon as he stops close enough, open your door. I'll meet you at your side to run into the crowd. Once we're gone, there's nothing he can do. He'll never find us."

I nuzzle her face a little more so Declan doesn't get suspicious, and when I draw back, the streetlight illuminates the inside of the vehicle through the sunroof. Her blush is perfect for Declan to think I just said something inappropriate.

A few minutes later, the bright lights of Times Square come into view. I squeeze her hand once when Declan gets stuck between a truck trying to back up and two taxis wedging him in on either side.

Sierra opens her door and Declan instantly puts the SUV in park. Then his gaze shoots to mine as I open my door. I feel bad for the panicked expression on his face as he watches me shut the door, but he can't get his door open because of the taxi pressed in close beside him. Sierra's thin enough to slip out, but Declan's too big.

He rolls down his window as I take Sierra's hand. "Sir!"

I wave to him and wink, which makes his face turn bright red. "Sorry. Don't wait up." Sierra laughs and I look at her. "Ready to experience a real date with me?"

"Completely."

I tug her toward Times Square, the millions of lights making it feel as if it's still daylight. We shuffle through the crowd of tourists and stop for a minute to watch a group of guys perform acrobatics. We pretend to be a normal couple on a date, her hand fitting perfectly in mine.

We end up watching a bunch of different acts working their asses off to make money from the tourists, but our Times Square experience is over too quickly. It was a great starting point to lose Declan, but for some reason, I want more alone time with Sierra.

"Tell me one thing you've always wanted to do in the city," I say as we weave away from the busyness of Times Square. The streetlights don't shine as brightly here, and it actually feels like we're in New York and not Las Vegas.

"I'm not really sure," she says, so we continue walking. We end up walking right into Rockefeller Center and she turns to me. "Ice skating?"

There's no tree up yet and it's early in the season, so the ice rink isn't nearly as jammed as it was the one year my mom brought us here. Of course, then they closed off the rink for our family.

"I feel I need to warn you that I'm pretty good on skates."

She smiles at me. "Is that so? Then I should warn you, I'm pretty good on skates too, and I'm not talking about man-made ice rinks my butler slaved over. I skated on ponds and basketball courts that just froze over."

She's adorable. How did I not notice this when she first walked into the room earlier?

"First of all, I live in the country, which means I too skated on ponds. And our butler answers the door and delivers drinks, thank you very much. It'd be the groundskeeper who's in charge of the outdoors."

She giggles, her body swaying into mine, and it feels natural for me to open my arms to her, welcoming her into my hold. Her deep-red hair tickles my nose and the scent of her shampoo has me wondering what running her hair through my fingers would feel like.

"Duly noted. I guess all we can do is get out there and see who's the better skater," she says.

We rent ice skates and sit down to change out of our shoes.

"I'd like to put a disclaimer out there," she says, tying up her laces. "I am in a dress."

I look over then down at myself. Yeah, this won't be easy. "No complaints if you want to do the Biellmann move." I wink.

"Biellmann move? Please tell me you weren't a figure skater at one point?"

"My sister. Felicia. All her life." I lean in. "Another secret, I love her, but she's not made for figure skating. The coaches are always barking orders. She wants to be the one barking orders."

"Your secret is safe with me." She stands, her feet wobbling before she gains stability. "I might want to put another disclaimer out there."

I stand, having the same issue at first, although I think my ankles just cracked too. "What's that?"

"It's been years since I've ice skated. Eighteen years to be exact."

I take her hand. "No worries, a prince always takes care of his lady first."

We reach the edge of the ice, and her hesitation is clear from Sierra's rigid stance. She doesn't even smile at what I said, so I step out first, holding out my hand for her to take.

"Ever have that hunch that you're about to end up in the hospital?"

"Where's the firecracker who was talking all that smack?" I joke, but she's pale and obviously unnerved about what was her idea in the first place. "It's like riding a bike."

My skates slide and I lose my balance for a second but luckily recover so I don't end up on my ass.

"Yeah? Tell me, do you know how to ride a bike?" she asks.

She eases her hand into mine and I skate backward, welcoming her onto the ice as I guide us to the side of the rink. "You assume I can't ride a bike?"

"I figured you always had someone drive you anywhere you wanted to go."

I shrug. I did. I can't lie about that. "My mom was pretty set on us having as normal of a childhood as we could. We learned to ride in our backyard."

"I've seen your backyard," she says.

I feel the line between my brows appear. "You have?"

"In pictures. I'm not sure I'd refer to it as a backyard."

"Sure, it is."

She raises her eyebrows. "It's bigger than all of Manhattan."

"Nooo." In truth, she may be right. And she's only been

able to see where the press snaps pictures they're authorized to.

"Let me ask you something? Are you modest, ignorant as to how you grew up, or just trying to lie to me?"

"Do you realize you've skated half the rink already?"

She looks behind her then meets my gaze. "Don't dodge the question."

I let go of one of her hands as she gets the rhythm of skating down. "Just like riding a bike. You're doing great. Even in that dress."

"I had to hike it up," she says.

"You think I didn't notice?" I grin at her.

A blush creeps into her cheeks and my dick takes notice. This woman, with her red hair and her blushes, is like a damn siren.

"You're still dodging the question," she says.

"I'm conversing."

"Answer the question."

A kid whizzes by her side and Sierra's arms flail, but she catches the side of the rink.

I stop right in front of her, ready to start over, but she shoos me away. "I can do this. Distract me by telling me the answer to my question." She smirks and one foot slides out while her other foot joins in. She's not smooth, but she's getting the job done.

I sigh, ready to bare the truth to who is essentially a stranger. "I know I'm privileged, and I abuse that privilege. Just my name alone gets me things. Things you can't even imagine. But lately I've wondered what it would be like to live a normal life."

She huffs. "Trust me, it's not what it's cracked up to be."

"Like right now. If anyone around here recognized me, they'd take pictures and wonder who you were. They'd do almost anything to find out. Misconstrue what's happening here and before dawn, your whole life story would be in the paper."

"Yes, but you get to vacation in exotic places. You have servants and bodyguards. Have you ever had to worry about parallel parking in the city? How far of a walk you'd have in four-inch heels after you got off the subway? How you'd make ends meet?"

"You speak from experience?"

She stares at me with a blank expression. "Yeah. I do."

"I guess there's the good and the bad, but lately all I've seen is the bad." I shrug.

"Ever wonder what it would be like to run away? Start fresh? Just hop on a bus to the first city it took you to, find a job, and start a brand new life?"

I observe her while she continues to concentrate on getting her footing correct. Truth is, she's doing awesome, but her last statement concerns me. Is her life so bad that she wants to run away? Then again, my life isn't *bad* per se, and I've had thoughts of disappearing too.

"A bus? And give up my private plane?"

She shakes her head at me. I'm glad she gets my humor because that moment was way too serious for me.

"So just me, huh?" The corners of her pink lips turn down.

I could be a douche and lie so that tomorrow she won't report that during her dream date with Prince Adrian, he admitted to being done with his royal obligations, but something tells me that what Sierra and I are doing tonight isn't her interviewing me to give the scoop to anyone.

"No. I've had those feelings ever since I was ten and realized the cameras weren't all that cool and the photographers behind them were assholes only out for themselves."

A look of remorse mixed with pity mars her beautiful features. "I'm sorry."

I hate that look, so I recover quickly. "Don't be. I'm a prince, remember?" I wink to show her everything is cool in my book.

Then a group of kids pass by and one of them smacks her ass, turning around and laughing after he passes. I'd go after the little jerk and ream him out but Sierra stumbles and grabs my jacket for support, which makes me lose my footing and all I can do is try to cushion her fall. I allow myself to go down first, my arm swinging around her waist so she falls on top of me.

Her head falls into my chest and she peeks up, her hair in her eyes. I brush it out of the way, and for a moment, our eyes meet, and it feels as if we're going to kiss. She laughs, her chest vibrating along my stomach.

"What's so funny?"

"Did you plan this? Saving me from falling down on the ice? What a princely thing to do. Are the cameras somewhere nearby?" She searches the area as she crawls to her feet, but she'll find nothing.

"Just like a fairy tale," I say.

She shakes her head as we skate off the ice. "There's no such thing as fairy tales."

I couldn't agree more.

Sierra

We return our skates and end up grabbing a taxi to drive us to the Brooklyn Bridge.

"You're different than I thought you'd be," I say after he pays the taxi and we head toward the pedestrian walkway.

He smirks, turning in my direction for a second. "How so?"

"More down to earth maybe?"

He nods as though he gets that a lot. "Did you expect me to be in my royal attire and force you to bow?"

"No, but for some reason I expected you to be crazy wild."

"How so?"

"I didn't think a night in New York with you would constitute you wanting to walk the Brooklyn Bridge and ice skate at Rockefeller. Especially after ditching your security."

His phone had buzzed a few times right after we left the

vehicle, but I think he must've silenced his phone because it's been quiet since.

"For me, the fact that I don't have to take pictures, and no one really knows who I am feels freeing. When you show up with a guy who looks like he's a professional wrestler and an assistant, people know you're *someone*, even if they don't know exactly who, which means they linger until they figure it out. You have no idea how many times I've taken a picture with someone only to be asked who I was after."

"Oh, your ego must've been crushed." I knock my shoulder with his and he captures my hand in the exchange.

"I've just always been different than my family."

My attempt at bringing humor fails, and we stroll hand in hand down the crowded walkway, the view of Brooklyn ahead of us and Manhattan behind. His admission only reminds me of how different I am from my family.

"Why?" I ask, curious to hear more.

"The cameras make me uncomfortable."

"You've never grown used to them?"

We stop halfway across the bridge and lean on the railing. He takes out his phone and snaps a picture of the Manhattan skyline. "I've learned to tolerate them. Haven't you noticed that most pictures of me are usually ones I had no idea were being taken?"

I recall the pictures I've seen of him online and he's right —him jumping off a cliff, him on his four-wheeler back home, him entering or leaving a nightclub in Europe. The only pictures I've seen of him where he's posed are the ones with his entire family or when someone he meets must request it.

"So living in the microscope isn't all it's cracked up to be? You'd give it all up to live a normal life where you have to make your own meals, do your own laundry, and work for every penny?"

He laughs. "Don't put words in my mouth."

I join in on his laughter. "Yeah, I imagine it'd be hard to walk away from all that, no matter how much you don't like the cameras."

"It's more my family. I can't leave them, especially right now." An awkward silence descends between us until he clears his throat. "Let's talk about you. I can't give away too many royal secrets to you."

Panic squeezes my heart. Is he expecting me to talk about my family? That's usually a no-fly zone for me. "There's not much to tell."

He positions me in front of the Brooklyn side and snaps a picture. I attempt to smile casually since this will be the only night I'll spend with him and this photo will probably be deleted in a month. Then again, maybe he'll keep it as a memory of a night shared with a stranger, exploring the city. A girl can dream.

We walk again, continuing on toward the Brooklyn side of the bridge.

"What about your childhood? Siblings? Parents?" he asks.

Of course we're going to start there. "No siblings."

"That's it?" he asks.

I normally spurt out the news about my mom having died in the Iraq War just to get the pitying looks over with, but I won't see Adrian after tonight, so I decide he doesn't need to know that sometimes I chew the same cinnamon gum my mom always had in her purse to remind me of her. Or that I buy the perfume she wore so that the memories I still have of her won't fade. Her voice quiets a bit in my memory with each passing year.

Tonight isn't the night to tell him my sad story.

"That's it," I say and shrug. Nothing to see here.

"What's it like growing up normal?"

I sputter out a laugh. "You mean not being followed around and having a list of royal duties?"

"Yes, I guess."

"I don't think it's as liberating as you think it is."

"Certainly more liberating than ruling an entire country." We reach Brooklyn and he flags down a taxi. "Where to now?"

I slide onto the bench seat and he follows, his large body occupying the majority of the space. His long legs are spread wide, his knee dangerously close to mine.

"Wherever you want," I say.

He smirks and shakes his head. "It's your choice. The bridge was mine."

"Bar?"

"Done." He leans forward to talk to the taxi driver. "Best bar around here."

The taxi driver glances to me in the rearview mirror like "that's not my job." But he pulls away from the curb.

"Aren't you worried?" I whisper after the driver puts his earbuds in.

"Worried about what? Oh, taking over." He shrugs. "I was brought up knowing it would be my role."

He's so forthcoming with me and here I am lying by omission, like I came from some great family. But this is only one night and it's not like he has the ability to hide anything. His entire life is documented somewhere.

"I meant being"—I glance at the driver, who's now having a conversation of his own with someone on the phone —"recognized."

"I've gone this entire night without it happening. I think the majority of the time, if anyone does think it's me, they talk themselves out of it. Because in their minds, a prince would come with an entourage and never be in their corner bar."

That makes sense.

The taxi pulls up to the curb in front of a neighborhood bar that looks like it will be filled with regulars, not outsiders. But it's probably better this way. His chances of being recognized here are less than at a club. I'm not the only girl in her twenties who follows the prince on Instagram.

I pull out some money, but Adrian shoos my hand away, pulling out his money clip and paying the driver. He wastes no time before taking my hand and opening the door to the bar, where "Pour Some Sugar on Me" by Def Leppard blares. I raise my eyebrows at Adrian, and he chuckles, pressing his hand on my back for me to continue.

We find a dark booth in the corner by a long shuffleboard, and an older woman comes over.

Pulling the pen from behind her ear and sliding on the eyeglasses that are hooked on by a chain around her neck, she prepares to take our order. "What would you like?"

I look over the menu in the middle of the table. "Martini with a lemon twist?"

She stares at me but writes it down and looks at Adrian. His good looks don't faze her in the least. "And you?"

Adrian's expression suggests he already likes her. I'm not sure what he likes. Her rudeness? "I'll have a Rusty Nail. But can we start with two shots?"

Her pen stays poised over the paper, waiting for him to give her specifics.

"Woman's choice," he says.

Both sets of eyes land on me.

"You want me to choose?" I ask.

"Yes."

"Okay…" I think for a moment because what would a prince like as a shot? Surely he doesn't want a girly one, plus I doubt this place would even have the ingredients for something like that. "Crouching Tiger?"

Adrian smiles and looks at our waitress—who never gave us her name, nor does she wear a name tag. She scribbles it down and walks away without a word, her glasses falling back down to her chest as she slides her pen behind her ear again.

"What's a Rusty Nail?" I ask.

"Scotch whiskey and orange peel. What am I in for with the Crouching Tiger?"

"It's a type of tequila shot."

He nods. "One where I get to lick salt off you?"

My body heats as I imagine his mouth on the most sensitive part of my body. Well, not the most sensitive, but the part he could lick in public anyway. "Sorry, it's a straight shot."

"And I thought we were getting somewhere here." He winks and my stomach somersaults.

Of course I'd imagined our date turning into a one-night stand, but could it actually be possible?

"And where are you hoping for it to go?" I raise my eyebrows.

He laughs, sliding out of the booth. "Shuffleboard?"

"Sure." I let him dodge the question because I'm not sure I want an answer right now. "I will warn you, I've never played this before."

He pulls the small disks from the side and puts them on the hardwood surface. "No talking shit like you did with ice skating? Admitting defeat before we even start? We've only known each other a short time, but I find it surprising."

I mock offense while sliding one of the discs back and forth. "Should I be insulted?"

He comes over and his hand covers mine. "Not at all. You just seem like a woman who doesn't take defeat easily. Someone who constantly strives for perfection and never admits when she's unsure."

His hand is soft under mine, but it's still large enough to remind me that he's a man. "You might be a little right."

"Don't change who you are on account of me. I'm a nobody."

"You're the Prince of Sandsal."

Then he removes his hand from mine and circles behind me, his lips right at my ear. "Not tonight. Tonight I'm your date, Adrian Marx. That's it."

His voice is low and sultry, and I clench my thighs before I can allow myself to swivel around and use my lips to shut him up.

His hand covers mine again and we're moving the disc thing back and forth. "This is a weight."

I nod, unable to find my voice.

"It's all about the pressure and force you use to release it. The goal is to get it to the last section without falling off. Bonus if you knock out an opponent's disc." He initiates the release, and I miss his touch as soon as the disc travels down the tabletop, stopping right before the edge.

I narrow my eyes at him. "Not even going to try to hustle me, huh?"

He chuckles and steps away from me, picking up the two shots that the waitress must've dropped off as I was lost in Adrian. Handing one over, he holds his up high. "To whatever tonight brings."

I clink his glass and we down the shots.

He flags down the waitress. "Two Big Bamboos."

She nods and heads to the bar.

"Are you on a mission to get drunk?" I ask.

"Nah, but I think we both need some nerves to disappear."

I try to decipher what he's talking about and why he would have any nerves. The man has a way of always appearing in charge and in control of himself.

"Ready?"

I nod, sipping my martini and stepping up to the board.

"Ladies first." He does the whole arm out and bow like you'd expect a prince to do.

"Man, you've perfected that move." I stand in front of the board.

"I watch a lot of Disney movies."

I try to keep the alcohol in my mouth, but it sputters out, dripping to the floor, when I laugh. "I knew you'd be fun to party with."

I grab a napkin and bend down to wipe up my mess. He crouches in front of me and our eyes meet.

Something's there.

It feels like a promise that says we're about to start the really fun part of our date.

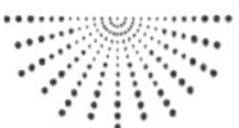

CHAPTER SIX

Sierra

My assumption is that Adrian's been playing shuffleboard since birth because he's beaten me five games out of five. Plus, I think he could outdrink anyone—including Chugger, the guy who was rumored to drink a pony keg on his own one night in college. Whereas my lips already feel tingly and my hands keep venturing over and touching any part of Adrian that's acceptable. He's not complaining though.

I slide my last disc and it tips off the table halfway down. "I'm out." Picking up my glass, I slide back into the circular booth. The next round of shots that Adrian ordered is waiting for us. "I might have to pass on this one."

"I never figured you for a lightweight." He slides in after me, another Rusty Nail in his hand.

"Unless you'd like me to ruin your outfit with vomit, I suggest we cool it for a little while." I flag down our waitress, who has smiled at us twice now. I think she likes Adrian's accent. "Water please."

She nods, picking up the empty glasses off the table.

Watching her so I can effectively ignore the feeling of Adrian's eyes on me, I spot a table full of girls. One of them is staring at her phone and then at Adrian.

"Uh oh," I say.

Adrian leans back, his drink in his hand. "I'm not going to lie, Sierra, I'd like you to spend the night with me at my hotel."

My head twists in his direction. His face shows no sign of joking.

"Um." Who just asks like that? Who does that?

A prince does that. A guy who's never told no. A guy who's probably slept with any woman he's ever wanted. And I'm sure there were a lot.

"You're not shy."

"There's no point in pretending I don't want you. Will you spend the night with me?"

I shake my head to clear it, thankful when the waitress slides the glass of water my way. My lips attach to the straw and I suck until the glass is half empty. He's still staring at me when I glance over.

He's wearing a cocky smirk mixed with a Cheshire Cat grin because he knows I want him. "I'll serve you breakfast in the morning, but then it's back to reality for both of us."

I nod, still taken aback. I'm not sure I remember having a conversation before a one-night stand. This is a first for me, but he's Prince Adrian Marx. The man I've been following for almost a year. A man I've masturbated to more times than any other man. Oh, how I want to know if my imagination is right.

"Excuse me?"

Our heads turn to find the girl I saw with the phone standing at the edge of our table.

The elation in my stomach sinks because she has her phone out.

Adrian's smile fades for a moment.

She looks over her shoulder at her group of friends, who are staring. "Are you Prince Adrian?"

He bites his lip for a moment. "I am."

Her entire face lights up like I imagine mine would have if I had accidentally run into him. She practically jumps up and down. Adrian looks at me from the corner of his eye but keeps his focus on her.

She waves her friends over and they all hurry off their stools, each one armed with a phone.

"Can we have a picture?"

Adrian slides out of the booth. "Sure."

"Oh no, we'll come in your way." The group slides in on his side. "Would you take the picture?" The girl who can't keep her eyes off Adrian hands me her phone.

"Please." Another girl hands me hers.

A not-so-nice reply sits at the tip of my tongue, but I can't destroy Adrian's reputation. Instead, I press my lips together, grab the phones, and slide out of the booth.

I stand on the edge as they snuggle in as close to him as they can get. Two of them are cheek to cheek. God knows where his hands are. As I snap the pictures, I realize that I'm right about why he's so bold to ask me to go home with him. He's never been told no. Not that I want to be the woman who holds the pin to pop that bubble for him, but someone should. One day. Just maybe not tonight.

After I'm done, the girls don't get up. They don't leave. They ask him a million questions about why he's there, what he's drinking, what his favorite thing to eat is, how his sister and brother are.

Lastly, the bold girl who had the guts to walk over here looks at me still standing at the edge of the booth. "Is she your girlfriend?"

Adrian's humored eyes meet mine and I can see that his mind is working overtime on how to answer that question. He's been so unpredictable tonight, I have no idea what will come out of his mouth. Will he tell them the truth—that I won a date? Or tell them that I'm his girl for tonight but slip this other girl his number for tomorrow?

Never did I imagine he'd answer, "Yes. This is Sierra."

All the overabundance of excitement at the table fades. The girls look at me and their eyes roam up and down, their smiles transforming into scowls. The "she's not all that" expression is apparent on their faces.

Damn, I'm getting an idea why Adrian's life might not be all it seems.

"If you'll excuse us, we were having a night together," Adrian says.

The girls all profess their apologies, but the first girl doesn't slide out like her friends. She pulls out a black Sharpie from her back pocket and unbuttons her shirt until the swell of her breasts shows.

"Can I have your autograph?" she asks.

Did I just transport to the backstage of some rock concert? Surely Adrian isn't at a caliber that makes women strip down. Next thing is she'll be leaving her underwear for him.

The ease with which Adrian takes the marker, tears off the cap with his teeth, and puts the tip to skin says it's not his first time. He's skilled at being the hot prince with the cap secured between his teeth as though he's teasing them to imagine what he'd be like in bed. Does he get some kind of kick out of this, pulling at a young girl's heartstrings with a dream that will never come into existence?

"Thanks." She gets out and huffs.

I sit back down in the booth.

"Sorry about that," he says.

"I feel bad for your future girlfriends." I laugh, looking at the girl's retreating form. But when all I hear from him is silence, I turn my head to find him facing straight, his penetrating gaze on me.

"They'll probably be used to it."

"Oh yeah, you probably can only date women of a certain lineage, right? Like princesses and stuff."

"No one tells me who to date." His face is completely void of any emotion and I wish I could ask him what he's really thinking about.

"Well, do yourself a favor and make sure she's very confident." I pick up my water and sip the rest until it's only ice.

"Want another?" he asks.

"Nah."

He downs his Rusty Nail and slides to the edge of his seat. "You're pretty self-confident. And you've yet to answer my request." His hand lands on my knee, sliding just under the fabric of my dress, his fingers running along my inner thigh.

I suck in a breath.

The door of the bar opens, and my eyes shift because I'm not sure how to answer his question. No doubt I want to sleep with him, but how will I feel in the morning? Because he isn't some random guy from the club who's been dancing with me all night. I'll have to see mention of him on social media for the rest of my life. If the sex is good, which I'm sure it will be, am I doomed to relive our night together over and over again in my head?

The big body in the doorway steals my attention and my mouth drops when I spot who it is.

"John Cena is here," I say.

Adrian's eyes scrunch up and a smile tips his lips. "Me and

John Cena at a corner bar in Brooklyn on the same night? What are the—" He abruptly stops when he follows my gaze to find his bodyguard scanning the room.

Adrian grabs my arm and slides us to the far end of the booth where we might be able to hide. He leaves a few hundred on the table, taking my hand and peeking over the edge of the booth. My heart races even though I have nothing to lose. He's the runaway. I'm a grown adult.

JC heads to the table with the girls, which makes how he found us click together. They posted pictures, probably tagging themselves at the bar.

Adrian uses the opportunity to escape the booth and lead us to the back hallway.

"We have to sneak out the back door," he tells me right before his back straightens and his shoulders rise. Like a transformer, the casual guy I was doing shots with and leaned lazily against in the booth vanishes and is replaced with a strong and confident prince.

He walks us right through the swinging doors of the small kitchen, sliding money to the dishwasher, and out the back door. Once we're in the fresh air, a sprinkle of rain lands on my face.

I stop walking, staring at the dark sky.

Adrian tugs on my hand. "Come on."

We jog up the stairs, down the small space between the brick wall and building, and step around empty kegs and garbage. When we reach the street, Adrian looks back and forth while the rain comes down harder.

"Why not just let John Cena take us back to the hotel?" I ask.

He stares at me for a moment. If only I could read what's transpiring behind those gorgeous blue eyes. "I'm enjoying this too much."

I smile because a small part of me is too.

We walk, and when car headlights light up behind us, Adrian turns down another street, but the car follows slowly.

"Fuck."

We both run like teenagers from the cops even though we've done nothing wrong, but it's exhilarating, and I can't stop laughing as he pulls me down different streets and over the fences of people's backyards.

Finally, an alcove of a building offers us a hiding place. Adrian practically tosses me in and covers my hysterical laughter with his hand over my mouth. John Cena drives by slowly, the car behind him honking until he speeds up.

"Hotel?" Adrian whispers.

For a moment, all those fears I had in the bar disappear because his strong body is pressed to mine. The skin of his palm is over my lips. Our soaked bodies and drenched clothes somehow make this more romantic than it should feel.

I answer, going with my instincts. "Yes."

I laugh again when he peers left and right as if we're criminals hiding from the law. He's a prince for heaven's sake. We walk to the corner, cross the street, and right into a hotel lobby as if he knew it was there the whole time.

I look down at our drenched clothes, droplets of water falling from the hem of his suit jacket and my dress.

"A room with a king bed please," he asks the woman working the front desk.

She nods, typing on her computer. "Perfect, and how will you be paying, sir?"

Adrian grabs a few more hundreds—which are now soaked—from his money clip. "Might have to let those dry a little."

I pull out my wallet and slide a credit card over to her, but Adrian holds his hand over mine. The woman looks at both of us. The more of a scene we make, the better the chance

Adrian might trigger a memory, so he hands me back my credit card, putting down another hundred for the security deposit.

We head over to the elevators and wait for it to arrive. Once inside, Adrian presses the button for the fifth floor, and it rises. I exhale a breath when the doors slide open, but it only lasts a minute until I step out into the hall and Adrian grabs my wrist, circles me back around to him, and smashes his lips to mine.

It's clear then that this was the right decision because I'd be stupid not to have the prince for a night. A saying I've heard my entire life rings in my head when his tongue slides against mine.

It's better to have loved and lost than never to have loved at all.

This time, it's just better to have had the prince than not at all.

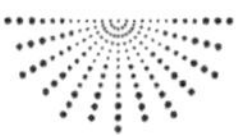

Sierra

ow. Adrian can kiss.

I shouldn't be surprised.

He's a prince. Of course he can kiss until I feel like my legs might give out.

As his lips slow and his hand entwines with mine, he guides me down the hall. "Let's get out of these wet clothes."

I find myself at a loss for words, a rare event. Usually I'm balls to the wall. I'll act how I want to act and if you don't like it, I don't give a shit, but as the light on the door lock turns from red to green, my stomach clenches and my throat squeezes.

We step into a typical hotel room. At least typical to me.

"Is this slumming it for you?" I say, shutting the blinds that reveal a view of a Brooklyn apartment complex.

"No."

I turn around to find his suit jacket already off and him

halfway through the buttons of his shirt. Someone's as eager as I am, I guess.

"Come on, you've really spent the night in a room like this before?" I slip off my heels and place my purse on the built-in desk.

"Can we forget who I am right now?"

His voice is low and sincere and respectful. He's probably practiced his entire life how to avoid losing his temper for no reason. Unlike me, who can lash out without notice.

"You want me to forget you're Prince Adrian Marx of Sandsal?"

He finishes unbuttoning his shirt, splaying it open and peeling the wet fabric off his skin. My gaze fixes to his taut stomach with a few small ripples. His bicep muscles aren't overly developed like his bodyguard's, but present and noticeable. It's obvious he takes care of his body.

"Yes, because tonight with you, I've never felt like less of a prince and I love it." He steps up to me. I hold my breath when his finger holds steady on the zipper at the back of my dress. "May I?"

I nod, my eyes locked with his.

"Stay in the bubble with me?" he whispers.

The sound of the zipper through the room is louder than a blaring television.

"Right now, I'm a guy who spent an evening with a gorgeous woman and wants to spend the rest of the night showing her how much tonight meant to me."

"You sure have your lines down."

He slides my dress off my shoulder. His hand warms my cool skin as the other side glides off my shoulder and the wet fabric falls to my feet. His breath hiccups and his gaze strays down my body, taking in my black bra and panties. A matching set I picked out just in case, back when my bravado was high, secure in the fact that I could handle what I assumed would be a cocky prince. He's so different than I ever thought he would be.

"I only speak the truth," he says and steps closer.

My nipples tighten and poke through my sheer bra when his chest meets mine. Warmth radiates off him while I'm still chilled from the rain.

Reaching around my body, he unlatches the clasp of my bra and he mimics the same movement he did with my dress, sliding my straps down my arms until it joins my dress on the floor. He takes me in for a second, sucking in a breath with wide eyes before he pulls back my wet red hair so it lays across my back. Then he tips my chin up with his forefinger and descends on my mouth, capturing my lips in a kiss that promises a night of cherished caresses and exploration.

I melt into him. It's impossible not to as our tongues and chests meet with the sound of rain hitting the window.

Ending the kiss too soon, his lips scatter across my chin to my earlobe. "Let's get you warm."

His hand tucks inside mine and he leads me toward the bathroom, never letting go of my hand as he turns on the shower and I watch steam filling the small space. He positions me by the sink, his hands sliding my panties down my legs and placing them on the counter. I swallow back my anticipation, watching him unbuckle his belt, unbutton and unzip his slacks, and finally push them down his legs. But there aren't a pair of black boxer briefs under his pants as I'd assumed. Instead they're black but with a genie pot with writing on the legs that says, "Keep rubbing. You might just get your wish."

A laugh bubbles out of me, which ruins our moment.

He glances down and laughs himself. "Hey, these are my favorite ones."

I step closer, my hand landing on the large bulge pressing against the fabric and rub down the hardness of his length.

"Make a wish, Sierra," he says.

I slip my hand past the waistband and close my fist around him. He inhales deeply, the smile falling off his face for a moment.

"I think it's already coming true," I whisper.

I have no idea if it's the fact that his cock is in my hand or if it's my words, but his hand snakes around my neck and he smashes his lips to mine in an unrelenting kiss that says something very different than the kiss earlier. This one promises me a night of screaming and orgasms.

"Let me help you there." His hands leave my body to take off his boxers, which he kicks out of the way, not treating them as preciously as he did my panties.

Opening the shower curtain, I step into the hot water. It removes the chill from my skin right away. Adrian joins me and positions the nozzle perfectly so that the water isn't spraying in our faces. He picks up the tiny bottle of shampoo and cups his hand while squeezing out a small bit. I laugh and he looks at me, a bit dumbfounded.

"I'll need practically the whole bottle."

He evaluates my long hair and nods, squeezing the bottle until it indents. I steal it, putting some shampoo in my hands and running them through his hair. For a moment, all I think about is how he probably uses more expensive hair products than me, but he asked that I don't treat him like a prince, so I keep my mouth shut.

His fingers run along my scalp as he rubs in the shampoo, massaging it into a lather. "Man, you do have a lot of hair."

To make it easier, I turn around and he steps closer until his body is pressed to mine, his dick pressed to the small of my back.

"It's beautiful. Your hair. I love the color."

"I'm surprised you didn't say anything about the rug matching the drapes."

It's not uncommon. Almost every man I've slept with said something the first time they saw me naked. Not sure what the fascination is. You don't see brunettes getting the same jokes about their bush.

"I'm more of a breast man." His sudsy hands slide out of my hair and up under my arms, molding to my breasts, his thumbs running over my nipples.

Leaning in closer, he takes the bar of soap, having to peel back the paper and toss it out of the shower. He runs the soap over my body as his lips press kisses to my ear, sighing every so often. The man drowns me in a wanton feeling.

"Let's rinse. I'm growing impatient, and I don't want the constrictions of a small hotel shower."

When I swivel back around, the cascade of water rinses the shampoo from my hair, and he helps with his hands.

We change places, and I take the opportunity to hand him the conditioner. "Next step."

He shakes his head. "Girls."

But he puts it in my hair, working it through the strands like a professional. The man's hair screams hair masks and moisturizer, so I know he's probably had this done to himself a bunch of times.

I sink to my knees with the bar of soap, running it along his muscled legs and up his torso, my tongue darting out and teasing his dick. His hands fall to my wet hair and he cups my face as I look up at him with the tip of his dick right at my lips.

"May I?" I ask.

"Always." A smirk appears until I take him into my mouth fully. "Shit."

Placing my hand at the base of his dick, I lick and suck him until his hands reach under my arms and he urges me up.

"You all warm now? Time to get out."

He changes positions with me and helps me rinse the conditioner while I laugh at his sudden urgency. I'd love to know how many blowjobs he's gotten from other women. Actually, I'm not sure I do want to know.

"I'm warm," I say.

He opens the shower and I step out on the small rug. He follows suit, leaving the water running.

"Water conservation?" I say.

"The steam will keep you warm until you're dried off."

I smile at his thoughtfulness as he wraps a towel around my body and works it over my skin, soaking up any droplet of water he finds. After he's dry too, he turns off the water, takes the towel from my hand, and picks me up so I'm straddling him, carrying me into the bedroom.

He stops briefly by his pants and pulls condoms from one pocket.

"There's some in my purse too."

His eyes find mine and I get rewarded with a kiss. "Good thing you're prepared." Laying me across the bed, he spreads my legs. His knuckles run up the length of my inner thigh, teasing me. "I love your skin."

"I love your touch." I quiver when his knuckles graze between my legs.

"I can't wait to find out every spot that drives you wild." His finger runs down the length of my center and back up.

My hips buck off the mattress, wanting him to press into me. But he only continues teasing me, the same finger running along my stomach, then up and around a nipple, until he slides it into my mouth. I swirl my tongue around his fingertip, so he's reminded of exactly what I'll be doing to his dick again later on. He watches with lust-filled eyes that only make me wetter.

Adrian brings the foil packet to his lips and tears it open, retrieving the condom and dropping the packet carelessly.

He slides the condom down his length and props one knee on the bed, followed by the other one. Bending, he casts kisses along my hot, waiting flesh.

When he captures my mouth, his tongue dives in and he eases himself into my center, my legs falling aside to make room for his hips. From there, our hands grip, our bodies clench, and every thrust feels more sensitive and more earth-shattering than the one before, increasing the tension in my body.

His lips leave mine but only to move along my jaw as his hands grab mine, raising them until he has them secured above my head. Something about not being able to touch a man has always made me hot. My orgasm crests, teetering over the edge until I plummet into bliss.

I have no idea how long I'm outside of myself when I hear his labored breath in my ear. "I'm going to fuck you no less than five times tonight, each one longer than the one before, each one in a different position. You're going to ride my cock *and* my face. I'm going to fuck you from behind, sideways, and on every surface in this place. Because I don't think I can get enough of you."

Holy shit, Prince Adrian is a dirty talker.

That's all it takes for my body to scream mercy. My eyes shut and stars fill my vision as the tension in my body slowly leaves me with the euphoria of another orgasm.

He pumps into me a few more times before stilling inside me with a groan. Seconds later, he falls onto his back, taking me with him, and we lay there until our heartbeats slow.

Hands down, the best sex of my life.

Now I wonder if his promises will be fulfilled post orgasm. That will show me what kind of guy he really is.

CHAPTER EIGHT

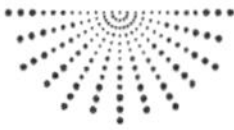

Adrian

My eyes open from under a curtain of red hair. Sierra's warm, naked body is plastered to mine.

I slide her hair off my face and slide out of bed without disturbing her. My suit is wrinkled but dry and I slide it on, checking to make sure she's still sleeping.

Once I'm dressed, I take her in one more time. She's definitely a force to be reckoned with. She was more than willing to let me fulfill my promise that spurred her second orgasm last night.

Memories of last night run through my head like a highlight reel of key moments—her kneeling in front of me, her straddling my face, her ass perched in front of me as I used our third condom on her bent over the bed.

I shake my head and walk out the door with the expert quietness of a thief.

Heading toward the elevators, past a housekeeper's cart, I dip my head just in case. When I get to the lobby, the same girl from last night is leaving with street clothes on, waving goodbye to her co-workers with what looks like relief.

When I walk outside, it's like a reset button was clicked with the morning sun. There's no sign of the rain from last night, not even a little puddle along the side of the road. I walk against the rush of families with strollers and couples walking hand in hand. The weight of my phone in my pocket is like a pinprick with every step. Sooner or later, I have to face the music. I can't hide out for the rest of my life.

My recurring dream of running away from my responsibilities dries up with the light of day. If I don't want to be found, I can't very well see my family when I want. I'd have to leave them behind and that's just not an option.

Eventually I'll be king, and I fear that time is coming sooner than I want.

Stopping at a park, I pull out my phone and press the on button. I start to check my messages. Yeah, no. I shove it back into my pocket and head across the street to a bakery. The line is long, and without a hat, I keep my head down, looking at the cement floor. I doubt they'd think I was a prince— what with me looking like I slept on a park bench—but you can never be too careful.

Ten minutes later and without anyone recognizing me, I'm armed with two coffees, a bunch of pastries, and bagels with cream cheese. When I walk into the hotel, my phone is vibrating once again. I stop in the lobby outside the gift shop and pull it out.

Declan: *You have ten minutes.*
Declan: *Ten minutes are up.*
Declan: *I'm calling Jean.*
Jean: *Adrian? Come on. Not again.*

Jean: *Sooner or later we'll find you. You're the prince. You can't hide forever.*

I scroll farther into the night after Declan had no choice but to call my mom.

Mom: *You cannot ditch security.*
Felicia: *Seriously Adrian, grow the fuck up.*
Mom: *What if something happens? People are crazy. Declan is frantically searching for you.*
Rowan: *Mom's crying. Something bad happened. Wanna play Xbox?*
Dad: *Your mother called. This adolescent behavior has to stop. Call Declan to pick you up NOW.*
Mom: *Please sweetie. Don't be upset about me contacting Dad, I'm worried and have no idea what to do.*
Felicia: *I need you and this isn't about you going rogue on security.*
Mom: *You were tagged. Declan's coming now.*
Declan: *Where did you go? I know you were at this bar. Stop running.*
Jean: *There's a hold on all your credit cards. Good luck going anywhere.*

Ha! Little did Jean know I had more than enough cash for a typical night out.

There's silence through the rest of the night, and this morning, there's only one text from my mom.

Mom: *I love you and I know you love me. Please don't make me worry. It's time to call now, sweetie. It's time to stop hiding.*

I leave the pastries and coffees on a small table and go into the small hotel store, picking out a shirt and shorts for

Sierra and me. Once I'm done, I sit in the chair away from any prying ears and dial my mother, prepared for her wrath.

"Adrian," she says, sighing.

"I just wanted one night," I grumble.

"I know, but when is it going to stop? When will it be enough? Declan is beside himself. Jean blames Declan. Felicia is doing everything she can to keep everything out of the press."

I sigh and pinch the bridge of my nose, my head down.

"Your father is here, I'm putting you on speaker."

I roll my eyes and pull my leg up to rest on my knee. This should be good. Him lecturing me on proper behavior.

"Adrian, I demand you return home right now."

"Yeah, thanks, but I don't think so."

"This is not a choice. I am prepared to cut you off. You think because you had a few hundred bucks to mess around with in New York City that you have any idea what it's like to not have the privilege this life offers you? Maybe it would do you some good to learn how blessed you are in this life you hate so much."

His authoritative voice doesn't make me want to comply. Not after he's the one who ruined our family.

My phone dings and I look to see Felicia is calling.

"I'll call you right back," I say.

"We need to talk—"

I cut my dad off and click over to Felicia. "Yeah, yeah, save the lecture."

"We have bigger problems than you acting like a runaway child. A reporter has figured out what's going on. I'm not sure if Dad's *friend* talked or not, but they want money to keep quiet."

My head rolls across the back of the seat. "It's going to come out."

"I'm doing everything I can, but you know if it comes out and they get a divorce… you know what that means, right?"

I might hate my life, but I know the royal rules that govern my birthplace. If my parents get divorced, I'm to marry immediately and take the throne. Only a king *and* a queen may serve.

"Yeah, I know."

"It means you'd have to marry Princess Adelaide."

Aggravation gnaws at my insides. "I know."

"You have to stop running away."

"I don't want to marry her. Look what happened to Mom and Dad. He cheated because he married a woman he didn't love."

"They love each other."

Felicia is a glass-half-full person, where I always see the glass as half empty.

"Like a brother and sister and still he could do that to her." I'm angry enough without having to see my dad with someone else. I can't imagine how Felicia does it, having seen it in person.

"I know. But rules are rules."

"For being such a tough bitch, you sure sit back and let the rules from centuries ago stick it to you."

She scoffs. "Don't take it out on me. It's not my fault I don't have a dick."

Felicia was born first, and out of the three of us, she's the only one who can't rule, even if she is the most suited.

"It's time to come home now. I gave you your night without cameras."

I tap my fingers on my ankle, staring at the two coffees and bag of pastries. The bag of his and hers *I Heart New York* T-shirts. "I'm not ready yet."

"I don't care."

"I'm going to call Mom and arrange a deal."

"Adrian? This is ridiculous. Just come home."

"I love you." I hang up and dial my mom back, but of course my dad picks up.

"Adrian, you do not hang up on us—"

I cut him off before he gets a chance to launch his lecture. "I'll come home and marry Princess Adelaide on one condition."

"No."

"What is it, sweetie?" my mom asks, always the one to give in to us. I think she secretly wanted to live a normal life before marrying a prince.

"We are not adhering to his demands," he says to my mom. "You are to contact Declan to alert him of your whereabouts and then you are to come home."

"I want two months. Two months."

"You're supposed to meet Princess Adelaide and her parents in a month. It's all been arranged. A short courtship and a quick wedding," my mom says.

The thought nauseates me, but I'll do it if they'll give me this time to just be myself, figure out who that really is.

"I want two months. You two need to look happy and get that woman to keep her mouth shut. If I'm going to sacrifice my entire life to rule Sandsal and marry a woman I don't know, then you can do it for two months."

Silence is all I hear from the other side of the phone.

I watch as a happy couple leaves the hotel, the man carrying a large garment bag. Their shirts are inscribed with bride and groom in white cursive letters and their smiles could brighten all of Brooklyn. Jealousy knifes me in the heart.

I hear my parents talking in low murmurs, my dad's seething voice a little louder than my mom's.

"Okay," my mom says.

My dad intervenes quickly. "Two months. But you're cut

off. Whatever money you have with you is all you've got from us. You do not have Declan or Jean. If you really want to do this, you're on your own."

As shallow as it sounds, I hadn't really thought about that part of it, but he's right. If I want to experience a life without the handcuffs my privileged life stifles me with, I can't have the gains of it either. "Fine."

"Where will you live?" my mom asks.

"I'll figure that out and be in touch."

"In two months, you are to return home and I never want one of these disappearing acts to happen again, is that understood? You come home, marry Princess Adelaide, and rule this country without any argument."

"I will." Elation wars with my acceptance of my eventual fate.

"I hope you find whatever it is you're looking for before you come home," my mom says.

"Thanks, Mom."

She sighs but doesn't say anything.

"Don't call us if you embarrass the family and end up in jail," my dad chimes in.

"I think you've embarrassed the family enough for all of us." The nerve of that bastard.

"Okay, you two, enough. Adrian, make sure you check in with us once a week. We love you."

"Love you, Mom." I click the phone off and sit in the chair for a moment. Did they really agree to allow me two months to live in the United States and do whatever I want?

I pick up the coffees and bags and head to the elevators. I guess I don't have to cut my time with Sierra short after all. As I ride the elevator to the fifth floor, I realize if I'm cut off and I don't have a job, I have no money for an apartment. But I can be inventive. I must have something to offer someone.

Using the keycard, the door lock flashes green and I open

the door as quietly as I can, but when I hear the television, I figure she's up. Walking into the room, I find Sierra still naked under the sheets, watching some reality television show.

"Good morning, beautiful," I say, holding out the coffee tray.

"I thought you left. You know, duty called." She tries to throw it out as a joke, even masks her face as if she couldn't care less, but I see her red-rimmed eyes.

I should've left a note.

"No, and actually…" I grab my coffee, toeing out of my shoes, and hop onto the bed next to her. The mattress bounces and Sierra rises, clinging to her coffee to avoid spillage before we both settle back down. "I got pastries and an outfit for you."

She eyes my suit. "You went out like that?"

I nod.

"Any pictures?"

"Not that I saw. What prince walks around in a wrinkled suit?"

"One doing the walk of shame."

I shrug. She has a point. "In essence, as of this morning, I've been stripped of my title."

Her eyes bug out of her head. "Because of last night? I'm so sorry. Do you want me to talk to someone? I could totally say I was sick, or I kidnapped you."

I laugh and shake my head. I appreciate that she'd go to such lengths for me. "I asked for two months of freedom to do what I want, and my parents granted it."

"Really?" Her jaw is slack as she stares at me.

I nod. "I was thinking on my way up here… you said your roommate is leaving, right?"

This could be a horrible idea because I might spend my

two months screwing Sierra because the sex was so good and never getting around to the finding myself part.

"Yeah. She's moving out today."

"Do you have another roommate lined up yet?"

She tilts her head as though she's following but doesn't believe I'm actually going to ask her. "No…"

"Want one?" I hold out my arms.

Her eyebrows shoot up to her hairline. "You?"

I chuckle. "Yes, me. The problem is my parents cut me off, so I was thinking that maybe I can swap a room for an exclusive interview? The only thing is, you can't run the interview until after I return home."

Her shoulders fall and she places her coffee on the nightstand. "You're serious?"

"Yep."

"You remember I don't even live in the city, right?"

I run my finger over the bedsheet along her thigh. "The way you talked about Cliffton Heights last night, and your friends? That's what I want."

She takes a moment to think it over and I worry she's going to deny me. Although we learned a lot about one another last night, I still don't know her well and I'm pretty much asking to move in with her.

"Okay." She nods. "But I want the interview. It'll help propel my career."

I take my finger and cross my heart. "Promise."

She laughs. "Be careful what you wish for, that's all I have to say."

I toss the bag of pastries onto the nightstand with our coffees, roll on top of her, and we spend the next two hours in bed before reality sets in and I find out that for normal folks, check-out times aren't merely a suggestion.

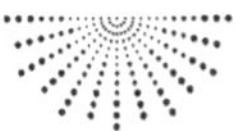

CHAPTER NINE

Sierra

We're wearing matching *I Heart New York* T-shirts and shorts like a couple of tourists. Luckily when we went back down to the store they had flip-flops for me, but poor Adrian has to wear his dress shoes.

His phone dings, pulling my eyes away from the rolling green landscape outside the train window.

"Jean said my luggage is being delivered to your place later today by carrier."

"It'll probably get there before us what with the whole royalty thing. You going to miss it?"

"I don't think so. I'm going to cut my hair and grow a beard with the hope that anyone who does follow me won't recognize me."

I run my fingers through his shoulder-length hair. "I love your hair."

"You loved gripping it last night when my face was between your thighs, that's for sure." He chuckles.

I love his laugh. It's so real and authentic and true.

I could pinch myself right now. How did I go from winning a date to now living with him? Though he says he's no longer a prince, he still is. Giving up your royal obligations for two months to play house isn't like abdicating altogether.

"So Rian is the other roommate. You think she'll be okay with me staying there?"

I laugh. Rian won't know what to do with him, but they both have easygoing personalities.

"She's a math textbook writer and she loves baking, so you might put on some pounds during your stay with us." I pat his stomach and he laughs, not taking my hand.

Actually, since we left the hotel, he hasn't shown me any affection at all. Where do we stand for these next two months? Do I even want to get attached to someone, knowing ahead of time there's a ticking clock on our time together?

"That's an interesting job. I was great at calculus. Maybe I'll have her test me." He gets lost in thought for a moment. "And the others? The guys who live across the hall?"

He's been quizzing me ever since we agreed he was going to live with us.

"Dylan owns the tattoo shop across the street from the apartment. Seth is a photographer still working his way up, so he takes boudoir pictures right now."

"Like glamour shots?"

"More like lingerie-clad sexy pictures."

"Of women?"

I laugh. "Yeah."

"Lucky man." He waggles his eyebrows.

"He doesn't think so. He aspires to be well-known in

other areas of photography. And then Knox is a police officer."

"And tell me about your best friend?"

I'd almost forgotten about her. I'll see her with Ethan every day, down the hall. Adrian will make that more bearable though.

"Blanca and Ethan, they're journalists and work at the same magazine. Write articles on opposing views of one another."

He nods. "Cool."

"I guess. Ethan has a lot of stuff, so maybe I can have her leave her bedroom stuff for you."

I pull my phone out and dial her, but she doesn't answer. She's probably busy with the move. But I'm sure it won't be a problem.

The train stops in Cliffton Heights and we descend the stairs, Adrian looking around as if he's in Disneyland.

"It's just a small city."

"I love it."

"It's not New York," I remind him for the millionth time.

"I know. Stop being so nervous. This was my decision." He knocks shoulders with me.

"Well, come on." I nod in the direction of the Rooftop Apartments.

He soaks it all in, pointing and asking questions about each store and restaurant, commenting about how he needs to go to the drug store to grab some toiletries. He wasn't even this excited last night when we ditched his security.

"Thanks, Sierra," he says as I put the key into the lock of my apartment building.

"You're welcome." I smile.

His fingers land on my ribcage, tickling me while we walk toward the elevator. The doors open immediately, and we file in, his hands slowing and moving along my body. He crowds me into the corner and his mouth draws closer to me, his lips meeting mine and his tongue sliding into my mouth. This feels so right, but the two-month timeline rings in my head like a warning bell, ruining the kiss.

As though he can hear my musings, his body presses harder, his lips firmer, his tongue faster as though he's trying to push that thought from my head. The doors open and we part, walking out of the elevator hand in hand.

The Mancini crew lingers between Blanca's new apartment and mine. I peek into my apartment, not seeing Ethan and Blanca, so I leave Adrian there and head down the hall, saying a quick hello to everyone in the hall. I pound on Ethan's door and he and Blanca groan from the other side. I do not want to know what they were doing because I'm fairly sure it's what I was doing in the elevator with Adrian.

"What, Sierra?" Blanca asks through the door.

"You're not taking your bed, right? Mind leaving it for Adrian? Maybe your dresser too?"

Ethan groans and the door swings open. Blanca's lips are swollen, and Ethan turns his back to adjust himself.

"What?" Blanca's eyes fly up and down my body, concern in her expression.

"Oh my God." I step into their apartment and shut the door. There's something about telling other people that a prince is moving in with us that I find so exciting. Blanca will know what this means to me. "He wants to live with us," I whisper as if he's within earshot.

"I'm sorry. Who does?" Blanca whispers back.

"Adrian." I cannot lose the perma-smile on my face.

"*Holy shit! Carm*, grab your camera. It's *Prince Adrian Marx*!" Bella, Blanca's soon-to-be sister-in-law yells from the hallway.

"I'm not getting shit. He's not that great, you know. Running a country isn't any harder than selling an overpriced penthouse in Manhattan," Carm, Blanca's brother, yells back.

Blanca opens the door and walks down the hallway which is now empty. Ethan and I follow, and when we reach my apartment, sure enough, Bella's mouth is hanging open.

Val, Blanca's very pregnant sister-in-law, is searching the pantry, uncaring.

Annie, the second almost-sister-in-law, is sitting, watching everything go down with rapt attention.

All the guys are on the couch, watching the football game.

Rian raises her eyebrows at Blanca. They both think this is crazy. Maybe it is.

Adrian turns on his charm with Blanca, holding his hand out to her. "Hello, I'm Adrian Marx."

God, his accent is so sexy.

Bella leans forward. "Prince. Adrian. Marx." As though she might need clarification.

He chuckles and turns his attention back to Blanca. "Where do I sleep? In your bed?"

Ethan's arm quickly hangs over her shoulder in a protective manner. "Not happening."

"Sierra mentioned I could borrow a bed while I stay here. Temporarily, of course. Would you like compensation?"

"That accent," Bella sighs.

"I have an accent too. A New York accent," Carm yells.

"No, no compensation. So you're moving in here?" Blanca clarifies, her gaze shooting from me to him to Ethan and to Adrian again.

"Yes. Sierra said that would be okay."

Blanca turns to me and I giggle like the schoolgirl I am right now. "Can you believe it?"

She shakes her head. "No. I can't."

Rian grabs my arm. "Excuse us, Your Highness." She curtsies, and Adrian laughs.

Blanca is quick to follow, and the three of us end up in Rian's room with the door shut.

"Explain this to me, Sierra, because I had this lovely girl coming for an interview tomorrow," Rian says, ever patient. She's never quick to react. I'm the time bomb in our friendship.

"He's taking two months off from being a prince."

They aren't nearly as surprised as I was. They actually seem indifferent.

"Okay, and why does that have anything to do with us?" Rian asks.

"Did you sleep with him?" Blanca asks, her eyes already casting judgment when her gaze dips down at my clothes.

"I don't kiss and tell," I joke.

"Sure, you do," Rian says. "That's all you do. Am I going to be stuck in a sexfest for two months?"

"No." Although I kind of secretly hope there is more sex. Only because he's so talented.

Rian's expression says she doesn't believe me. The unbreakable smile on my face probably doesn't help with her assessment.

"Okay, I'm not sure. But he asked if he could take the spare room in exchange for an exclusive interview. You guys know how much I've wanted to move up to anchor. Maybe if I score this interview, I have a chance. I can't be a beat reporter for some local station forever."

Blanca's shoulders fall because unlike Rian, she understands the work thing. Rian is happy writing textbook questions and baking in her free time. She's content in that facet of her life, whereas Blanca and I are on a quest to climb the ladder as high and fast as we can get there. Fuck any glass ceilings along the way. We'll bust through them.

"How is the prince paying for rent?" Rian asks.

"I'm paying the first month for sure. In exchange for the interview."

Blanca balks. "Can you afford that?"

I nod. I have money tucked away from my mom dying in action that I hardly ever touch.

Blanca says nothing because she doesn't have a say. She doesn't live here anymore. But a line forms between her brows as she leans forward and lowers her voice. "I don't want to see you get hurt. What happens in two months?"

"He returns to Sandsal and has to carry out his royal duties."

Rian's head falls into her hands. "This is insane. We're living with a prince?"

"Thanks for understanding, Rian." I should have called her before agreeing to it, I know that, but I was caught up in the moment. We're roommates *and* friends. "It was wrong of me to agree to it without speaking to you first."

She shrugs. "It will be a little uncomfortable at first like when…"

We still walk on eggshells sometimes when it comes to mine and Ethan's past relationship, even though Blanca and Ethan are together now.

"I know, but there's no relationship between Adrian and me, so there shouldn't be any fights or anything."

Rian nods, but I can tell she's worried. "I guess I should go meet him and get to know him a bit." She stands and heads for the door.

Before Rian can open it, Blanca almost plows me over with her arms wrapped tight around me. "Be careful, okay? He has those family obligations he'll never walk away from, and I'm sure there's no Sandsal version of Barbara Walters you can replace there."

"I will."

"I do expect a full report on the sex at a later date though." Blanca smiles, releasing me.

"Definitely," Rian adds. "And if you have sex, do it in your bedroom. That way you're at least a room away."

I grin. "Noted."

I couldn't ask for better friends.

We walk out of the bedroom to find Adrian on the couch with a beer in his hand, sandwiched between Enzo and Carm, Blanca's brothers. They hammer question after question at him about his royal life. Bella sits next to Carm, perched on the arm of the couch in rapt attention as her boyfriend rubs her ass as though there's no one else in the room.

Val and Annie talk at the kitchen table while Val eats the last of the oatmeal scotchie cookies Rian made a few days ago.

Dom approaches Blanca. "Are we ordering food? Val needs fuel for the baby."

"I can order something." Blanca goes to the drawer with the menus. "What do you want?"

"Don't mind your brother. I'm fine. These are good." Val holds up half-eaten cookie.

"Babe, the baby needs something besides sugar," Dom says.

She leans back and rubs her belly. "Sugar makes baby happy." She takes his hand and rests it on her swollen belly. His face lights up with a smile that probably matches mine at the moment.

"Is she kicking?" Annie's hand shoots across the table.

"Who said it's a she?" Dom asks.

Annie laughs. "A hunch."

"Mama thinks it's a boy, but I think that's wishful thinking," Blanca chimes in.

I stare at the Mancini family. A family I always wanted to

be a part of. Ethan swings his arm over Blanca's shoulder and kisses her cheek.

"Oh, I felt it!" Annie screeches, earning Enzo's attention for a moment. "The little girl is kicking."

"Watch it, Annie," Dom warns with the same razor edge tone he's had since we were younger.

"Don't talk to my fiancée like that." Enzo stands.

Adrian and Carm turn around. Adrian's gaze meets mine, and as the Mancini family do what they do best—bicker—I'm lost in the sea of blue in his eyes.

Will I be able to get through two months without falling head over heels in love with this man? What did I sign myself up for?

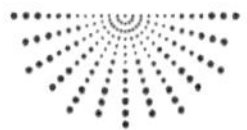

CHAPTER TEN

Adrian

I'm used to having my own space. Not that I'm not enjoying spending time with everyone, but I thought that moving in with Sierra meant Sierra and Rian. After Blanca's family left, the three guys from across the hall never left unless it was to grab something and come right back. And Blanca and Ethan keep coming by to ask for a screwdriver or a hammer or some other tool.

The buzzer from downstairs sounds and Rian answers it since she's in the kitchen. From what I can tell, she's always doing something in there, whether it's cooking, baking, or cleaning. If this was my apartment, my friends would assume she was my servant.

"I have a delivery for Athos Dumas," the crackling voice of a woman says through the speaker.

"Oh, I'm sorry—"

"That's me." I stand and all eyes land on me.

Rian's head tilts, but she presses the button. "Come on up."

"Athos Dumas?" Sierra asks from her spot on the couch.

"It's my fake name for hotels and stuff. It's a nod to the *Three Musketeers*. Don't ask."

"You have to check in under a fake name like movie stars?" Seth asks, his jaw slightly open. "Do women stand outside your hotel room, chanting your name?" His smirk says he can't imagine that's the truth.

"Women never chant my name, no. But after my grandfather was assassinated by some woman's spiked heel in his throat, all the men in our family have to use pretend names at hotels. And any woman who enters our room must be barefoot."

"Spiked heel to the throat?" Seth asks, wide-eyed.

Sierra says nothing, but she knows I'm lying. Which makes me wonder if she's aware of the fact that my grandfather is alive and celebrating his seventy-fifth birthday next year.

"Yes, there was blood everywhere. My grandmother thought it was his mistress. The press was all over it."

"Seriously?" Seth asks.

"No." I shake my head, and it takes a moment for him to realize I was lying.

"Bastard. I thought for sure you were telling the truth. It was going to make me look at those sexy spiked heels differently the next time I see them on a hot woman."

"No, it wouldn't," Sierra says, hitting him in the thigh with her foot.

He shrugs. "Probably not. You should pick a cool name to go by."

"You should've used Ben Jergen Hoff," Dylan says, laughter sputtering out of him.

The rest of the gang joins in.

"And your girlfriend can be Ivana Humpalot," Seth adds.

"I went to college with a guy named Ben Dover," Rian says from the kitchen.

Dylan slaps his thigh and points at her while he laughs. Her cheeks redden.

"What about Willie Stroker?" Knox points at Seth and he points back, almost spitting out his beer.

"I forgot about that guy. I always felt bad for him," Seth says once he's swallowed the beer in his mouth.

"He should've gone by Bill Stroker, or really just anything else." Knox sips his beer, shaking his head as if the guy is in the room.

"That's what I'll never understand. Why wouldn't these people change their names?" Dylan asks. "Not to mention, do parents never think about their kids going to high school?"

They all laugh, and I look around at the group. I like the way they're so close.

A knock sounds on the door, and I open it to find three bags and a woman heaving for a breath. Her dark hair is pulled back in a ponytail under a black baseball cap.

"Want some water?" I ask her.

"Thanks." She steps in.

Rian grabs a bottle from the fridge, hands it to me, and I pass it on to her. I dig into my pocket to get her some money for a tip, but she waves me off.

"I've already been tipped by the guy. *Oh.*" She nods as if she just remembered, digging into her back pocket. "He told me to give this to you."

The envelope is white and thick. I should send Jean a huge thank you since my parents have denied me all access to family money.

"Thanks."

"No problem. He's lucky, you know. It doesn't take a rocket scientist to figure out what's in that envelope. Most people would've run away with your luggage and your money, Athos." She snickers at my name, which means she's figured out it's not my real name.

"Leilani?" Knox says from behind me.

The water bottle pauses at her lips. "Knox?"

The room behind me is silent now. I'm obviously not the only one who doesn't know this girl. Or maybe they all know exactly who she is and that's why they're quiet, waiting to see how this plays out.

"I can't believe it's you." His large frame brushes past me and his arms wrap around her small frame, lifting her feet off the floor.

The woman's eyes briefly shut as her arms lock around his neck.

They've obviously shared more than a friendship in the past.

I glance at Rian because she's the closest to me, but she shrugs. Her gaze floats to the other side of the room to meet the other confused faces.

"Who's your friend, Knox?" Dylan asks.

Knox lowers her to the floor and asks her, "Where have you been? Last I heard you were on the west coast."

The woman nods but her smile is timid, as though she doesn't want to go into specifics.

"We need to catch up. My apartment." Knox takes her hand and escorts her across the hall.

When the door shuts, we all stare at one another, looking dumbfounded.

"I guess we're not getting an introduction," Dylan says.

I pick up my three pieces of luggage and head to my room.

"Want help?" Sierra asks.

"Nah, I've got it."

Once I'm in the room that still has Blanca's girly light-pink-and-white comforter on the bed, I open the envelope Jean added to my belongings.

ADRIAN,

HERE ARE your belongings from the hotel. Declan and I have been filled in on your decision and are returning to Sandsal in the morning. This is all the money I had for our trip. Enjoy your two months.

"Your greatest responsibility is to love yourself and to know you are enough."

~ *JEAN*

JEAN HAS this insistent need to recite quotes and write them on things I'll find. He thinks I doubt my ability to be king, but truth is, I don't want the position. I fold up his letter and stuff the cash into my dresser, laying my boxers over it.

Unpacking three suitcases doesn't take long, so I enjoy the quiet of the room a bit more before rejoining everyone. But I didn't leave my life in Sandsal to hole myself up in a stranger's apartment, so I walk out and join the group. Everyone except Knox is still there. Apparently the guys from across the hall never leave.

"When is Mama Mancini coming back? Why isn't she here to help Blanca move?" Seth asks, groaning as he holds his stomach.

"The 'rents aren't very happy with the 'living in sin' situation," Dylan says, not taking his eyes off the television.

"Really? Don't her brothers live with their girlfriends?" Rian asks.

"They do," Sierra says.

"That's shitty," Seth adds.

"Yeah, but to be expected. She's the only daughter and youngest in an Italian family." Sierra chuckles and slides over on the couch to make room for me. "All unpacked and ready to live a life of boring normalcy?"

All eyes are on me and I feel like a petri dish science experiment. "I might go out and buy a few things."

"Want me to tag along? I could show you more of the town."

She's so excited that I hate to turn her down, but I need to come to grips with what I did in a spur-of-the-moment decision because I was pissed off at my parents.

"Nah, you stay with your friends. I won't be long." I head toward the door.

They all say goodbye, none of them enthusiastic. More like they think I should've let Sierra come with me.

"Wait, a key!" Sierra hops up off the couch. "These were…" She waves. "Doesn't matter. They're yours for the next two months."

Her smile suggests she's not angry with me for needing a little alone time, so I take the keys with a thank you and leave.

Cliffton Heights is quaint and reminds me of one of those small towns depicted in the majority of Hallmark movies. Thanks to Felicia, I know all about those movies and how wrong they get royalty.

My phone vibrates in my pocket, and I pull it out to see my brother's name flash across the screen.

"Hey, bud," I answer.

"You're not coming back from America?"

I anticipated his call once my parents told him. If I could

ship him over, I would, but Mom would never allow that. "I am, but not right away."

"Two months! Mom said two months!"

"Yeah, but I have my Xbox. We can play together here."

"Why? Is it Dad?"

How do you tell a ten-year-old that our dad isn't the man we thought he was? "No, I just need some time away."

"I heard Dad and Mom fighting. They said you'll have to step up and be king."

God I hope it doesn't come to that. At the same time, my mom deserves better than my father.

"We'll see what happens. Right now, just keep going to school and doing your thing. You have my number. Call me whenever."

"I hate the way everyone thinks they can keep secrets from me."

I laugh. Sometimes I try to find all his hiding places when he eavesdrops on conversations. The kid knows more about what goes on in our castle than even our servants.

"Well, they're trying to protect you."

He says nothing for a moment. "Am I going to have to marry someone I don't love?"

"No, because when I'm king, I'll change that rule." I kick at a small stone as I continue down the sidewalk—where to, I'm not sure.

"Hate to break it to you, but I'm not sure you have the power."

"We'll see."

The kid is right, but I'll try my best. No one should be shackled to someone else just because we were born into two royal families. My parents are an example of that.

I reach a parkette with a large gazebo in the middle and make my way over, sitting down inside to take in my new home for the next two months. I listen for a few minutes while Rowan fills me in on a game of *Fortnite* that he and his friends played yesterday.

When I spot Blanca struggling with a box down the street, I say, "Listen, I gotta go. I'll call you soon, okay?"

"Wait!"

"Yeah?"

"Are you, like, going to get a job and stuff? Mom told Dad he shouldn't have cut you off but..." He stops talking, probably because he doesn't want to give me a reason to hate my father more.

"I'm not sure, why?"

"I just wonder why you'd want to move to America and work when you could be here?"

I have no response. At ten, I thought my life was pretty fantastic too.

"I'll call you tomorrow, okay?" I say.

"Okay." The disappointment in his voice squeezes my chest.

We hang up, and I jog down the steps of the gazebo toward Blanca. She stops in front of a store, putting down the big box and blowing out a breath.

"Need some help?" I ask.

She smiles. I saw the difference between Blanca and Sierra the minute I was introduced. Blanca is much more easygoing.

"Of course a prince comes to the rescue."

"I'm no longer a prince. At least not for two months." I pick up the box and see from the label on the outside that it's a bookcase. "Furniture in a box?"

She giggles as we head toward the apartments. "Yeah, that's what us poor folk do."

"I'm poor now too."

"You're temporarily poor."

I shrug. She's right, I suppose. Maybe Rowan is right, and I should get a job and take advantage of this opportunity.

We pass a storefront with a Help Wanted sign on the door. Stopping, I place the box next to the door and my hand moves to the handle.

"Are you hungry?" she asks, and I look up to see it says the Bagel Place. "Because Seth—"

I open the door and walk into the small cafe-type restaurant. A few tables are filled with families and couples.

A woman with dark hair comes out and wipes her floured hands on her apron. "How can I help you? We're mostly out of everything, but I'm making some more if you'd like to wait."

"Adrian," Blanca says from behind me.

"Hey, Blanca," the woman who works here says. "I haven't seen you in a while."

Blanca's cheeks pinken. "Oh, I've been swamped and haven't had time to stop for a bagel."

"I get you. I've been living off bagels for the last week. We had two people leave us this week. I'm desperate."

Desperate is good. "I'd like to apply for the job," I say.

Her gaze falls over my body. Maybe I should've stayed in my *I Heart New York* shirt. She looks skeptical.

"Evan, this is Adrian. He just moved in down the hall from me."

The woman puts out her hand. "Do you have any work experience?"

"None."

She looks at Blanca at my side, and the two appear to have some sort of conversation without words. "You're hired."

CHAPTER ELEVEN

Sierra

"*Blue Bloods* night!" Dylan walks into our apartment unannounced with a pizza in hand.

Before the door closes, I hear Adrian's voice in the hallway.

"Was that Adrian?" I ask him.

"Yeah, he and Blanca were just coming in."

I stand. Rian's face tells me to let it go, it's nothing, but unease washes over me. "I'm going to see if they want to join us."

"You know Blanca still has to catch up," Rian says.

Blanca hasn't joined us to watch *Blue Bloods* because she keeps saying she wants to catch up from the beginning. But there's nothing wrong with a friendly visit to ask her if she wants to join us though, right?

Blanca and Ethan's door is open when I reach their apartment. Inside, Ethan's talking to Adrian, so I stop to listen for a minute.

"Babe, why didn't you call me?" Ethan asks Blanca.

"Because I had it," she says.

"She's too proud to ever ask for help," Ethan says.

Both men laugh.

"Happy to help," Adrian says.

"Adrian found a job," Blanca says from somewhere deep in the apartment.

A job? I hadn't thought of what he would do, but for some reason, a job never occurred to me.

"That's great. Where at?" Ethan asks.

"The Bagel Place."

Shit.

"Oh shit. Babe? The Bagel Place?"

Ethan's worried tone is right on the mark. Why would Blanca allow him to get a job at Seth's family's archnemesis?

"I figure it's only two months, and Evan was desperate for help."

"You're on a first-name basis with her?" Ethan asks.

Yeah, how did I miss that one too?

"I thought we talked about this," Ethan says.

Now I'm too curious to just eavesdrop. I have questions to ask and answers to find out, so I step out of the hallway into the doorway of their apartment.

Ethan does a double-take. "Hey, Sierra."

"Did I hear you got a job?" I pose my question to Adrian.

Ethan laughs, probably knowing I was eavesdropping and heads into their small galley kitchen. "Beer?"

"Sure," Adrian answers.

"Nah. *Blue Bloods* is starting," I tell Ethan.

"I promised to wait for Blanca to catch up before I watch any more."

Ugh. Of course he did.

"What about you, Adrian? Want to watch *Blue Bloods*?" I ask.

"Is that a show?" He accepts a beer from Ethan, quickly taking a sip.

"Yeah, we watch every Sunday," I say.

"Donnie Wahlberg is in it," Ethan says as though that should be clear enough.

"The boy band guy?" Adrian asks.

"That's the one." Ethan tips back his own beer to draw a sip.

"I think I'll pass."

"Blanca and I are heading up to the roof tonight. You're welcome to join us."

Adrian shakes his head. "I wouldn't want to impose on your date night."

Ethan laughs. "You're not imposing. We work together, man. Which means we commute together and now we live together." His eyes widen with the admission as though it's too much time together.

I punch him in the shoulder.

"Ow. What the hell?" Ethan gives me a dirty look.

"Don't disrespect my girl like that," I say.

Adrian turns his head in surprise. "That was all bullshit?"

"Yeah, sorry. I was just trying to make you not feel like the third wheel because you're new here and they're all going to watch a television show that's in its seventh season."

"Oh." My cheeks redden that my overprotectiveness shined through in front of Adrian.

Adrian laughs. "Let me buy the pizza."

Ethan nods. "Sure."

"No. We have it." Blanca comes out of the closet she's been in this whole time. "You're like a guest."

"He moved in, so not a guest," Ethan says, the cheapskate he is.

"Please, it'd be my pleasure." Adrian smiles.

"See, babe, we can't deny the man his pleasure." Ethan puts his arm around her.

Blanca's eyes fall to me with a heavily implied smirk and I have no time to stop her before she says, "I think he got a lot of pleasure last night. Right, Sierra?"

Ethan's eyebrows raise and a flush heats Adrian's face. I give her my best evil stare.

"Let's go to the roof, man." Ethan heads to the fridge and takes out a few more beers.

Adrian smiles at me, so I'm guessing he's not mad. Which, why do I care? It's not like we're a secret or anything.

"I guess I'll be on the rooftop," Adrian tells me.

"Have fun."

"Babe?" Ethan nods toward the door.

Blanca's gaze stays on me and she lifts her finger. "One minute."

Ethan shakes his head.

The minute the door closes after them, Blanca grabs my hand and pulls me to the couch. "Spill."

"Spill what?"

"You know what! You guys obviously had sex. I knew you were bullshitting us earlier. You had sex with a prince!" She's almost happier than I was.

Okay, not quite. The man knows how to please a woman —which only reminds me of how many women probably came before me. "And?"

"And he's a prince. You owe me details."

I raise my eyebrows. It feels kinda weird to talk to Blanca about my sex life now since it might lead to her talking about hers. With her dating my ex, I'm familiar with Ethan in the bedroom even if it makes me shake in disgust now. We've yet to share in that way since she and Ethan got together.

"Okay, you don't owe me, but I know you and it's killing

you not to get it out."

I bite my bottom lip. She's right. I do want and need to talk to someone about this. How do I go from what I assumed would be a one-night stand with a prince to living with him?

"I have no idea how it happened. One minute he's this slob who put no effort into getting ready for our evening together and then he's showing me a few vulnerabilities. And we ran away from security—"

The apartment door opens without a knock.

"*Blue Bloods,* guys!" Rian yells but spots us on the couch and opens the door farther, stepping into the apartment. "What's going on?" She sits on the floor at our feet.

"Sierra is giving me more details about her date with Adrian." Blanca waggles her eyebrows.

Rian slides her ass closer, straightening her back like a good-mannered kid ready for storytime at the library.

"It wasn't a fairy tale date, but…" I rehash the night—running from security, falling on the ice rink, the bar with Adrian's fans, getting caught in the rain. Then I get into the really interesting parts and tell them about all the places we had sex—the shower, the bed, the dresser, and the bathroom countertop.

By the time I'm done with my story, they're both staring at me with huge smiles.

"And then he decided he wanted to move in?" Rian asks.

"After he talked to his parents and they agreed to let him do what he wanted for two months, he had nowhere to go. We agreed that he'd give me an exclusive interview in exchange for living here for two months."

Their smiles dim.

"So where does that leave you two?" Blanca asks.

"I have no idea." I purposely keep a lightness in my tone as though I haven't wondered the same thing all day.

"Are you going to be sleeping together? Because I just want to say public places are off-limits. No shower or bathroom countertops, okay?" Rian says.

Blanca and I laugh.

"I have no idea if last night was it or what. I mean, even if we do sleep together, it's not like there can ever be a future. He's a prince and has to go back to Sandsal in two months."

They both stare at me.

"What?" I ask.

"Sierra." Blanca takes my hand. "The man you've been following online and have been infatuated with is sleeping in the bedroom next to yours. You had sex multiple times with him last night. You can't just live the next two months in the dark. Nor can you allow him to come and go from your bed without some kind of agreement between you guys."

I slide my hands from hers, heading into the kitchen. "I'm not like you guys. I don't expect to become princess and get my happy ever after. Is it crazy that I met him in person and even crazier that we slept together, and he asked to move in here? Sure, it's like an out-of-body experience. I'm not sure it's completely soaked in yet, but I'd never expect something serious from him." I pull a bottle of wine from her fridge. "Cool if we open this?"

Blanca stands and Rian follows. "Of course. Opener is in the drawer by the dishwasher."

As I open the bottle of wine, I'm aware of their silence. It weighs heavy on my shoulders. "Will you two stop worrying? Sometimes people just have fun. If we sleep together again, then great. If not, I'm cool."

They look at one another then back at me. Blanca is more of a straight-shooter, so she takes charge. "You deserve more than that. Talk to him. Figure out where you stand, because in two months, you could end up devastated if you're not careful."

I pour a glass for each of them and slide them over the counter. "You guys are worried for nothing. It's me. I can have sex with a guy and not become emotionally invested."

Blanca sips her wine while Rian twirls her glass at the stem.

"But this is different," Rian says. "This is Prince Adrian Marx of Sandsal. A guy you already had a thing for. Not some stranger from a club you'll never see again."

I pat her hand. "You guys know I can handle myself."

They both release exasperated breaths.

"I think you should talk to him," Blanca says.

The apartment door opens before I have to repeat my argument again.

"Hello! *Blue Bloods*. The pizza is getting cold." Dylan peeks his head in but enters when he spots us all huddled together at the counter. "What's the gossip, hens?"

"You're always in on the gossip," Rian jokes.

Dylan swings his arm around her shoulders, leaning in. "Are we talking about sex toys, masturbation, or porn?"

Rian pushes on his stomach. "None of the above."

Dylan laughs, assuming we wouldn't be talking about any of those things. He doesn't need to know that girls have those conversations too.

"We're talking about Sierra living in the dark," Blanca says.

The attitude she's copping is grating on my nerves now.

"What does that mean?" His forehead wrinkles for a second, then his head falls back. "Ah, the prince."

"Yes, tell them, Dylan. You don't have to sign a contract with someone before having sex with them." I slip out from behind the counter to head to the couch. I'm positive the three of them are probably exchanging some look behind my back.

"Can't do that," Dylan says.

I whip my head around to find him sipping out of Rian's glass. I narrow my eyes at him. "You are not a Boy Scout, Dylan."

He passes the glass back to Rian then raises his hands. "I know and I never said I was, but I don't bring my one-night stands home to live with me for two months either."

"We made a deal. I get an exclusive interview. You know how huge that is for me? I mean, Kay is all up Jack's ass and he's going to give her the next anchor job. I get an interview with a prince who disappeared from his responsibilities for two months? Game changer."

Kay and I started at the station at the same time. She does the weather and I'm a beat reporter, but we both want the anchor position. With Georgia retiring, Adrian's interview could give me a leg up or make it more probable that another station might hire me.

"Hey, it's none of my business," Dylan says, "but I think it's best for all if intentions are laid out on the table, so no one gets blindsided."

Seth opens the apartment door and pops his head in. "Someone tell me why I'm sitting in an apartment all by myself with a pizza and a paused television?"

"We're coming." Rian stands to join him.

"I'm out for tonight. I'll catch it later this week." I sit on the sofa, taking into consideration all the advice being thrown my way.

Dylan is similar to me. The most serious relationship he's ever had was with a dog he found on the street. I've never seen him so depressed as when the family came to pick him up.

Maybe he's right though. I can't live with the man who gave me the best sex of my life without making it clear that this is just a bit of fun. In two months, he's free to go back to his life as a prince and I'll be one step further in my career.

CHAPTER TWELVE

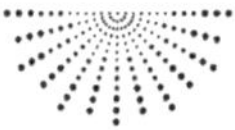

Adrian

The rooftop has a table with six chairs, a few stools, lights hung from one edge of the roof to the other, and a grill in the corner next to a small garden that appears it was probably used in the summer months. One of those standing propane heaters near the seating area takes the edge off of the chill of the autumn night.

"Is the entire building welcome up here?" I ask.

Ethan slides a chair down and sits. I do the same.

"Technically yes, but it's pretty much just ours. At least we seem to be the only ones who hang out up here." He leans his head back and stares at the sky.

"What do you do?" I ask. I'd like to veer the conversation as far away from Sierra and him dating as I can.

"I'm a writer at a small magazine called *Mars and Venus*. Blanca and I write articles with opposing viewpoints." He tips back his beer.

As I often do, I try to imagine myself in his shoes. A man who's comfortable in his skin and his abilities. At least from what I can tell. "That's a lot of time together."

He stretches his legs out on the chair in front of him and laughs. "Yeah, but we're not sick of one another yet. It's funny, you know, how dissimilar different relationships can be."

Oh shit, here we go. He's going to talk about his relationship with Sierra.

"I mean, when I moved in with Sierra, I felt suffocated, but I can spend all this time with Blanca and only want more. That's not a dig on Sierra. I think she felt the same way. 'Cause she can be..." He glances over, probably forgetting I just met Sierra. Other than knowing every inch of her body and the spots on her body that drive her insane with want, I don't know her well. "Sorry, I shouldn't have said anything."

"No, it's okay. I'm aware you guys had a relationship prior."

He nods. "I'm not surprised she told you."

"And why is that?"

He shrugs, taking another pull of his beer. "That's Sierra. She's straight-up and doesn't keep a lot close to the vest. Actually." He shakes his head. "That's not true. She keeps a lot to herself if it has to do with her, but you never have to worry about what her opinion about something is."

I consider what he's saying, but an ex-boyfriend always has a different view of his ex-girlfriend post-breakup, so I push what he says to the back of my mind. I've never met exes who can co-exist without some bitterness.

I'm not sure if it's my face or something else, but he raises his hands and shakes his head. "Forget that. Change of topic."

Before he can say anything else, the door opens, and Blanca and Sierra join us. Ethan drops his legs and slides the chair closer to him while Blanca looks at him as though he's the best boyfriend ever. What must that be like? To know someone loves you for you and not for what you represent?

Sierra slides out another chair and sits down. I should have stood and pulled out the chair for her. I do it for women I have no respect for. I should definitely do it for her.

"No television show?" I ask.

She shakes her head, her gaze falling to Blanca. "Not tonight. I'm not in the mood."

I hook my hand on her chair and slide it closer to me. "Good."

Then it's me who gets the best boyfriend smile, but the difference is, I'm not her boyfriend.

"Hey, E, I have something to show you." Blanca stands and holds her hand out for Ethan's.

"Nothing bad can follow that sentence." Ethan accepts her hand.

"Unless it's a pregnancy test," Sierra calls out, laughing.

"Bite your tongue!" Blanca says.

They disappear on the other side of the building where we can't see them. I wrap my hand around Sierra's neck and pull her to me for a kiss. Just like last night, the pull between us is there from the moment my lips brush hers. She sinks into my hold and I slide my tongue through her parted lips. Her breath now tastes like the sweetness of white wine.

"I've been wanting to do that all day," I murmur with our lips millimeters apart.

"Why didn't you?"

With my hand still resting on the back of her neck, I draw back to see her eyes. There's self-doubt there, which surprises me.

"Is something wrong?" I ask.

She leans back in her chair, my arm falling down. With her concentration on her wine glass, she talks to it more than to me. "My friends think we should set things straight. What's happening between us?"

I sip my beer, the coolness coating my now-dry throat. I should've figured this would be a complication when I asked to move in. Truth is, my life is so fucked up, the last thing I should do is get involved with someone.

"What do you think is happening?" I ask, being a coward and throwing it back at her.

The legs of her chair screech back on the cement, and she walks to the edge of the roof, looking at the night sky. "Please don't do that."

"Do what?" I follow her.

"Try and deflect."

Giggling on the other side of the rooftop can be heard and her eyes fall shut for a moment.

"Do you still have feelings for him?" I ask and find myself holding my breath, waiting for her answer.

Her forehead wrinkles. "No."

"Are you sure?"

She huffs. "Yeah, I'm sure."

"Good." Why is that good? I have no idea, but I didn't like the idea that Ethan and Blanca seem to bother her.

But jealousy can't be the reason I fuck her tonight. I live in a world with no consequences, but there are some here. The fact that I slept with this girl last night and now she's my roommate is a consequence that never occurred to me when my only goal was not to go home to my dysfunctional family.

"You leave in two months," she says.

"I do."

"So I'd rather not get serious with you."

"Okay. Me too." I fail to mention that the reason why is because I've been promised to someone else.

"Friends then?"

"Friends who kiss?" I push, knowing two months in an apartment with Sierra will lead to a serious case of blue balls.

She shrugs. Something crosses her eyes. It looks a lot like pain. "I'm not sure that's a good idea."

I sigh and turn her toward me. "So just friends?"

"I think that's best."

Although I would have loved to see what would transpire between us, she's right. I can't promise her a future. Sleeping together would be fun, but where would that leave her when I return to Sandsal and get married?

"Okay." I hold out my hand. "Friends."

She slides her hand into mine and I refuse the urge to yank her into my arms and kiss her until she's begging me to take her to bed.

"Friends." She turns her head away from me and sips the rest of her wine. "I need a refill."

I watch her back retreat as she leaves the rooftop and the door shuts. Disappointment seeps into my chest at her departure, but I turn my attention to the city of Cliffton Heights lit up in lights below and finish my beer.

I'm not surprised when Ethan and Blanca return from the other side of the roof and Sierra has yet to return. Maybe I should see if they have a spare room I can stay in, because I have no idea how I'm going to live alongside Sierra without actually having her.

My phone buzzes.

Felicia: *Mom and Dad will be divorcing when you return. Congratulations King. FYI, Princess Adelaide thinks you're doing a top-secret humanitarian expedition.*

So that seals my fate. The universe is telling me I should only be friends with Sierra, because in two months, I'll rule as king—after I marry a woman I don't know and don't love.

I take another glance at the stars before I leave the rooftop.

Fucking universe.

CHAPTER THIRTEEN

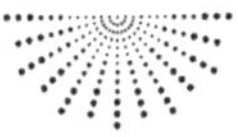

Sierra

Walking into the station to start my day, I'm already aware that it's going to be a shitty day. My day started by coming face-to-face with Adrian as I stepped out of the shower. He's not used to sharing a bathroom or he was still half asleep when he opened the door just as I pushed open the shower curtain. I watched his eyes light with flames as his gaze moved over my naked body until his already morning wood became stiffer in his boxers. I shut the curtain and turn on the cold water.

Then Andrews Bagels was out of my jalapeño bagels because of some shortage. After Mrs. Andrews apologized and laid on the guilt that she hadn't seen me in a while, I had to spend ten minutes convincing her that I'm really okay with the Blanca and Ethan thing.

Then I walk into my office and end up in an elevator with Kay and Jack. I swear they're having a secret relationship.

"Sierra!" Kay's overdramatized announcement of my arrival says I probably caught them making out or something equally gross.

Kay's at least thirty years younger, freshly out of college, while Jack has been divorced four times over with six kids between his four ex-wives. If she's looking for a sugar daddy, I can assure her it's not with a man who has to pay three-fourths of his check to child support.

"Good morning." I smile because I can't very well call them out on it.

Jack's cheeks are red and he's dodging any eye contact with me.

Yup, they're fucking and that means I'm fucked. An interview with Prince Adrian Marx doesn't come close to twenty-three-year-old pussy to a man in his fifties.

The elevator opens and I exit with a sigh, happy to be free from the uncomfortable ride.

"Hey, Mick." I wave to our receptionist, who holds up his hand for me to stop while he presses buttons, asking people to hold.

I wait until he puts down the receiver and falls back in his chair. "I can't do the job of twenty, you know what I'm saying?" He says it loud enough so Jack hears it as he walks by.

Kay stops as well. "Any messages?"

She smiles at me with a grin that says she's happy I discovered she's screwing our boss.

Good for her. Does she want me to do a cheer?

"No." Mick's tone is annoyed, and if she wasn't standing right here, I'd totally high-five him.

"See you at the staff meeting, Sierra." Her hand brushes my shoulder and I fake a smile back.

"They're screwing," I tell Mick, my work BFF.

"I told you they were last month, and you wouldn't

believe me." He crosses his arms and raises one eyebrow. It's impressive how he can do that.

"You can't trust Gill saying he saw Jack's hand squeeze her ass after a segment. The man told you he could do that eating six saltines challenge and what happened when I brought in saltines?"

"He almost choked to death," Mick deadpans.

"That's right."

Mick's eyes widen. "But in this case, Gill was right."

"Most likely." My fists clench. "*Ugh*, I mean if Georgia retires now while their relationship is all hot and steamy, I'm screwed."

" Yeah, you are."

"Thanks for the vote of confidence."

He puts one hand up in front of him. "Hey, a work spouse should not lie."

I put up my hand to match him. "True that. Thanks for always saying how it is."

He gives me a high-five. "Lunch at Hilda's? It's baked potato soup day."

My body warms just thinking about that soup. It's the best she has to offer, but she only offers it twice a month. I think it's some marketing ploy, but it works. The line can be out the door. "Let's leave fifteen minutes early just in case she runs out."

"I'll have my coat on." Mick winks.

I wave, heading down the hall, only to pass Kay walking out of the small kitchen, carrying two coffees.

"Jack's?" I ask.

"Yep, he asked me to get him a cup. With the shortage of assistants here, it's the least I can do."

I'd love to yank her by the inch-long roots of her dyed blonde hair and tell her she's a disgrace to all women, but instead I smile sweetly. "You're such a company asset. Make sure Jack thanks you the way you deserve." I wink and turn, heading to my cubicle.

A half hour later, my phone buzzes with Jack's number.

"Hey, Jack."

"Can you come to my office for a moment?"

"Sure thing."

During the one-minute trip down the hall to Jack's office, I half wonder if he's going to ask me to keep the relationship quiet. Maybe he'll try to barter, and I can say I want the anchor spot. A girl can hope, okay?

I knock lightly on his open door.

His salt-and-pepper head lifts from the paper in front of him. "Sierra, please have a seat."

I walk into the room.

"Shut the door please."

Cue my stomach squeezing so tight I might throw up. The only other time Jack has asked me to shut the door was when he asked me about a segment I did about penis implants. Can we say awkward?

Nothing good will come from this closed door situation. But I shut it and sit in the chair in front of him, leaning back to appear relaxed, as if all my insides aren't contracting.

"Thanks." He picks up his pen. "Georgia has decided to retire. This is quiet news because she's not going to announce it for a month, but I told her I needed to get things in place in the interim. I know you've been here the same amount of time as Kay and you two are next in line for a promotion. But I want to be transparent—I like having you in the field. You find interesting stories that pique people's interest."

I literally bite my tongue to keep from saying that's only because he's fucking Kay and my legs are sealed shut where he's concerned.

"I'm going to decline outside interviews, so it's really just between you and Kay, but I can't give you an answer—"

"I've got an interview with Prince Adrian Marx," I ramble before I remember I can't actually air it until after the two months are over.

He looks up from his desk with surprise. "How did you manage that?"

"I won a date with him through a charity."

"And he agreed to an interview?" I nod. "Sounds like the date went well."

I think for a moment back to that night. Unless the audience wants to know how long and thick the prince's dick is, then I need to sell the interview and not what happened on the date. Too bad just thinking about Adrian's dick has my core pulsing with longing.

"Oh, well, it wasn't a big deal. He was all proper behavior and practiced answers. But he did agree to an in-depth interview that we can do in two months."

"Two months?" His bushy eyebrows rise.

"Unfortunately, but we could tease it out. Pique the viewers' interest in the meantime."

He nods, his gaze shifting out his window at the view of the lake. "This is my problem, you understand that, right?"

"What?"

"The fact that you get people others can't. You're a go-getter and don't know the word no. If I replace Georgia with you, I fear you'll die a slow death in that job. You're meant for the action, not a boring teleprompter job."

Bullshit. With anchor, there's a shit-ton more money growing in my bank account.

"I'm sure you can find someone to replace me. Have you thought about making Kay a reporter and taking her off weather? She's resourceful in her endeavors to rise to the top as well."

His stare holds mine for a moment.

Is he going to take my bait and confront me on it?

"Well, I just wanted to let you and Kay know that you're both being considered for the promotion, but I won't make any announcements about Georgia publicly for a while. Back to this prince thing, get with the art department and tease the public with the interview. You'll have to decide what angle you're taking."

"Angle?" I stand and rest my hands on the back of the chair.

"What's the edge? We need a story to go along with the interview. If they wanted to know how he lived, they'd google the man. You need to dig up something interesting."

I nod. Right. He's so right. Though I don't have anything with a hook right now. The only thing I really know about him is he's amazing at sex and wanted a reprieve from his duties for two months.

Maybe that's where the story lies. *Why* did he want the reprieve?

THE SCREECH of the fire alarm and a billow of smoke nails me in the face when I open the apartment door. Waving at the smoke, I spot Adrian with a smoking cookie sheet in his hand.

I put down my bags and open the windows before grabbing the broom from the closet and hitting the smoke detector over and over again, unable to see the button due to the smoke filling the room. "What are you making?"

He takes the broom from me. "What are you doing?"

"I have to hit the button so the sound stops."

He finds it the first time. Lucky try.

Once the sound stops, the ringing in my ears subsides too.

"I was trying to make bagels. Evan said she wanted me to try all the different kinds, but I think I put them in too long or something."

"You think?" I wave at the charred bagels on the sheet. "Have you ever cooked?"

"Yes, of course." He shrugs.

I wait for the real answer.

"Well, no. I eat leftover pizza, but that's cold."

"Let's go get you some bagels to try." I dispose of the cookie sheet in the sink and leave a note for Rian on what happened. "Also, there's a toaster in the cupboard if you ever want to toast something again."

I show him where it is, and he appears a bit chagrined. It's a cute look on him.

We leave our apartment, and it's not until we're in broad daylight that I notice he cut his hair and didn't shave today.

At the stoplight, I run my fingers through the short hair at the back of his head. "I can't believe you cut it."

He nods. "Knox took me to his barber. I wasn't going to get it this short." His hand falls to the barely-there hair.

I chuckle. "Mistake number one. Don't go to a cop's barber."

He laughs. "You're right again."

"Well, what can I say." I examine his scruff and realize it might make him even sexier, but I keep that thought to myself. "I'm starved, so this is a good thing. I've only eaten a muffin since this morning."

"No lunch?"

We cross the street.

"No, the deli I go to was out of the baked potato soup I wanted, and acting like a pure brat, I refused to eat anything else." We reach the other side of the road and I look at him. "It's been a bad day."

"Bad from the start. I had a raging hard-on all morning."

We share a smile, and my belly warms that I wasn't the only one affected by our encounter this morning.

We walk into the Bagel Place as I feel the need to glance over my shoulder like maybe Seth will see me. I have no idea if the girl behind the counter is Evan or not, but since she doesn't say anything to Adrian, my assumption is she's not.

"We'll have one of everything and an extra jalapeño," I order for us, and Adrian's hand moves to his wallet. "No, I got this. Save your money for Rian's new cookie sheets."

He laughs and allows me to pay.

"Also all the flavors of cream cheese. He's starting here tomorrow." I point at Adrian.

The girl looks at him as though he's available. I guess he is, but she should consider that he might be with me. "Evan didn't tell me she'd hired someone. I don't usually work here, but she made me. I'm Elsie, her sister."

Adrian shakes her hand. She's definitely younger than us, by about a decade.

"She's making you try each flavor, huh? She makes every new employee do that. Don't throw up." She slides the tray over, and Adrian takes it, his dreamy smile on display.

We find a booth in the back corner, and I eat both jalapeño bagels after Adrian tried it and said it wasn't for him. He allows me to vent about Kay and Jack and all my drama. Once we're finished and he has all his notes—yes, he took notes about the bagels on his phone—he puts away our tray and we say goodbye to Elsie.

His hand falls to my lower back, and we walk out like a normal couple even though we're anything but.

CHAPTER FOURTEEN

Adrian

It's my first day of work and Evan has been patient and understanding, though I'm not sure that will last now that I've burned a second sheet of bagels.

"Hey, Evan!" I call out to her mid-morning, well after the rush—during which she only allowed me to fill boxes and cream cheese containers for the customers.

"How is it goin—" She waves her hand and opens up the back door again. "Another batch, huh?"

There's a bite to her tone, but she's yet to yell or really raise her voice at me.

"Are you sure the temperature is reading correctly?" I ask.

"Yep, ever since we got them last year."

"So they're new ovens, huh?"

"Sure are." She picks up the tray and tosses it into the large industrial stainless steel sink. "So let's go over this again. Four hundred twenty-five for seven minutes. Turn and another seven minutes. Should you write it down?"

I grab my pen and paper. "You know, my roommate and I came by last night and I tried every bagel. I really like the garlic and salt ones and the onion ones."

"My sister mentioned that you came by with your girlfriend."

"Oh, she's not my girlfriend. Just my roommate."

Evan makes round balls of dough into rings. She's skilled. "Elsie's at that age where any two people who are the opposite sex and even remotely close must be a couple. I didn't mean to assume."

"It's okay." I pick up a ball and try to mimic what she's doing.

"No." She moves her hands along the dough, showing me the spinning action again instead of my sad attempt.

"You've done this a long time, huh?"

She chuckles. "My entire life. I think I've been making bagels since I was three. It's my parents' shop, but they haven't had the time lately, so I've kind of taken it over."

"Have you always wanted to run this place?" I've never in my life had a job like this.

She balks. "No." Another small laugh comes out of her. "But I knew early on in those teen years when people ask you, 'What do you want to be when you grow up?' that this was my destiny."

"What would you want to be if you had a choice?" I ask.

"Good job." She nods at the bagel I made. "I have no idea. I feel like I have no time to think about it. But can I really complain about running a business at twenty-seven? My parents trust me with something they worked on building for years."

Yeah, I want to tell her, you can kick and scream because

it's not fair to people like us, people who have their futures decided at birth.

"Do you have a boyfriend?"

She laughs harder now. "No."

"Why not?" I try again to make my bagel look as good as hers, but it's not happening.

"Who has time for one? And all the guys around here are just…" She picks up another ball of dough, her natural movements faltering when she doesn't get the shape she wants.

I tilt my head and study her. "I feel like you're hiding something."

She looks at me and plops the bagel on the tray. "That can be made into bagel bites."

"You can trust me."

"I don't even know you." She picks up another ball, but the same thing happens again. It turns into a square bagel with hardly a hole. Whatever she's thinking about, it bothers her.

"Exactly. Aren't those the best people to tell things to?"

She seems to think about it for a minute, messes up another bagel, and as she goes to pick up another ball, I steal it from her.

"I get that the Bagel Place is going to be my life until one day maybe one of my kids wants to take it over, but does that mean I have to take on my parents' fight in order to be in charge of this business?"

"I'm not sure I follow," I say.

"Promise me whatever I say stays here?" From the seriousness in her eyes, I can see that this girl might need someone to talk to as much as I do.

I nod. "Promise."

"Okay." She pulls up a stool and puts one out for me. "There are two bagel places in Cliffton Heights. Us and Andrews Bagels."

I know that from the conversation with Ethan and Blanca, but I don't think now is the time to tell her he's my next-door neighbor.

"So I've hated the Andrews family since I was nine." She waves me off. "Forget it. It's stupid."

"You don't want to hate the Andrews family?" I pry a little.

"My dad and Mr. Andrews were best friends, and I was pretty good friends with their son, Seth. And then something happened…" She stares at the stainless steel table. "Since then, they hate each other. The families hate each other. So Seth hates me, and I pretend like I hate him." She stares at the tray of messed up bagels. "Ugh. Please distract me from my pity party and tell me something about yourself."

The one plus to working here is that Evan doesn't know who I am. If I tell her we have something in common—that we were both destined to walk in our parents' footsteps instead of blazing our own trail—it would ruin us sitting here shooting the shit while making bagels.

"I slept with my roommate and now she's put us in the friend zone."

"Ouch. Sorry." Her scrunched up nose says she's sincere.

"Yeah. She's doing the smart thing. We shouldn't get involved with one another."

"Why? Obviously if you slept together, there's something there."

There's a spark with Sierra that I've never felt with anyone, but the fact that I care about her is the same reason I refuse to sleep with her. Not to mention I have nothing to offer except a life of scrutiny even if we could somehow be together. Then there's Princess Adelaide. Am I supposed to leave her high and dry?

"I don't want to hurt her."

She narrows her eyes to me. "Why do you think you'll hurt her?"

Because I can't give her a normal life.

"I'm not ready to settle down yet." I shrug as though that's all it is.

She knocks her shoulder against mine. "What is with guys? Why is settling down so bad? If you find that person, you're one hundred percent yourself around and who makes you happy you're not *settling* for anything. I think "settling down" was some stupid name made up by a perpetual bachelor. Just because you fall in love doesn't mean you're *settling* for anything. I can imagine my husband and me traveling together and seeing the world. Of course, then who will run the bagel shop?" She frowns.

As I watch the reality of her dream splitting open at the seams, it confirms that some of us can't live our dream life and that's just a fact.

"Maybe you could find someone to run it for you, or maybe your sister will want to take over." I try to close up that seam for her because I want one of us to get what we really want.

The chime on the door rings and she stands from the stool. "Okay, so four hundred twenty-five for seven minutes, right? Turn and then another seven?"

"Got it." I nod.

She laughs and heads out.

I hope she gets everything she dreamed of. I also feel like an impromptu meeting between her and Seth needs to happen. Though I usually hate meddling.

I SMELL LIKE SO many flavors of bagels that I need to strip

these clothes off and give them to my… well, I guess *I* need to wash them.

When I enter the apartment, Sierra is sitting at the table with her checkbook out and her laptop in front of her.

"How was your first day? Rian made you a cake even though you ruined her baking sheets." She points at a small round vanilla-iced cake on the table, a multitude of colored sprinkles along the sides and top.

"That's nice of her." I smile. "Would you like to go shopping with me to buy replacement cookie sheets for her?"

"Sure, right after I finish confirming that I can't quit my job." She closes her laptop. "Why do you want to live a normal life? It sucks."

I open a Coke from the fridge and sit down with her. "I owe you for the rent."

"No, I got it. We made a deal."

"We made a deal that I could live here."

"But your parents cut you off?"

"They did, but Jean sent me money when he sent my things. Plus I have a job."

A smile tips her lips as though she thinks I'm naive. "It's minimum wage."

"True, but it's something. Hold up." I go into my room, lift my boxers, and count out the cash needed for two months' rent. When I return to the kitchen, I lay it on the table in front of Sierra.

"All cash?" she asks, staring at it.

"Yes. Listen, I have a question."

She counts the cash. There was a time I would be insulted by that. "Yeah?"

"Will you teach me how to do laundry?"

She stops counting and stares at me for a moment. "Just put your stuff with mine and I'll do it."

I finish off the Coke. "I'd rather learn."

She studies me for a second. "Okay, grab your laundry." She shuts her checkbook. "Let's go."

Fifteen minutes later, I walk out of my bedroom with my suitcase full of dirty clothes.

Sierra laughs. "That's one way to carry your dirty clothes."

"I need to buy one of those things." I point at her duffle bag thing.

"We'll get you one. In the meantime, let's go before it gets too crowded. Nothing worse than having your clothes wet in the washing machine and not being able to find a dryer."

We hit the street and pass Ink Envy, walking down one block.

"Hey." I stop us after the third time she switches the big sack of clothes from one arm to the other. "Trade me."

I give her the handle of my suitcase to pull behind her and put her duffle on my shoulder.

"Thanks," she says, but there's a surprise in her voice that I hate. Has this woman never been cared for like she should be?

"It's the least I can do, what with you teaching me all these domestic acts."

"Oh, it's not that bad. I kind of like showing you the ropes of being an everyday Joe."

We walk into the laundromat and she's right, there's a man and a woman near the back, fighting over a dryer.

"Do they not have enough dryers?" I whisper once we find two washing machines next to one another.

"Drying can take longer than washing." She opens up her duffle bag. "So, we'll do ours together if you don't mind."

"So our underwear gets to slide around together but not us, huh?" I tease.

Her tongue slides across her bottom lip and I fixate on it, my dick chubbing in my pants. "Keep up that talk and I'm going to sit on the washer during the spin cycle and torture you with my moaning."

I inhale a quick breath and stare at her. The more I'm around her, the harder it is to keep my hands to myself.

"So we split the whites and darks." Sierra is all business now. How does this electricity that sparks between us not bother her? She looks at my suitcase. "Unzip your luggage and start putting all your whites here and colors there."

I watch a pair of her white panties go into the washer, then the dark pair I stripped off of her that first night we met.

"Why do you think women's panties and bras are so sexy and men just get boxers, briefs, or boxer briefs?" I sort out my laundry as she watches.

"I think there's some sexy underwear for men out there. You could get an elephant trunk pair." She chuckles.

"Yeah, no."

"Then don't complain. Plus I think a woman's private area is much prettier than a man's, so we get pretty things to cover them."

I lean in close to her, her perfume like an aphrodisiac. "So you didn't find my private area pretty?"

She laughs and turns her head so that our faces are nose to nose. "Would you really be happy if I said you had a *pretty* cock?"

Damn. The word cock coming from her mouth has me picturing her mouth around said cock.

I lean back. "True. Very true. Let's start this conversation over again."

She laughs. "I think someone has sex on the brain."

"And you don't?" I ask because please tell me she's in as much pain as I am when we're around one another.

"I never said that, did I?"

Before I have the chance to respond, she cuts the conversation short and rambles on about detergent and payment.

Once the clothes are in the washer, she turns to me. "Now we wait."

Oh great, more downtime with Sierra when all I really want is to take her into the bathroom in the back and get dirtier than the clothes we put in the washing machine.

CHAPTER FIFTEEN

Sierra

I never knew someone could have so many sexual jokes regarding laundry. Wasn't he in agreement up on that roof that we should remain friends and nothing more? Because from the way he keeps looking at me, he wants me on my knees with my mouth open.

"Grab that dryer!" I tell him, hurrying to put our wet clothes in a bin.

He stands in front of it with his arms crossed. Seconds later, a little old lady walks up to him.

"Excuse me," she says, her hand on his hip, pushing him out of the way.

"I'm sorry, we're going to use this one."

He's so polite it kills me. Can he really tell a little old lady no?

"It's first come, first serve. You should tell your lady

friend to move a little quicker." She pushes him some more and he stares at her as if she's crazy.

I'm so distracted by the scene until I realize I need to get the clothes out faster.

"I was here first," he tells her, using that smile that gleams. His prince smile.

"You're not here unless you have clothes in the dryer. You have no clothes, so you have no dryer." She pushes her cart into him a bit.

"Ma'am," he says with practiced sincerity.

I roll my cart over, but the woman keeps hitting him until he finally raises his hands in defeat.

"You need to learn the rules!" she says, angrily putting her clothes into the dryer on the low level. "Tall people use the top ones!"

I bite my lip to keep from laughing and Adrian huffs, staring her down. I'm not sure his size intimidates her at all.

"I guess she doesn't recognize you," I say.

"Man, this place is ruthless."

"It's okay. We'll wait for the next one."

The lady looks at me, goes back to her clothes, then turns back in my direction and stands to her four-foot-eleven stature. "Sierra Sanders?"

I look around the room. How many other people will circle around us because they think I'm some popular celebrity before they realize I'm not? "Yeah."

"I watch you every night." She takes out her clothes and nods in Adrian's direction. "Is he yours?"

I can't stop the smile as I look at Adrian and back at her. "Kind of."

"What the hell does kind of mean?" she says with a scrunched up face that highlights her wrinkles.

"It's complicated," I answer.

"Truth is she put me in the friend zone," Adrian leans in

and stage-whispers so the entire laundromat hears him. I elbow him and he fakes hurt. "She's brutal, I tell you."

A few people laugh around us.

I roll my eyes at him. "He's messing around."

"Take the dryer," she says, wheeling her cart away. "I'm sure you have to get to a new story. When you unveiled that social security scam, the entire floor was in awe."

"No. Please." I lead her back to the dryer.

"Nonsense. I don't have anything but my crosswords to do."

I eye Adrian and he puts her clothes in the dryer. She catches me looking at him and quickly snatches her bra out of his hand.

"I appreciate it, but you can't be touching my delicates." After she's put a few items in the dryer, she looks at him. "That was sweet of you though. She's pretty and all, but she's not very smart if she's letting you stay out in the wild."

A few more snickers from the other patrons.

"I treat her like a princess," Adrian carries on with a shit-eating grin. "I have a jet plane to sweep her off to my big castle, but she doesn't want any of it."

Little does this woman know that it's true.

"She's foolish. You two would make some beautiful kids," she says.

"I think so too." He stares at me as if he's proposed and I've turned him down.

The woman shuts the dryer door and Adrian quickly puts change in the machine. "That's for trying to convince her to snatch me up." He gives her his prince smile again.

I shake my head because we agreed that we'd be friends. In less than two months, he's leaving on his jet plane back to his big castle. It's not like me going with him is even a possibility. Uproot my life just to have to rebuild it again when things fall apart between us? No, thank you.

She pats his cheek. "Oh you. I'd marry you if I was fifty years younger."

"What's age but a number?" Adrian says.

Laughter at his not-funny jokes from the people around us once again commences.

"That's what I say all the time. But..." She crooks her finger for him to come closer. "Have sex as much as you can when you're younger. The hips lose something after the first replacement. So do the Kama Sutra stuff when you're young."

Adrian tries to fight his smile because she's dead serious. "Will do." He nods at her.

A dryer opens up and I hurry to get our clothes inside it.

Adrian comes over and helps me. "What do you think about her advice?"

"I'm curious as to why you threw me under the bus."

"What do you mean?"

"I mean we *both* agreed to do the friends thing. You made it sound like you're ready to get down on bended knee."

A look I can't decipher crosses his face before it vanishes with the emergence of his cocky smile. "I haven't been shy that I want you."

"You want me for two months, and then you'll take your jet plane home. Where does that leave us?"

He's silent because he doesn't have an answer either.

"So from now on, no throwing me under the bus." I grumpily shove the last of the wet clothes into the dryer.

He holds up his three fingers.

"Do they have Boy Scouts in Sandsal?"

"We sure do." He lowers his hand. "But I was kicked out in Webelos."

I laugh. "How does the prince get kicked out of a group?"

"Because I was a terror. I've never been good at following rules."

"Still, I thought the prince would get special treatment."

He closes the door and puts change in the dryer. "Not always."

"Ice cream?" I change topics because I need to get out of here and into the fresh, crisp air before I suffocate and make a bad decision by sleeping with Adrian again.

"My treat for you helping me." He takes my hand.

The old lady winks at him when she sees our physical contact.

We're not even a week into this thing and I'm already halfway to convincing myself that I'd be fine with sleeping with him for two months and saying goodbye.

It's been three weeks since Adrian moved in. I come home from work, exhausted from the game of who will get Georgia's position. I passed Kay getting coffee for Jack once again, then I spotted them returning from lunch in his car.

Probably went to make out somewhere.

Gross.

I hear the television as I put my key in the door, which puts a smile on my face because I forgot this was Adrian's day off. He's really become used to normal life lately. We frequent the laundromat together every week. He even baked a cake with Rian the other day. It might've been lopsided and a little dense, but he gets an A for effort.

I open the door to find *Blue Bloods* on. Adrian isn't alone.

My stomach sinks as the two of them turn around to face me.

"Blanca?" I ask.

"Hey, I caught Adrian on my way home from work this afternoon. I took a half day because it's... you know." She looks down at herself. Her period. Got it. "And we were talking about how we both need to catch up, so we figured an afternoon of watching *Blue Bloods* was in order."

There's a pizza box on the coffee table, and they're both dressed in sweatpants and T-shirts. I close my eyes for a moment to quiet the jealousy. She has Ethan. This is a friends things. I wouldn't care if she was here with Dylan, Seth, or Knox.

"Oh, that's nice. How far did you get?" Acting as if I'm not freaking out isn't working.

"Not far." Blanca comes over to the kitchen. Adrian pauses the television and picks up the pizza box. While he's distracted, she runs her hand down my arm. "We were just watching television."

"I know," I whisper, not looking at her.

And I do, don't I? I can't be jealous. The man flirts every chance he gets. I've had to stop myself so many times from kissing him, knowing he'd kiss me back.

"Okay. I should get home anyway. I had a fun day, Adrian."

He waves goodbye. "Me too. Next hooky day, me, you, Donnie Wahlberg."

"Definitely!" She slips out and shuts the door.

"I didn't mean to spoil your day," I say, grabbing a water from the fridge.

He puts the pizza box on the kitchen table, a puzzled look on his face. "You didn't."

"Make sure you clean up after yourself. You've been leaving stuff around lately and Rian is getting annoyed."

He stops all movement and looks at me. "Did she tell you that?"

I turn and walk to my room. "I can tell. We've been friends a long time. I have to lie down." I shut my bedroom door and flop onto my bed.

Better to lock myself in here before he gets an upfront view of my jealousy.

A soft knock on my door tells me I was too transparent out there.

"I'm going to lie—"

"Talk to me," he says, coming in and shutting the door.

Me, him, and a bed is not a good idea. Not right now.

"I just had another bad day. I think I need to quit, honestly."

He sits down beside me on the bed.

Bad idea.

"What's with the attitude?" he asks.

"I don't have an attitude."

"You do realize that I don't want anyone but you and that if I can't have you, I'm not going to resort to being with someone else?"

I didn't.

"Why do you keep putting it out there like there's some hope for us? If we sleep together and then get annoyed with one another, we have to stay living together. Not good. And if we try to make a go of it, you're leaving anyway and going back to a life in a completely different country with a million obligations that don't include me."

"Save me the speech. I've heard it a million times." The irritation in his voice is clear. "I'm just saying that I'm not going to fuck your friend, okay?" He heads toward the door.

I hate that he's angry. "Why are you mad?"

He faces me and I notice his hands are clenched into fists. "Because I want you so badly. Every night when I go to bed, I beat off to the memories of the one night I had you. I beat off to images of me taking you on every surface in this apartment. And you seem to just take it in stride like it doesn't bother you until you see me with your friend."

I pop up off the bed. "You think I don't want you? My body physically aches for you. I lie in bed and imagine you beating off with the hope it's to me. But in a little over a month you're going to walk out that door and I'll never see you again. I can't risk it."

He crosses the room, his finger landing under my chin and bringing my face to his. "Who hurt you?"

I close my eyes, trying to hide the tears building.

It was just a bad day at work. Shut it off. Push down the emotions.

"Sierra, open your eyes." When I don't open them, he leans closer. "Open your eyes, baby."

I open them and two fat tears roll down my cheeks. "Let's go for a walk."

CHAPTER SIXTEEN

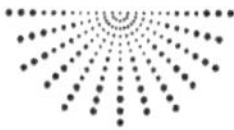

Sierra

"I thought we would walk around downtown Cliffton Heights," I say after we step off the train in Manhattan, only to hop into a taxi.

"We got to know each other so much the night we met in Manhattan that way. The apartment is great, and I thank you and Rian for letting me stay there, but it's crowded. I get no alone time with you."

"You want alone time with me?" My chest feels buoyant from his words.

He quirks his eyebrow at me and shakes his head. "Who told you you weren't important." He isn't asking it as a question, but more a statement to himself.

Pain and sadness seep into all those wounds that are exposed like the parched desert floor.

Not because anyone told me I don't matter. Quite the

opposite actually. But wounds don't always come from words; they also come from actions.

We arrive at the Brooklyn Bridge and I laugh. "We're heading back down memory lane, huh?" I climb out, and he joins me after paying the cab driver.

"Shall we revisit our first date?" He holds out his hand.

"I'd love to."

We walk hand in hand, but the weather is colder and it's not quite as enjoyable as that perfect fall night the first time we were here. There are fewer pedestrians and the ones who are braving it are wrapped up in scarves and gloves.

"I feel unprepared," I say.

"Yeah, I'm used to my servants telling me if I need extra attire," he says so convincingly. He checks me out from the corner of his eye. "I'm kidding. I didn't realize the weather would be so much colder here."

"It's the river," I say but snuggle closer to him for warmth.

"Listen, we made a deal to be friends and that won't change when it's time for me to return home. I wanted to talk to you about something… I've noticed these past weeks that you hold a lot in."

"Please don't say you brought me here for some Psych 101 discussion to discover the hidden secrets of Sierra Sanders?"

He chuckles. "I have a shit-ton of secrets and I need a confidant, so I figure we should dish all our crap to one another, promising to never repeat it."

"So, what? Neither one of us can tell anyone else how screwed up we are?"

"Pretty much." He stops us midway over the bridge and we look over the railing at the dark water below that matches the blanket of dark sky above us. "So talk. Blanca made an off-the-cuff comment about your mom passing away when you were young. And when I looked at her like I didn't know what she was talking about, she shut up quick." He pauses, I think to give me time to digest what he said.

If I tell him, he'll know. I'll no longer be the woman he slept with and lived with. I will forever be the girl whose mom died in war.

"She's a good friend, you know? Shitty what happened, but she's definitely got your back."

I nod. I've known that my entire life. Even when I was upset that she went to a different college. I knew it was what was best for her future, but instead of being happy for her, all I saw was that she was choosing to leave me.

Maybe Adrian is right. If I vomit out all my problems, maybe I'll feel better. Worst case scenario, he's not attracted to me anymore afterward. Maybe that will help relieve some of the sexual tension we've been living with.

"I was born to Sergeant and Sergeant Sanders." I turn to him. "Is this what you expected?"

His smirk says he enjoys my sense of humor. "Military parents?"

I bite my lip and nod. I want to get this over with quickly so I can tell him my mom died and he can give me the sad eyes and we can move on. "Yep. Both fought in the Iraq War, but only one sergeant returned home."

He releases my hand and touches my forearm. "I'm sorry." He's sincere.

Of course he is. Everyone always is.

I glance at him. It's like the moonlight was made to cast down on Prince Adrian Marx. He's beautiful and sexy and kindhearted. Nothing like I thought he'd be when I stalked him in those magazines and online gossip blogs.

"I know."

There it is, the moment when the eyes grow even sadder

because losing a mother is thought of as worse. I lost the nurturer, the caregiver. The woman who was to teach me how to put on eyeliner, to talk about womanhood, go prom dress shopping.

Turning on my heels, I walk down the path, but coming closer to the Brooklyn side after talking about my parents only makes it harder for me to breathe. "Everyone is always sorry."

He catches up to me. "What's it like?"

I glance at him, not understanding what he's asking.

"I don't mean to pry. Sorry." He stuffs his hands into his pockets because I've opted to wrap my arms around myself.

I'm sure he feels the rapid chill coming off me. It always happens when I talk about my mom.

"It's fine. I was ten. The government allowed my parents to be deployed at different times. My dad went first, and my whole family hoped the war would be over quickly and he would return safely. The war continued, so one month after my dad returned, my mom went. Six months later, she died when her Humvee was ambushed." Repeating the details is easy. It's like a speech I've rehearsed a million times.

When someone hears that my mother died when I was ten, there are questions in their eyes. Some pry and others try not to, but I can tell they want to know how because they want her to have died in a way that they can't. After they hear the details, it's like they think they'll be safe as long as they don't become a soldier and go to Iraq.

He remains quiet as we walk.

"Anyway, my dad raised me, but truth is when they say it takes a village, in my case it truly did. I owe a lot to the families who took care of us. Afterward, my dad didn't reenlist, and he fell into a depression for a few years."

"Are you close?"

He probably assumes we would be. Wouldn't the shared

grief over the woman we loved most in the world bond two people together? Maybe in some families, but not mine.

"Not really."

"So he's not depressed anymore?" His voice sounds almost hopeful.

I laugh from thinking about the last time I had to witness his new girlfriend making herself comfortable in our kitchen. The one where my mom would make us meals with love. "Not at all."

We reach Brooklyn.

"Let's go." He raises his hand for a taxi, and one stops for us. I can't imagine he would ever have a problem getting one with the authority he exudes.

"Where are we going?" I ask after I crawl in.

"We're in Brooklyn. Let's go to your childhood house. Show me where you grew up."

My eyes narrow as I wonder why he wants to know so much about me. "Why?"

"I'm curious how the other half lives." He laughs and knocks his shoulder to mine in the back of the cab.

"Okay, but it's not that interesting. We don't have gold plates and a servant to make us a late night snack."

He shakes his head, but his smile says he's amused.

We arrive in Carroll Gardens before I'm prepared. The taxi asks for a specific address, but I instruct him to pull over.

"We'll walk," I say.

My footfalls on the pavement of my old neighborhood while Adrian pays the taxi driver.

"Which way?" Adrian asks when he joins me on the sidewalk.

Although it's getting later, there are still a lot of people out on the streets, coming from dinner or wherever they were. We walk down the sidewalk, and I point out the bakery that has the best black and white cookies, wishing they were open for me to share one with him, then the cafes and small Italian restaurants. The neighborhood has evolved, with Brooklyn becoming a more popular place to live, but there's still a sense of the neighborhood I grew up in. The people who care for and look out for one another.

"Where did you live? Does your dad still live there?"

I point forward. "Four blocks and a left."

He tugs at my sleeve. "Show me."

"Unless you want to be stuck in a conversation with my father, I suggest we stick to the common areas."

He shrugs. "I'll talk to your father."

Just the thought has my heart constricting. "And tell him what?"

"How enamored I am with his daughter. Come on." He tugs my sleeve. "Are you embarrassed of me?"

"No, but—"

"Then come on." He walks backward in front of me, almost taunting me. Unfortunately, nothing good comes from when people challenge me.

"You asked for it."

We walk the four blocks, stopping at a liquor store to buy a bottle of wine because Adrian doesn't believe in showing up empty-handed. This entire thing seems weird and awkward and I'm thankful I never lied to him about my childhood. I might have omitted some things, but my dad won't talk about my mom anyway. That's a taboo subject in our house.

Turning down my street, the same feeling that washes over me every time I visit envelops me. My heartbeat races, but at the same time, my heart feels as if it weighs as much as an elephant. After my mom died, I lost my sense of home. The house became walls and floors and a roof—shelter.

I see a sign in the distance that looks as though it could be in front of our house, but I squint, unable to tell through the darkness.

There's no way.

My feet move a little faster, though Adrian's able to keep up with his long strides.

"You have to be fucking kidding me."

CHAPTER SEVENTEEN

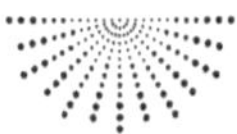

Sierra

We stop, and my eyes zero in on the For Sale sign. All the reluctance to come to my childhood home and introduce my dad to a man he'll never see again is replaced with anger, heating my veins until my skin burns and I'm stomping up the walkway, digging in my purse for my keys.

I was here last month, and he said nothing. So help me God, if this is his new girlfriend's idea, there's going to be a hair-pulling girl fight.

Adrian is oblivious, waiting for me to get my key—I half wonder whether it will still work—into the lock and open up the door. "Did you not know your dad had it up for sale?"

Guess he's not oblivious.

"No," I say, seething.

The door opens and it's complete darkness inside. My dad's been an insomniac since my mother's death, so I'm pretty certain he's not sleeping. When I flick on the lights, my footsteps stop and Adrian runs right into my back, his large hands on my biceps to prevent me from falling forward.

New furniture, new paint. Where are all the pictures? Adrenaline pumps through my veins and I step out of Adrian's hold, flicking on light after light, inspecting every room and every surface.

He's erased *her*.

He's erased *me*.

Every picture is a flower or a destination he's never been to. All the army signs and "proud to be a soldier" stuff has been stripped away too.

"Sierra?" Adrian calls when I open the basement door and pound down the steps. "What's going on?"

He follows me, but my search only becomes more frantic. Where did he put them? He doesn't deserve them anymore if he's going to stuff them in a box in the basement.

Then I spot them. Three boxes filled with pictures of our family. The only remembrance of my mother is her folded flag that's still on the mantel upstairs.

The vault I've locked up so securely cracks as if someone pounded it with a sledgehammer, and a tear falls down my cheek. Part relief that they're here, part pain that they are.

"Take this one." I pick up a box and shove it into Adrian's arms. Picking up the second one, I put it on top of the other one in his arms. He staggers for a second to handle the weight but gets a hold of the boxes. I pick up the third. "Let's go."

"Sierra, let's talk to your father."

I shake my head. "He doesn't deserve to have these anymore. They're coming home with me."

Adrian doesn't move, so I pass him and go up the stairs.

"I honestly think you should talk to your father." Adrian follows me.

I place the box on the kitchen table and rush upstairs to see what else my dad has done to the house. All the pictures that my mom perfectly placed up the stairs—my birth to ten, the first day of school, our first family photo, my first visit with Santa—every framed picture has been stripped from the wall. There's not even a sign of them. No rectangular patch to show how many years it was there because... wait.

I flip on the light switch on the stairs. Sure enough, he painted my room too.

"*Ugh!*" I scream, my feet unable to move fast enough for me.

I open my dad's bedroom door, and there's all the proof I need that he's erased her from his life. Their wedding picture no longer stands on the corner of the dresser. Her jewelry box that held her wedding ring that she didn't want to wear into combat and all the heirlooms of her family gone. Packed away somewhere as though they're meaningless.

"Hey." Adrian's hand runs down the length of my arm.

My throat tightens the more I realize that it no longer feels like my mother in this room. And all I can think about is how *she* sleeps here. Fae. The fake-blonde I'm beginning to hate.

Tearing away from Adrian and the room that holds good and bad memories, I head into my old room. He's vanquished any sign of my life in this house as well. My purple bedspread has been replaced with a gray one. My track medals no longer hang next to my dresser. Pulling open the closet door, I see that my Girl Scout uniform no longer hangs on the rack with my prom dress and other memories. There are boxes labeled "Sierra's room" stuffed in the corner of the closet, so I sit down and pry one open.

"Sierra," Adrian says.

I know he doesn't understand my reaction. He ran away from his family. I did too, all those years ago. I abandoned my dad as soon as I was old enough, but I never thought he'd do this without talking to me.

I look up and Adrian's standing in the doorway of my walk-in closet, sadness in his eyes. I hate that look and everything it represents.

"You know what? I'm sorry, I'm gonna stay here. You should probably go." I stand and walk out of the room, knowing he'll probably follow me.

"What? I'm not going anywhere without you."

"There's no reason for you to stay. I'm just going to figure this all out and I'll probably move this stuff somewhere, a storage locker or something. I'll see you back at the apartment, okay?" I open the front door, but he stands in my dad's new living room.

"Sierra?"

"I'm fine."

He inhales a deep breath and his gaze bores into mine.

"What?" I ask.

"You're hurting."

"I just need to handle this. Please go home."

"No." He shakes his head and sits in a chair I don't recognize.

"Adrian."

He raises his eyebrows from the bite of my tone. "I'm not five and you're not my mother. You can't force me to do something I don't want to do." He crosses his leg, his ankle resting on his knee. Relaxed as though he's waiting for a drink to be delivered so he can have a long conversation with an old friend.

"This isn't your business." I swallow the lump forming in my throat. Will he leave so I can do this by myself and break down alone?

"Kind of is."

"How do you figure?" I ask.

A couple walks by the house, looks through the open front door, and continues on down the street. I used to know everyone who lived on this block.

"I'm your friend. It's a friend's duty to make their friend feel better when said friend is upset."

I almost laugh at his absurd way of bringing up this topic up now. "Friends know when friends need space."

"Friends give hugs when said friend is about to cry." He slides up to the edge of the cushion and holds out his arms.

"Said friend needs to go home so the other friend can deal with her family."

He shakes his head. "Said friend wants to help the other friend."

I hold up my hand. "Please stop with the friend talk."

"So friend stays?" he asks.

"No." I stomp my foot like a toddler.

He leans back in the chair again, exuding patience. "Yes, said friend is gonna stay until the other friend is honest."

I slam the front door, my amusement morphing to anger that he won't leave me be. Let me grieve, let me be angry without an audience. "Said friend is annoying the other friend."

"Said friend is sorry." His smirk says he's not going to go anywhere.

I move my hand to where my dad always keeps the remote—in the basket on the end table—but it's not there. Looking down, all I find is a folded up piece of paper. I open it to find the itinerary of a trip.

"You're shittin' me," I say, reading how Dad and Fae are on vacation in Tahiti right now.

I drop the paper and scour for the remote, finding it on the other end table. It's not even positioned in my dad's military OCD, pointed in the direction of the television. It's all cockeyed.

Picking it up, I press the power button and toss the remote to Adrian. "Said friend can watch television while the other friend handles things upstairs."

Without waiting for his answer, I run upstairs, refusing to look at the now-blank stairway wall. Sitting on the floor of my closet, I open a box and find my mom's jewelry box.

When did this become mine and not his?

I slide both hands along the edge of the jewelry box, my knuckles running along the rough cardboard as it easily slides out of the box. I place the jewelry box on the floor and brush my fingertips along the inscription.

Nothing in here is as beautiful as you.

MY HANDS SHAKE as I open the box. Tears overflow, seeing her wedding ring in the slot next to her high school class ring and the emerald ring my dad gave her on their anniversary.

I sort through her earrings and necklaces, some heirlooms from her grandmothers, and other pieces she bought on her own—some expensive, some cheap. The small round hoops she wore on a daily basis except for the weekends she had to go to the Army Reserve.

Lifting the first tray, I gently place it on the carpet. The bottom is filled with jewelry boxes. Boxes I don't remember from when I was younger and would sneak a look at her jewelry as she got ready for dates with my dad.

I open the dark boxes one by one, finding medal after medal, ribbon after ribbon. Everything she earned during her time in the Army Reserve. The last box I pick up is more worn than the previous ones, as though it's been opened more than the others.

My heart hammers, knowing this is something important, something he looked at often. Because it's with the rest of her military accolades, I'm not surprised when her dog tags lay on the cotton in the box. The last time I saw them, they were clenched in my dad's fists after he'd passed out.

I pick them up, reading the hammered out lettering, my thumb running along the length.

SANDERS
Abigail M
134 50 8920
O Positive
Catholic

HE'S ready to let her go and leave all her memories, all of our family memories to me? How could he do that? How can he forget her? Is Fae that great of a lay that's she stripped the deep love my father had for my mother? The love that made him lay in that bed day after day? The love that paralyzed him from being the father he was for the first ten years of my life?

One tear tumbles down, catching another tear until streaks form down both cheeks. I pound my fist on the floor, clutching her dog tags and falling forward as I hold them as close as I can to my chest.

"Help me remember her. Don't ever let me forget her. Don't ever let me do what my dad is doing and let her rot in a box," I murmur, hoping the universe or God is listening.

My breath is labored as reality sets in like it did when I

was ten and realized she was never returning. Somehow, the fact that my dad is stripping her from his life makes me feel as though I'm losing her all over again.

As if someone is listening to me, two strong arms pick me up off the floor and carry me to the bed.

A memory floats up from the back of my mind of a time I was in a different set of arms. There was a storm and I sneaked into my parents' room, but my mom walked me back, saying Daddy had an early morning. I was terrified she was going to tuck me in and say it was just a storm and I'd be fine, but after she laid me down, she slid into my twin-size bed and held me until dawn.

I feel as safe in these arms as I did then.

CHAPTER EIGHTEEN

Adrian

I'm partly responsible for the fact that Sierra's tears are staining my shirt. I forced her to talk to me, to get everything out in the open. Never did I think we'd uncover all this.

I tried to let her sort through her things upstairs. I tried to concentrate on some reality show drama where people were arguing about stupid shit and forget that whatever she was doing, she was hurting. But I couldn't. She needed to know I'm here for her.

As night went on, she fell into a deeper sleep, nestled into my side with her arm draped over my stomach. I can't remember the last time I slept with a woman. Clothed, that is.

Being a prince, I never tried to have a long-term relationship, mostly because I never knew what a woman's intentions were. It's hard to trust anyone when people view you as a means to an end. The title of queen being the ultimate end.

Now that dawn sneaks in through her open curtains and lights her childhood bedroom, the aftermath of her tears and her heartbreak are more visible on her sleeping face.

An overwhelming sense of admiration hits me square in the heart. She's so fierce and feisty, but under all that hides a little girl who lost her mom. Those wounds aren't healed. The fact her father told her nothing of the sale of the house says her relationship with him is strained at best.

Earlier, I picked up the piece of paper that says her father is in Tahiti until next week sometime. I didn't get the impression Sierra knew anything about that either.

She stirs, stopping all my rambling thoughts. I brush back her beautiful red hair, and she tries to slyly wipe the drool that fell from her mouth. I laugh and she looks at me, her cheeks turning my favorite shade of pink. I love to make that blush appear. If she was ever mine, I'd have fun making her blush all the time and discovering new ways to do so.

"I'm sorry." She sits up and my hand lazily runs circles on her back.

"Why?"

"Because. Look at me. You had to lie in bed with me all night. I swear this isn't me." She pulls the blankets off herself, but I lock my arm around her waist and force her back down. "What are you doing?"

"I'm enjoying this. It's okay to be vulnerable with me."

"What are you talking about? This all just took me by surprise." She looks off in the distance instead of at me.

I use my finger along her chin to bring her eyes back to me. "I understand how you feel."

She scoffs.

Her reaction takes me by surprise.

"I hate when people say that. People who have both parents still."

I nod. "True. You're right. Maybe I don't understand exactly how you feel, but hiding your grief isn't going to make it disappear."

She gnaws at her cheek, pulling her legs up to her chest and locking her arms around them. "I'm not hiding it. It was seventeen years ago."

"But yet, you're mad at your dad for moving on with his life."

Her head whips in my direction. "You don't know anything about it." She unhooks her arms from her legs and stands from the bed. "I'll pack these things and come back later before he returns."

"You gotta stop running. You have to face this." I sit up in her bed, leaning forward and resting my forearms on my thighs.

She turns and looks at me over her shoulder from the floor of her closet, tucking her mom's dog tags in a box as though they weren't what broke her last night. How many layers of denial are packed over that raw open wound of hers?

"Why do you care?"

She has the right to ask the question. I laid up most of the night asking myself the same thing. Most of the time, the minute things get more than fun with a woman, I remove myself from the situation. I have no idea if it's what's going on with my own family or the fact that she let me move in with her, but I do care.

"How come you let me move into your apartment? Was it because you were infatuated with me?"

Small wrinkles form on her forehead. "I wasn't and I'm not currently *infatuated* with you."

I shrug. "I saw the magazines, and you were able to answer all those questions to win the dating contest."

Her scowl increases for a second, but she forces it down. "Infatuated is not the same as intrigued."

I shrug. "Okay, however you want to describe it, but how come?"

"I wanted the interview."

I stare at her long and hard, hoping my glare is enough to crack her.

"The sex then."

I raise my eyebrows. "And yet you played the friends card immediately?"

She huffs, her attention shifting to the box, putting the jewelry box back in the cardboard box and crisscrossing the edges to close it.

"What do you want from me?" Her voice is strained and tired and angry.

I wish I could figure out why I'm forcing this. Why I want to make sure that when I leave here in five weeks, she's whole so she can find someone to love her. As much as the thought of another man's hands on her spurs a bout of Hulk-like anger, I want her to be happy.

"I want you to admit that you're hurting. It's only the two of us here. No one else will witness it. Just be straight with me."

She stands and heads toward the door, but I beat her there to stop her.

"Adrian," she says as though she's warning me.

"No, Sierra, admit it."

"What?"

"Admit how scared you are. Admit how much you miss your mom. Admit whatever you want but hiding the wounds won't make those feelings go away."

She tries to slide around me, but I grip her arms and bring her back in front of me.

"I'm going to kick you in the nuts."

"Fine, but you're ruining your chance at having kids then."

She pauses. "Will you stop saying things like that?"

"Like what?"

She steps back. "Like there's a chance for us. Acting like you want me. You're here for another month and then you'll go back home. Stop trying to act like we could be together."

I step toward her and she steps backward until her bum hits the dresser. "Maybe we could."

Fuck. What am I saying?

Stop talking. You know you can't make these promises.

My hands grip her waist. "But first I want you to be real with me."

She turns away like an indignant child, purposely avoiding eye contact. "And then you'll stop this whole us being together bullshit?"

I nod, fully aware that I'm probably lying.

"I already told you. My mom died. My dad fell into a depression. Most of my teenage years I spent at friends' houses. Now he's packed her up in boxes like she's an old sweater he doesn't want anymore." She looks me square in the eye, no sign of tears, her back ramrod-straight.

"Those are facts," I say. She places both hands on my chest and pushes me, but I grip her wrists in my hands. "Tell me how you *feel*."

"There's nothin—"

"Just tell me," I persist.

"I have no idea what you're talking about." She wiggles and I release my grip, wanting her to be willing to open up and let me in.

"Tell me. You can trust me."

She stops fighting to get away and closes her eyes with a ragged sigh. "I miss her. I'm scared every day that I'm forgetting her. Every day after her death when I'd walk into this house, I felt her. Like she could be in the kitchen waiting for me. Or in the basement packing up her gear. She used to be here, and last night I didn't feel her anymore." A tear runs down her cheek. "He packed her up and now she's really gone."

I pull her into my arms as tightly as I can, holding her head in the crook of my neck. She sobs, her back vibrating as tears coat my skin.

"I wish I could take this pain from you," I whisper, meaning my words right down to my soul.

I care for her. More than a friendship. I thought it was just sexual, that we could sleep together and say goodbye to one another in five weeks, which is why I keep bringing up the friend zone she's so aptly assigned me to. I'd leave and marry Princess Adelaide like my parents want and she'd find some guy that who'd give her a happy life.

Right now, I want to take her pain so that it spares her. So I can see that smile that spurs my own. I want her to joke around with me, so I have an excuse to tickle her, because her squirming in my arms is better than not being able to touch her.

The weight of her body falls deeper into my own.

"Hey," I whisper, brushing her hair out of her face.

She draws back, not apologizing for breaking down and not trying to free herself from my arms. Have I finally gotten her to admit to herself that she's hurting?

"I promise everything will be okay."

A small smile creases her lips. "I'm not your responsibility but thank you for staying last night."

Her vulnerability feels like a nail piercing my heart.

"You are," I say.

Confusion fills her eyes.

"I know things with us are complicated and right now is a shitty time for me to tell you this, but I really like you."

"What?" Her head jerks back.

"I like you, Sierra Sanders, and I want you to be my responsibility. Not in some caveman alpha male way. But I want the responsibility of making your day a little brighter, making you laugh on the bad days and holding you on the horrible ones. I want the responsibility of feeding you when you're sick and planning celebrations for milestones in our lives. I want to be responsible for making you smile, laugh, feel safe, feel secure, and of course, I want the sole responsibility for your orgasms."

She laughs, and her head falls to my chest. "But there's so much against this, against us."

I place my finger on her chin and bring it up so she's looking at me, as I have so many times before, but my heart grips tight, waiting for her response more than any other time before. "We'll figure it out but answer this question. Do you like me?"

I've never in my life asked a woman that question. Not even when I was in middle school. Nor have I ever held my breath, waiting for the answer.

Her smile is promising, but I want the words. "But…"

I put my finger over her lips. "It's a yes or no question."

Her eyes lock with mine and my answer is there before she verbalizes it. "Yes."

My hand runs up her back until my fingers are weaved through her vibrant hair, and I lean down, pressing my lips to hers. A kiss has never been such a perfect mix of sweet and hot.

CHAPTER NINETEEN

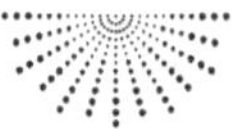

Sierra

Adrian's lips meet mine and our kiss is a stark difference from the first time weeks ago, when he stole my breath with a kiss. Then it was filled with lust and urgency. This time, his lips almost skim over mine at first, as if he wants to double-check that I'm in this.

And I am.

All the worries of how we'll make this work still scare me, but the feeling of waking up in his arms this morning and his overwhelming concern for my well-being have me answering yes.

The scariest part is that my feelings for him transcend way beyond what drew me to him in the first place. The fact that he's a prince doesn't matter. In reality, it only makes things between us more difficult.

His tongue slowly licks the seam of my lips and I open my mouth, my hands reaching up around his neck, running over the now-short hairs. I'm half able to realize we're moving, but it isn't until the backs of my legs hit the bed that I recognize that he's moved us over to the bed. He lowers my body down, his lips leaving mine briefly until he slides his body on mine. His lips find mine once more and our hands run over each other's clothes.

My head spins. This is really happening. Adrian and me.

I let all the worries of tomorrow drift away so I can be present in this moment. Him and me basking in the wondrous state of electric attraction that runs between us.

"I've never wanted anyone more," he whispers, his thigh sliding between my legs.

I lose myself for a moment, the sensation of his weight on me overwhelming my body. When I open my legs, his hips fall between them and his arms fall down on each side of my head, lips crashing to lips. He grinds into my center and I raise my legs, not wanting the feeling to stop. I grip him to my body, and we dry hump until I can't take it any longer.

"I need to feel you," I whisper and nibble on his earlobe.

He sits up, resting his ass on his heels, and strips off his shirt, revealing his defined chest. His hands slide up to help me remove my own clothes.

After a few awkward positions of stripping off jeans and socks and underwear, we're naked with our mouths attached again. The tip of his dick breaches my center while his lips cast kisses down my neck.

"Shit. Condom," I say.

He rips his lips from mine, gets up from the bed, and the look he gives me says we're screwed.

I close my eyes. "You didn't refill your wallet after our first night together?"

"Give me a break, who would think I was going to sleep with my win-a-date girl, and believe it or not, my intentions of walking the Brooklyn Bridge last night did not include this."

"Can you please never call me the win-a-date girl again?" I sit up and stare down the hall. "There's only one option."

He follows my line of vision. "Tell me you have some in your purse downstairs."

"Nope." We used those ones too. His fingers push through his hair, and I fall to my knees in front of him. "We could do other things then." I hold him at the base of his dick, licking up his length until my mouth covers the tip of him.

When I look up at him, his vision is locked on me and his hand grips the headboard of my bed. I've never had a guy in my childhood bedroom before, and I never thought I would at twenty-seven years old.

He groans and his free hand moves to the back of my head, but instead of pushing me onto him, he guides me to stop and motions for me to stand. "As much as I love that, I need to be inside you. I want to see your face when I push inside you."

I swallow and nod. "Side table, second drawer, my dad's bedroom."

He cocks his head at me.

"It's not what you think. He's a military man and a creature of habit. They were there when I was younger. I took one and tried to blow it up. I doubt he moved them."

"Blew it up?"

I put my hands on his shoulders and turn him around, smacking his ass. "Get moving. I'll be here, naked and waiting."

He walks down the hall, looking around as if my dad's going to pop out from somewhere. According to the itinerary I found, he's not due home until next week.

A few minutes later, Adrian returns holding a row of

condoms as if they're a first place trophy for a soapbox derby and he's eight years old.

"Aren't you hopeful," I say.

"No, I'm just confident in my stamina." He takes no time tearing off one and placing the rest of them on the nightstand by my bed. But he doesn't slide it on right away. "Now let me get back to seducing you."

"I won't complain about that."

His lips move along my skin and his breath teases the wetness left behind by his tongue. The way his fingertips skim along my skin, running around my back and gliding down to my ass, has me moaning. His large palms grip my ass and pull me against his very hard dick.

"I need you now," I pant, stripping my lips off his only for his mouth to travel to the side of my neck.

He gets up on his knees. "I had all these plans."

"Next time." I grab the condom out of his hand and tear it open, pulling out the latex.

"Nope. You are not taking charge… at least not this time around." He pinches the tip and rolls it down his length. "Lie down, babe."

My back falls on the lumpy old mattress and he positions himself at my center, holding the base of his shaft. Just as he said earlier, his eyes are steady on mine as he slowly slides into me inch by inch. Once I'm completely filled with him, he lowers his body and captures my lips in a kiss that holds so much intensity, I never want to leave this bed, or him.

The torturously slow grinding of his dick moving in and out of me accompanies his tongue teasing my lips. I hold the back of his head and my other hand grips his hard bicep.

Unable to handle much more teasing, he falls down on me, his rhythm growing faster and faster. Our bodies collide and shift against one another's. Moans, whimpers, and groans bounce against the walls of my childhood bedroom.

"I'm so close," I say.

He speeds up until the pressure of my orgasm builds like a brick wall—layer by layer—until the weight of keeping it back is too much and I let go. Pure glory spreads through my body, lighting up every nerve ending. My eyes drift closed, but Adrian drills harder into me and I clench my thighs tighter until he stills and grunts, pumping into me as his orgasm swells over him.

The fear sets in as we catch our breath, lying limp in my bed. What does the future bring now? Will one orgasm really change his mind, or will he leave me behind anyway? Although I hate myself for thinking it or doubting him, I can't help it.

As if he's worried too, he gets up on his elbows and his eyes search mine for some sign of whatever I'm looking for in his. "We're good?" He places a chaste kiss on my lips.

"We're good," I say.

"I'll be right back." He slides out of me, holding the base of the condom, and stands.

As he cleans himself up in the bathroom, I realize that I miss him already. Although that feeling scares the crap out of me, I stay rooted in place.

Until the front door downstairs opens.

Obviously, one of the things my dad didn't fix is the squeak that door has made since I was sixteen. He said it was his way to ensure I didn't sneak out in the middle of the night. I refrained from saying that there are windows and a back door, and he usually wasn't in any shape to hear a squeak.

"They'll get that squeak handled. So it's a three-bedroom with two and a half baths," a woman says.

Adrian comes out of the hallway completely naked and freezes when he hears little footsteps coming up the stairs.

Oh shit, they have kids with them.

"Don't touch anything, Caleb!" the mom screams.

Adrian looks as if he's seen a ghost, but he can't move fast enough to get into my room and shut the door. I scramble out of bed and toss him his pants while shuffling around to grab my clothes.

The kid pops into the room and screams at the sight of Adrian's naked ass.

The kid would be lucky to have an ass like Adrian's when he grows up.

"What the hell?" Adrian whisper-shouts.

Lucky for us, the kid runs back downstairs, giving Adrian and I time to get dressed.

"Hello? Is someone here? Mr. Sanders?" the realtor says, her shoes landing on the hardwood floors.

"It was like a moon!" the kid says to his mom downstairs, and I bite my lip to stop from laughing.

Adrian glares at me.

"Hello. I'm sorry, it's Sierra Sanders, Greg's daughter," I call then pop out the bedroom into the hallway.

The woman stands on the landing. She's older, with dark hair cut in a stylish bob, but her lack of a smile at this unusual situation says this isn't going to go smoothly and she'll probably tell my dad.

Great.

"Oh, I wasn't aware you were staying here. Your father and Fae told me I could bring anyone around whenever I wanted this week." She tilts to the side to look behind me at Adrian.

"This is my…" I'm unsure of what word to use.

"Prince Adrian Marx!" The woman gasps and her face lights up.

I glance behind me.

"Yes, ma'am." He steps up and puts out his hand. I do my

best to refrain from thinking that those fingers were rubbing my clit only minutes ago.

She shakes his hand. "What are you doing in Carroll Gardens? Here?"

He chuckles. "Sierra is my girlfriend," he says with pride that makes my shoulders straighten under his arm.

"Oh." Her attention turns to me. "Your father said nothing about you dating a prince."

My mouth opens, but Adrian beats me to it. "It's hush-hush, for obvious reasons. I haven't had a chance to tell my parents, so if you could keep it between us, I'd greatly appreciate it."

The woman is quick to answer. "Of course. I'd never want to ruin such a wonderful surprise."

"Thanks. That means a lot." He winks and gives her that prince smile.

"My pleasure."

Jeez, she's practically swooning like a schoolgirl.

"If you want to give us a minute, we'll clean up the room and be out of your hair," I interrupt her blatant staring at Adrian. I mean, he's gorgeous and all, but she's old enough to be his grandmother.

"Yes, that'd be great. Thank you."

I nod and she heads back down the stairs, leaving us alone.

"I'm your girlfriend, huh?" I ask to his back as Adrian straightens the comforter.

Breaking the distance, he pushes me against my desk. The desk I sat at and daydreamed about whether I'd ever be swept off my feet and thinking that was probably never going to happen to me. I was too crazy, too negative, too cold.

He wraps his arms around my waist and tugs me closer. "Is that a problem?"

I shake my head. "No problem."

"Good." He kisses my lips. "So no more friends crap, right?"

"Right."

He kisses me then releases me, sits on the bed, and puts on his socks. I wait for some crashing cymbal to sound, but it doesn't come.

Holy crap, my boyfriend is a prince.

drian

IN THE PAST WEEK, I haven't slept in my bed once because I've been in Sierra's. All the friends, including Rian, took it well that we're a couple now, although I catch Rian staring sometimes. I think she's apprehensive about my intentions.

When I return from a run, Rian's in the kitchen. Sierra said she'll be late due to some water crisis down by the river, which leaves some time for bonding with my other roommate.

"What are you making?"

Rian quirks her eyebrow at me, plugging in a mixer.

"What?" I ask.

"I'm baking Sierra's birthday cake."

My stomach drops. "It's her birthday? I didn't know."

She pulls out a stool and climbs it, opening a cabinet.

"Let me help you."

"Uh, no. It's my job to bake her cake."

"Come on. I'd love to learn so next year I can bake her cake." I sit on the chair and give her my best puppy dog eyes.

"And what will you teach me in return?" she asks.

"I can teach you how to curtsy, or how to speak French, the language of love. Or how to dodge security. Let's see, what else?"

Rian laughs. "That's okay. This is for Sierra after all. First thing you should know is that her favorite cake flavor is vanilla."

"Really? Why did I think it'd be something exotic, like pineapple or something?" I ask, taking the containers of flour and sugar from her arms and placing them on the table.

"Probably because there's nothing vanilla about her personality. I'm probably more the type of person someone would assume loves vanilla."

I say nothing because I'm not sure what to say. She kind of does seem like a girl who doesn't ask for a lot or go after her dreams. Sierra is the type you envision actually taking a bite of this world and claiming it as hers. Rian is the type to chip away for years and then hand whatever she has to someone she feels is more deserving. But now isn't the time to tell her this, so I stay silent.

"Her all-time favorite is vanilla with vanilla buttercream and a layer of strawberries, but I have no strawberries, so this time—"

"I can go to the store."

"I can use strawberry flavoring. They aren't in season right now."

"This is my first time making a cake for my girlfriend— we're not half-assing it. Do you need anything else?"

I grab my jacket and wallet while Rian watches me with confusion. "You're going to the store just for the strawberries that probably aren't all that good this time of year?"

"Yes, don't do anything without me."

She stares blankly. "Okay."

I shut the door of the apartment. I don't know why she's surprised that I want to impress Sierra. I mean, if she likes strawberries, why would I make a cake without them?

I pass the Bagel Place on the way to the grocery store, and I glance in to see who's working. Evan is there, helping a customer. She catches me looking and waves me in. I don't really have time, but she's my employer, so I walk in.

"Adrian!" Her voice is more chipper than normal.

"Hey, Evan."

A woman comes from the back and smiles at me. "You're Adrian?"

"Adrian?" A boy sitting in the corner stares at me. "You're the employee of the month?" He has a sweet demeanor and it's clear at first glance that he has Down syndrome.

"Eli!" Evan playfully scolds. "It was going to be a surprise."

Eli laughs. "Sorry." He covers his mouth, and Evan shakes her head.

"You cannot keep a secret."

Eli laughs harder. The exchange between them is sweet and endearing.

"Hi, Adrian, I'm Jenny, Evan's mother." I shake her outstretched hand and she looks me over with scrutiny. "You look familiar."

"Probably because his picture is on the wall." Evan widens her hands like Vanna White on *Wheel of Fortune* at a plaque with my picture on it. The one she told me she took the day we were slow so she could morph us with weird filters on her phone. "I know it's not the best picture, but we wanted it to be a surprise."

I walk over to the plaque and read the words Employee of the Month under my picture. My insides turn slightly gooey seeing people honor me for something other than being born into the right family. Something I've done entirely on my own and earned through my own hard work, not because of my royal heritage.

"Thank you." I bow my head slightly.

"You deserve it. I mean, it took a little while with the training, but you've really picked up your game. I think you make better bagels than me now," Evan exclaims.

Jenny glances at her daughter with skepticism, probably wondering why Evan's being overly complimentary. I kind of wonder too. I find myself speechless.

Jenny takes off her apron and disappears into the back, returning with her purse and coat. "It was great to finally meet you. Come on, Eli."

"Bye, Eli," Evan says.

"Bye. Congratulations, Adrian," Eli says and raises his hand.

"Thanks, buddy." I smack his high-five.

I can't stop taking glimpses at the plaque, and Evan laughs at me.

"So where are you on your way to?"

"To get strawberries. I'm baking a cake for my girlfriend."

"Oh. I didn't know you had a girlfriend?" From her tone, I think maybe she thought our friendship was leading somewhere else.

"It's new."

"That's great, and it's very sweet of you to make her a cake."

"Well, our other roommate is helping me."

She laughs and holds up her finger. "Hold up one second." She turns and heads into the kitchen.

I turn around while I wait and see Seth walking by slowly, staring into the windows. He stops when he sees me, ushering me with his hand to come outside.

"Here, take—" Evan returns a second later, and I turn as she must see who I'm staring at. "Oh, that little spy!" She rounds the counter, shoving a bag of strawberries into my chest and heading to the door.

I follow her.

"Seth Andrews." I'm not sure I've heard a more disgusted tone in someone's voice before.

Seth stuffs his hands into his pockets and chews his gum harder. "Evan. Looking good."

Her eyes narrow. "Stop spying on us."

"I was walking by." He shrugs.

Even with the obvious anger between them, they seem to almost soak each other in. Seth's eyes don't stop roaming and there's a softness Evan is trying to hide.

"Still taking pictures of half-naked women?" She sneers.

"They're called boudoir, and I'll clear my schedule for you. You just have to ask."

I shake my head.

"You're disgusting," she says.

"You're jealous because I'm not the one stuck running a bagel shop."

Evan scoffs. "Yeah, I'm jealous that you leave your poor parents to run that bagel shop all by themselves. That's exactly it."

Seth clears his throat. "Adrian, let's go. This isn't a *real* bagel place."

Evan glances at me. "You two know one another?"

"He lives across the hall from me." Seth waits for me to come, but he realizes Evan knows me too, and he scowls. "How do you know him?"

"He's my employee," Evan says. "At least he was until I found out he hangs with you."

"You work at the Bagel Place?" Seth asks. "You're a fucking prince. Why are you working?"

It's in this moment I regret not telling the guys I got a job. They're usually not around during the day anyway, and it seemed easier to keep this quiet once I heard about the situation between Seth's family and Evan's.

The door falls from Evan's grip. "You're a prince?"

Fucking Seth.

I sigh and shift the bag of strawberries to my other hand. "I am."

"Like prince of what?"

"I'm surprised you don't recognize him. You were always into all that gossip."

Evan cuts her eyes to Seth. "Go away, we're closed."

She steps inside and I follow, then she locks the door and flips the sign to Closed.

Seth mouths, "Sorry" and laughs, walking down the sidewalk.

"Please tell me that's Seth's idea of a joke?" Evan asks, her hands shaking.

"Listen. I wanted a job and if you didn't recognize me, that's a good thing. It's not like I'm the Prince of England. It's just Sandsal. I needed a job. But my title doesn't change who I am."

"You lied."

"I omitted."

She shoots me a look that would make a lesser man's balls shrivel up. "There's no difference to me. Not to mention you're friends with my worst enemy. How do I know you're not giving him our recipes?"

"Evan, I would never do that. You saw yourself, he didn't even know I worked here."

She glances at the plaque. "Just go. I have to think about this, because if the Andrews find out any of our secret recipes, my parents will lose their shit and their store."

I step closer to the counter. "I told you, I wouldn't do that."

"How do I know? I feel like I don't even know you now."

"That's unfair."

She's busy writing down the morning orders. "Just go. I'll tell you later tonight if you should show up to work tomorrow."

I shake my head and hesitate, but when she doesn't look up, I figure I might as well go.

So I leave the bagel shop like an overfilled balloon that just got popped. I was at the highest of highs with being named employee of the month, and now I'm not even sure if I have a job.

I stop and buy the strawberries, and on my way back to the apartment, I run into Seth coming from Ink Envy.

"I can't believe you've been working for my parents' competitor." He sounds less pissed off than Evan was though.

"I needed a job."

"My parents would've hired you."

I shake my head. Evan and her family needed me a lot more than Seth's did. "I think I'm fired anyway."

"Oh, well, believe me, you don't want to work with Evan. I've known that girl since birth and demanding is an understatement."

We step into the elevator.

"Did you guys ever date?"

He balks. "No."

He's not even a little convincing.

"Never?" I ask.

"No. We haven't even really talked since we were, like, nine or something."

The fact that he recites the same age Evan told me suggests that they might have never dated but they still like one another.

"Well, I feel like an asshole now," I say. "She's hurt I didn't tell her I know you, and she's worried I'll share the recipes with your family."

Seth bites his lips, looking at me. "There's a lot of history between our families. I'm sorry you're stuck in the crosshairs."

"It's fine. I have to leave in a month anyway, but I wanted to finish out the month. They need it. Evan practically runs the place by herself." I can't stop myself from talking, although I'm sure Seth is the last person who would care. "She works all the time, has no social life. She said her mom and dad are busy with her brother."

Understanding shows on Seth's face. "He has Down syndrome."

"Yeah, I met him earlier."

The elevator hits our floor and I step off, but Seth doesn't.

"Are you coming?" I ask holding the door.

He steps forward then back again, pressing the button for the first floor. "Shit. I forgot something at Ink Envy. I'll catch you later."

The elevator door shuts, and I walk to my apartment, trying to push away the thought that I might be fired so I can make a cake for Sierra to celebrate her birthday—even though she didn't mention it to me.

I think about Evan's words about an omission being the same as a lie. After four weeks, I feel like my omissions are catching up to me. It's time I tell Sierra about Princess Adelaide before that blows up in my face too.

CHAPTER TWENTY-ONE

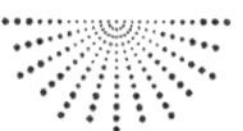

Sierra

My day was long and shitty, in part because of the knowledge that my dad is due to return home tomorrow and I know he's going to ask about my birthday. I haven't even told Adrian about my birthday yet. Not that I care to celebrate—unless it's him and me in a hotel room with its own Jacuzzi.

Opening the apartment door, the lights are off, and when I flip them on, the apartment is empty. Not that I thought it could be a surprise party. Okay, I thought it maybe only because Rian threw me one last year. But my birthday isn't for two more days anyway.

I hang my keys on the key ring near the door and kick off my shoes before picking them up to take them into my bedroom. I put my shoes in my closet and drop my computer bag on the chair by my dresser. A chair that's only there to hold clean clothes until I put them away, or for any other use besides sitting. Except for that time a few days ago when Adrian had me spread eagle on it. The bubbling sensation stirs deep in my belly at the thought.

It isn't until I unbutton my blouse that I notice the outfit on the bed. It's a Wonder Woman costume with a small note on top.

Put me on and meet the rest of the superheroes up on the roof.

I SMILE and dig into my purse for my phone to check for any missed messages. None.

Always one for a costume party, especially one where I get to be Wonder Woman, I quickly strip and morph into Wonder Woman.

When I walk up the stairs to the door that opens onto the roof, the music coming from the other side tips me off that the party is already going.

The door is locked or there's something pushed against it, so I have no choice but to knock. The music shuts off and I hear Rian telling everyone to hide. I chuckle.

A minute later the door opens and it's Adrian dressed as Superman, tights and all.

There's no time for me to give him a flirty comment about his bulge before everyone jumps out, screaming surprise. The lights we hung years ago illuminate a table with a cake and pizza.

Blanca jumps out as Catwoman with Ethan behind her as Batman, not nearly as excited about acting out his character as she is.

Rian is Supergirl, looking cute as ever, with Seth as Green Lantern and Knox as Aquaman.

"Ironman?" I point at Dylan with a cringe.

Everyone shakes their heads in disappointment at him.

"Apparently Ironman isn't a DC Comics character? It had man. I thought they were all the same thing." Dylan shrugs, downing half his beer.

"It just feels like a compliment that you dressed up."

We've tried years of Halloween parties on the rooftop only for Dylan to come in his regular clothes with the lame joke that he's a tattoo artist.

"Well, I love yah. Happy early birthday." He kisses my cheek and hugs me.

"Thanks."

After I say hello to everyone, I find my Superman by the ledge, talking to Knox and a girl dressed as Poison Ivy. I think she's the same girl who delivered Adrian's luggage, but it's hard to tell because she's outdone herself by painting herself green.

"Hey, you," I say to the group. "Do you mind if I steal Superman for a second?"

Adrian's hand falls into mine, and he leads us to the other side of the rooftop, the side people usually go to make out.

"Did you plan this?" I ask.

"I did. I wasn't sure about the theme, but I liked the idea of you in that costume, so I went with it."

"I had a Wonder Woman party when I was nine. Did Blanca tell you?"

"She mentioned something after I told them the theme. So it's cool?"

I smile and nod. "Definitely cool." I lift on my tiptoes and press my lips to his. "So do I get both Clark Kent and Superman tonight? Do you have a pair of dark-rimmed glasses to change into later in the bedroom?"

"Is it not enough you get a prince and an everyday guy? I kind of feel the pain of Superman having more than one identity on days like today." There's a melancholy look in his eyes.

"What happened?"

He's quick to shake his head. "Nothing. Let's enjoy tonight. We can talk about it tomorrow."

He takes my hand again, kisses the back of it, and leads me away from the make-out area where I thought we'd have a little fun before returning to the small party.

"Did you look at the cake?" he asks.

We head over to the table so I can check it out. Vanilla with sprinkles. My favorite. "Rian did a great job."

"Actually, Adrian helped me, so next year when you celebrate your birthday, it's all on him." She pats him on the back, her smile suggesting she's not second-guessing his motives anymore.

"You did?"

"I did." He pulls me into him.

I love the fact he's done all this for me, and I let my hand roam down his chest. "How can I ever thank you?"

"I have a few ideas for later on." He waggles his eyebrows and I playfully smack his puffed out chest, but I'll be more than happy to fulfill those wishes tonight. His laugh dies down and he sets his gaze on mine. "I told you, I want the responsibility for these things. I want to be the one to put that smile on your face by planning a birthday party and making your birthday cake. Now, it would've been easier if you'd told me that your birthday is in two days. I found out today and wanted to surprise you, so I threw it all together last minute. Thank God for same-day delivery."

I swear I must have cartoon heart eyes right now. "Now you know."

"Now I know." He kisses the end of my nose. "Go have fun with your friends."

"Great job on the cake, Adrian," Blanca says as she comes over.

"Thanks."

Eventually Adrian and Ethan start up their own conversation, and Blanca, Rian, and I are huddled in the corner of the rooftop.

"So he's all that and a prince, huh?" Blanca asks.

I nod, my eyes finding his across the dark rooftop. "I guess so."

"And you guys are, like, legit a couple?" Rian asks.

"Yeah, I guess." He winks and my stomach somersaults.

"You've fallen for him," Blanca says.

"No." I shake my head. "I mean, I have, but it's not love or anything. It's just heavy like."

"And what's going to happen in a month?" Rian asks.

She's the most concerned about my heart. I love her for being such a great friend, but I knew what I was risking when I agreed to be with him. I understood that he might dupe me and I'd end up in the fetal position on my bed when he decides to go back to Sandsal.

I sigh. "I don't know. We haven't talked about it. Yet."

Rian purses her lips. "He definitely has all the moves of a prince."

"He definitely does," Blanca agrees, but her words come out in a dreamy tone whereas Rian sounds more like a detective looking at her first suspect.

"Relax, Rian. I'm a big girl." I put my hand on her shoulder.

All three of us look at Ethan and Adrian talking. A man who I thought was my future at one time and now dates my best friend is talking to the man who's occupying my bed and quickly stealing my heart. I don't tell either of my friends that though, because if they knew how much I care for

Adrian already, they'll know how badly it will hurt if he leaves me.

~

THE PIZZA BOX IS EMPTY, and the cake plate has been licked clean by Dylan.

"Strawberries and everything," I say to Adrian as we lie on a blanket under the stars.

To make my night even dreamier, he set up an air mattress and candles all over the roof, the heater to our side. He even blocked the entrance to the roof like he did earlier so no one can bother us.

Pulling out a bottle of champagne, he pops the cork, and nothing sprays out. A perfect pour into two flutes later and he's on the mattress with me, handing me my glass.

"Happy birthday, Sierra," he says, holding up his glass.

"Thanks for all this," I say for what I feel is the millionth time. But not many people have gone to this much trouble for me.

"I'll always celebrate the day you were born. It's like a national holiday to me." We clink glasses and sip our champagne.

I nuzzle into his chest and try to remember the names of the stars.

"What are you thinking about?" he whispers.

"Just my last birthday with my mom. She did the super-hero thing. She was big on celebrating birthdays. I'd wake up and she'd tell me about the day she found out she was preg-nant and how horrible of a delivery she had, but how when she saw me, it made up for all the pain. The usual mom stories. But she'd come up with the theme for my birthday months in advance. I'd been so into Wonder Woman when she planned that party, but when my birthday got closer, I didn't want it anymore. Some girls at school said it was lame." I laugh, remember Blanca telling one of them off at the lunch table.

"I didn't want to ruin it for her, so I went through the day, not as happy as I should've been. When she tucked me in that night, she asked me what was wrong. I told her about the teasing, and she told me never to be afraid to tell her anything and we could've changed the theme."

"She sounds amazing," Adrian says.

I nod and clear my throat, resting my chin on his chest. "I don't want to relive those memories and get sad. I want to celebrate my twenty-eighth birthday with you." I run my hand down his cheek.

I get up, set our champagne glasses to the side of the air mattress, and straddle him, his hands landing on my hips. "I think I need to thank you properly for the party."

His hand moves to my chest, finding the zipper and lowering it down the bodice of my costume, making the top fall down between us. He flips me on my back and his hands make quick work of my costume.

"I'm not done with the birthday gifts yet." He slides down my body, sprinkling small kisses on my stomach. "And the boots are staying on," he orders, licking a path from my navel to clit.

"Oh, Adrian," I moan, my head falling back so I'm looking at the night sky.

He picks up his head. "It's Superman tonight."

"By all means, show me how super you can be."

A devilish expression lands on his face and he dives between my thighs.

Then Adrian, or Superman, gave me a birthday I'll never forget.

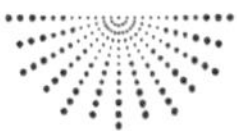

CHAPTER TWENTY-TWO

Adrian

A knock sounds on Sierra's bedroom door. She grumbles and rolls her naked body off of mine. "What?"

"Um…" Rian clears her throat. "There's someone here to see Adrian."

Sierra peeks one eye open at me, and I shrug.

"I have no idea," I whisper to her. "Give me a minute," I call to Rian.

I fling my legs off the bed and grab a pair of sweatpants while dread settles in my stomach. I talked to my mom the other day and everything was still a go for another month. The boulder gaining weight in the pit of my stomach says this is bad. That the hesitation in Rian's voice is a warning.

Sierra whines but sits up.

I rush to her side. "Just sleep, babe, I'll be right back."

"Who could it be?"

I shake my head. "I'm sure it's nothing. I'll come get you if I need you."

She falls back down to the bed, more hungover than I am.

Grabbing my phone, I take one last look to see if something there will warn me of the surprise waiting for me on the other side of the door. There's a text from Evan.

Evan: *You're not fired. Come in for your afternoon shift tomorrow. See you then.*

I hammer a text right back, but as I'm in the middle of "cool, I'll see you then," another knock lands on the door.

"Adrian!" Rian yells.

Sierra stands, and I salivate from watching her stretch her naked body. I'm not sure I'll ever grow tired of that visual. She grabs her robe off the hanger in her closet, covering up her beautiful self.

"Let's see what this is all about," she mumbles and opens the door.

After snatching a T-shirt from the foot of the bed, I follow her. I'm throwing it over my head when my omission comes crashing down on me like Mount Vesuvius.

"Who are you?" Sierra asks.

"I'm Princess Adelaide, Prince Adrian's fiancée."

Oh fuck.

Rian is in the kitchen, preparing breakfast loudly, every movement exaggerated.

"Rian, can you please keep it down? I have a headache." Sierra rubs her temples.

Did she not hear Adelaide?

"Are you a telegram or something? I mean, this has to be a joke." Sierra looks at me over her shoulder. Her face falls when she takes in my stricken expression.

"Excuse me. A telegram?" Adelaide says in a haughty tone.

She's wearing a conservative dress that lands mid-calf and doesn't mold to her curves. Her hair is blonde, straight, and sleek. Studded earrings and a single chain necklace with her family's emblem on it. She couldn't be more opposite of Sierra if she tried.

"What are you doing here? How did you find me?" I ask.

"I knew it!" Rian points her spatula at me. "I knew it was too good to be true. 'Oh, Rian, I'll go get strawberries.'" She mimics my words from yesterday in a horrible version of my accent. "'Let's do a surprise party for her.'"

Sierra sits on a chair and I'm worried she hasn't even processed this.

Adelaide raises her chin and looks down her nose at me. "Declan."

"Declan told you where I was? What kind of security is that?"

She smirks and her hands run down her dress as if she's preventing it from having even one wrinkle on it. "The kind who understands that you disappearing for a month has everyone in a frenzy. Your parents said you were volunteering in Uganda or something. I knew when there were no pictures of you that something was fishy, but I didn't think I'd find you in bed with another woman."

"Whoa." I hold up my hand for her to stop. "For the record, we are *not* engaged."

"We are *promised* to one another, so we might as well be. But I will not go through with it if you think you'll be sleeping around on me."

"So what, you're marrying her next month?" Sierra asks, too calm for my liking. I worry that she's going to snap when reality sets in.

"No," I say at the same time that Adelaide says, "Yes."

"I knew it. I could give some pointers to *Blue Bloods*. I can pinpoint the creeps and you're one of them, Adrian Marx." Rian points her spatula at me.

"Who are you making breakfast for?" I ask, knowing she's probably already been up for hours.

"Me," Adelaide says. "I asked her if there was anything to eat here."

"No. Go to a hotel or something. This is my life and you're fucking with it." I step closer to her.

"Sierra! What is wrong with you?" Rian screams when Sierra continues to sit there and not say anything.

The apartment door opens, and in waltzes Dylan in his boxer shorts, scratching the back of his head. "Damn, Seth was up early, banging around in the kitchen. Do you guys have—" He stops cold when he spots Adelaide. "Who's this?"

"Adrian's fiancée," Sierra answers.

I circle around to face her. She's cool and calm with an almost smile tipping at the corner of her mouth.

"She's not my fiancée," I say.

"That's not what she says." Sierra points at Adelaide and I turn back to see Dylan giving her an appreciative gaze.

"Get her out!" Rian yells.

"Ri, come on, my eardrums, babe." Dylan sticks his finger in his ear and sniffs. "Oh, whatcha making?"

He wanders over to her as I sit on the coffee table in front of Sierra, my hands on her thighs. She doesn't move, though her gaze shifts from Adelaide to me.

"Give me ten minutes to clear this up and then I'm coming back here so we can talk, okay?" I say.

Sierra nods. "Okay."

I hate to say this because I know it makes me sound like an asshole, but it's a little offensive that she hasn't shown any sign of jealousy like she did when she found me watching TV with Blanca.

"Follow me," I tell Adelaide.

She huffs but follows me toward the door. "Oh, darling, I do not eat pancakes. And I like my egg whites soft, not hard. Do you have Greek yogurt?"

Rian's eyes narrow and Dylan smiles, chomping down on a pancake.

"Sorry," I say to Rian and tug Adelaide's arm to move her out into the hallway. "You cannot ask my roommates to cook for you."

"Roommate? I thought she was your servant." Adelaide's heels click on the hallway floor as I lead her to the door to the rooftop, the only place we can probably find some privacy. "I'm not going up there. Don't they have terraces or something?"

"Nope, this is it."

She huffs. "Fine."

She climbs the stairs one at a time, like a toddler who doesn't have long enough legs to go from one stair to the next. I'm practically vibrating with anger by the time she makes it onto the roof.

"Who else knows you're here?" I ask.

"No one. I came here by myself."

"Why? Where are your assistants?"

She shrugs. "Are you running out on our marriage for that woman down there?"

At least she cuts to the chase.

"I was going to inform my parents after I return that I will not be marrying you, if that's your real question. As far as what's going on with Sierra, that's none of your business."

Her eyes narrow. "If you're going to embarrass me by calling off our marriage so you can marry a commoner, then it is absolutely my business."

Being away from all the royal bullshit for a month, I forgot how ridiculous it all sounds. A commoner? Like people who aren't royalty are beneath us somehow?

"I'm not sure why you came here," I say. "My parents granted me another month of freedom and I fully intend on living here and enjoying it."

"I'll stay as well then."

"No, you will not." I shake my head and fist my hands.

"Yes, I will. If you want me to keep your little secret."

"What?"

She pulls out her phone. "See, people are wondering why Prince Adrian hasn't updated his Instagram account for so long. There's actually a hashtag of #missingprincespotted where people post photos of men they think are you. Imagine if I tweeted your real location. They'd believe me too, since I'm a princess."

Her voice is sweet, but her words are evil.

"You cannot stay at my apartment. Sierra is my girlfriend and she's not going to understand. Not to mention I won't be marrying you in a month."

She's unfazed by my news. "Newsflash, I don't want to marry you either."

So Adelaide doesn't want to marry me, and Sierra doesn't care that I'm betrothed to someone else. Excellent self-esteem boost.

"Then why would you want to stay here?" I ask, pinching the bridge of my nose.

"Declan said you wanted to try a normal life. Maybe I wouldn't mind trying it as well."

I run my hands through my hair and grip it tightly.

"What do you do here?" she asks.

"I work."

"Well, I'm not sure about that, but I want to stay anyway. And just so you know, my dad is going to be very upset if the marriage is called off."

I nod. I figured I'd be pissing everyone off when I announced that I'm in a relationship and will not be marrying anyone. It means my brother will rule and he's just a kid. But the one thing I've realized while living here is that I'm not going to live by ancient rules any longer.

"So it's decided? I'm staying?" she asks.

I inhale a deep breath. "Just wait here for a second."

How are my two lives colliding right now?

"I'm not waiting here like some peasant. I'm going with you."

She follows me, so I hold open the door and let her head down the stairs first, regretting it as soon as she takes the steps again at the pace of a sloth.

On the way down, I say, "I can't talk to Sierra about you when you're there."

"That girl is making my breakfast and I'm hungry."

I blow out a breath. "Her name is Rian, and you can go into Dylan's apartment."

A line forms between her eyebrows—as much as it can with all the Botox that's probably been pumped in there. "Who is that?"

"The man with all the tattoos."

A look of disgust crosses her face and a part of me wants to laugh. It's the first time I've seen a woman have a reaction like that after seeing Dylan.

We walk down the hallway and I open the guys' apartment door, funneling Adelaide in and telling her to stay seated on the couch.

She looks at it as if she smells something rotten. "I'll stand."

"Whatever."

I'm about to shut the door when Seth comes out of the bathroom with a towel wrapped around his waist. "Am I dreaming? I beat off and the visual comes to life like that movie *Weird Science*?"

"Excuse me?" Adelaide asks with a hand to her chest as if she's been scandalized, and I shut the door.

They can work that out themselves.

By the time I walk back into my apartment, Sierra isn't sitting in the chair anymore. In fact, she's nowhere to be found. Rian and Dylan are eating breakfast at the table, both of them shaking their heads at me.

Ignoring them, I cross the room and open the door to Sierra's bedroom. She's sitting on the bed, her phone in her hands. No sign of tears or anger. Just indifference. The same emotion I've seen between my parents for the last five years.

"Sierra." I sit on the edge of her bed.

She looks up from her phone. "Do you need help packing?"

I stare blankly. "I'm not going anywhere."

"But…"

"I'm not going to marry Adelaide. There's a shit-ton I have to tell you, but first and foremost, you need to know that I'm not marrying her. I'm going to tell my parents after this month is up, but…"

Her armor cracks and a bit of her cold demeanor seeps out. "Why didn't you ever say anything?"

"Because I was scared. I never wanted to marry her. I wasn't sure what we were and it's still so early for us. But I should have. I know that. There's a lot you need to know, and if you hate me afterward, I completely understand, but please know that my feelings for you are real and deep and I don't want to ignore them."

She nods.

So far, so good.

"First I need a favor."

"What's that?" she asks.

"She wants to stay here. Live here with us for a short time."

The small crinkles on her forehead indent. I really wish I hadn't lied by omission all these weeks because it might cause me to lose the one person who means the most in this world to me. And what would be the point of all this if I finally found what I needed, only to lose it?

CHAPTER TWENTY-THREE

Adrian

"I think I need a lot more explanation," she says.

At least she's out of the comatose state she was in a moment ago, the one in which she'd shut down her emotions. I hate that. I'd rather have her breaking shit than go dark on me.

"Right. Okay. Let's get dressed and get out of here."

"And what? Leave your fiancée in the living room with Rian? She might shove the spatula up that woman's ass. Oh, that's right, she already has one up there."

I laugh and grab her, pulling her into my chest.

She scowls. "What is so funny?"

"You. I mean, you care about me. Losing me." I draw back, my hands still on her upper arms.

Those small wrinkles on her forehead are still there. I've confused her. "What are you talking about?"

"I wanted a reaction from you. You have nothing to worry

about, but for a moment, it seemed like you didn't care. Like you were willing to toss me aside and that what's been transpiring between us means nothing to you."

Her hand runs down my cheek. "It scared me," she says in a soft voice.

"Don't be scared. I'm not going anywhere."

She nods, but I wish I could be in her head to know if she truly believes me. From what I've witnessed, she hasn't had a lot of people on her side through the years, telling her how special she is.

"Okay, but I'm not sure Rian will agree to your fiancée staying with us. Not to mention I'm not comfortable with it."

I nod, knowing she's right. "She's threatening to out me on social media. Supposedly there's a hashtag, #missing-princespotted, happening."

Her teeth nibble on the corner of her mouth and she looks… guilty.

"You knew?" I ask.

She giggles and nods. "Yeah, I'm following it. It's great though. They've spotted you so many places not even close to where you really are. I wanted to be prepared if someone actually did find you."

"Prepared for what?"

She shrugs, but we both know for what. I wish I could strip her insecurities away, but that's going to take some time.

"Let's just get dressed and I'll figure Rian out. We'll figure it out." As she gets up off the bed, I grab the tie from her robe. "On second thought."

"Nope. You have a fiancée to deal with."

"Stop calling her that."

She allows the robe to fall open and cascade down to the floor.

"Nice ass."

She chuckles and disappears into her closet, so I resort to leaving the room. The apartment door opens as I'm walking from Sierra's room to mine, Adelaide walking in with Seth following close behind.

"Someone thinks I'm her servant and wants breakfast," he says.

Dylan and Rian glare at me.

Rian stands and dishes out a plate of pancakes before dropping them on the table. "We have pancakes. Eat them or starve."

Adelaide sighs and sits. "I haven't had a pancake since I was five."

Dylan blatantly checks out her body. "It looks like you haven't."

"Deal with it," Rian says to Adelaide.

"Hey, Rian, do you mind if Adelaide hangs around here while I take Sierra to breakfast?" I ask.

Adelaide turns to face me. "Breakfast? Like yogurt, eggs, and fruit? I cannot eat this." She picks up her pancake with her fork.

"You're kidding me, right? You want me to handle your problem?" Rian jams her hands on her hips.

"She's not my problem, but yeah, I need to talk to Sierra. Please. It's really important."

"I'll watch her. Do you need to shower after that long flight?" Dylan asks.

"We won't be long, and I promise to explain everything once we get back," I say to the group.

Rian blows out a breath. "Fine, but you are on my bad list, Adrian Marx." She points at me.

"You sure like to point," I say then snap my mouth shut. She's doing me a favor. "Adelaide, be good."

She rolls her eyes. "I'm not a dog."

I shut my bedroom door and throw on a pair of jeans and

a T-shirt with a sweatshirt. Grab some cash from my drawer and decide to actually hide the money in a sock in case Adelaide snoops. By the time I'm out of my room, Sierra is coming out of the bathroom with her hair in a messy bun, wearing yoga pants and a large sweatshirt.

Dylan is asking Adelaide questions about where she's from and what her plans are.

"Thanks again, Rian," I say.

She puts a heaping forkful of pancakes in her mouth and gives me a curt nod.

THE DINER down the street seats us in a two-person booth that's so cramped, we might have more privacy at the apartment than we do here, but I'm done stalling. Sierra has to know what I'm up against when I go home. Especially if I want her by my side when I do it.

We order our meals: mine an egg skillet and hers an egg white omelet with a muffin on the side.

I take her hands, wishing I would've told her last night as we lay under the blankets under the stars. But my procrastination ruined that. "The reason I took this two-month break is because my father cheated on my mom. My sister, Felicia, found him in his office with a woman in lingerie sprawled over his desk."

She grips my hands. "I'm sorry."

"Thanks. I was already arranged to marry Princess Adelaide," I whisper so no one will overhear. Then an idea comes to mind because I cannot chance that these details of my family's turmoil will be heard by someone in the public. "So in the story, the king was found with a woman who wasn't the queen in his office by his daughter."

Sierra doesn't pick up right away on what I'm doing, but she looks around and finally nods.

"The queen hasn't been seen with him in public since. The press knows something is going on, but they have no idea what. The royal family is desperate to keep it hidden because in their country, you cannot rule unless you're married. There has to be a king *and* a queen. So if the king and queen don't reconcile, their oldest son must take the crown and be married immediately."

"Are there rules as to who he has to marry?" She seems almost shy when she asks, and it pains me to give her the answer.

I nod, and she squeezes her eyes shut. "Of course, but the prince hasn't ever wanted to rule his country."

"Why?" she asks, seeming more interested than I thought she'd be. I actually feared she'd run out on me.

"He's just not interested."

Our food arrives and she picks up her fork. "Do you think the prince is underestimating himself?"

"No."

"Do you think the prince doesn't want to live by the rules?"

Man, she knows me well. "Maybe."

She smiles. "But if the prince is the king, can't he change the rules?"

"But he must marry before those rules can be changed."

Her shoulders sag a bit and she forks her omelet, putting it in her mouth as though she's thinking. When she's done chewing, she asks, "And what about Princess Adelaide?"

"What about her?"

"Where will she go if the prince doesn't marry her?"

"She'll stay in her country until she finds another prince to marry her, but it will hurt the ties between the two countries."

We eat in silence for a moment. The tables around us are emptying and filling again.

"Does the princess want to marry the prince?" she asks.

I shake my head.

"But she traveled a long distance to see him."

I shrug. A little girl from across the way leans over the booth, trying to hear us.

"She did, but it's more out of embarrassment. She's afraid the prince will make her look unworthy," I say.

"Oh." Her lips tip down. "That's sad."

"Which is why she wants to hide out until he goes home."

She forks another piece of her omelet off her plate, and silence fills the space between us for a minute. "So what does the prince want to do now?"

"That's easy. He wants to stay where he is and enjoy every day with his new girlfriend."

The little girl's mouth hangs open. "The prince has a girlfriend!"

Sierra turns to look at the little girl who's probably eight years old.

"Sweetie, sit down." The mom tries to divert her daughter's attention.

"That man is telling a fairy tale and the prince doesn't want the princess."

Her mom looks over her shoulder and smiles politely, but there's a scowl hidden under the fake facade.

"I think the monarchy and the royal family might feel a lot like the girl behind us," Sierra says, the smile that crested her lips moments ago vanishing.

"The prince isn't changing his mind."

Sierra puts down her fork, balls up her napkin, and puts it on her plate. "Sometimes even princes get pushed into corners. I have to think this prince will be too."

I shake my head. "Not the prince I'm talking about."

She nods, but there's disbelief all over her face, which means I'll have to prove it.

"I'm fine with her staying, but you'll have to get it past Rian."

"Thank you for understanding."

She nods. "We all have family drama. Most of mine's in the past. I can't lie, I'm scared what all this will bring, but I'm willing to see where it takes us."

I drop cash on the table and offer her my hand. "Let's go."

She accepts my hand and slides out of the booth.

"Princes and princesses live happily ever after," the little girl says as we pass her booth. She sticks her tongue out at us.

"I'm terribly sorry," the mom says, clearly embarrassed. "I told you he was just telling a story. Now sit down." She smiles at me once.

Sierra and I end up outside, and instead of heading toward the apartment, I lead her toward the park.

"I need something from you. Something I know isn't easy for you to give." I squeeze her hand and guide us to a bench.

"You need more? What?"

"I need you to trust me on this. Trust that I know my family. Trust that I know the royal system. It's not going to be easy." I turn toward her on the bench.

She nods. "Okay."

"I'm serious. I promise you from this point forward there will be no more omissions from me. I will tell you how it is, but for the next month, let's enjoy one another. Enjoy life without having to deal with the monarchy while we can."

"That's hard to do with a princess living under the same roof as us," she grumbles.

"I know it's not ideal, but we have no choice. If we don't, she's going to out me."

She nods. "Trust isn't one of my best personality traits."

I chuckle. "I know, but try for me?"

She nods, though apparently reluctantly. "I'll try."

"And we can enjoy these four weeks?"

"That's the only part I'm fully prepared for."

I stand and offer her my hand again. "Then let's go home. You're filthy and in need of a shower."

"Is that so?" We walk hand in hand out of the park.

"Yes, and I need to dirty up that delicious body of yours a little more before I clean it."

She grins. "And do I get to wash your body too?"

"That's a must."

She moves closer to me, her hand gripping tighter. Maybe we're both in denial about what's coming over the horizon in thirty days, but right now, I'm not ready to face the thundercloud headed our way. I want to enjoy the clear skies for another month before the storm starts.

CHAPTER TWENTY-FOUR

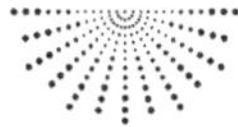

Sierra

Adrian and I return from breakfast to find Blanca and Rian with Adelaide in the living room. Adelaide's on the phone while the two of them whisper to one another.

"What's going on?" I ask.

Blanca stands and rounds the back of the couch. "The princess is talking to her parents. Telling them she's headed to a friend's house until you're found." She nods at Adrian.

He closes his eyes and shakes his head.

Rian doesn't wait to join our huddle in the kitchen. She jabs Adrian in the chest with her finger. "I hope by *friend* she's not talking about you."

I've never seen Rian this upset with someone before. Except for the short stint when Dylan was dating that one girl. But Rian just gave her the cold shoulder, not outright death glares.

"Well…" He grimaces and grips the back of his neck.

Blanca leans in. "You're going to have the princess move in?"

"Absolutely not," Rian says, crossing her arms.

"Listen, if we don't let her stay with us, she's going to post on social media where Adrian is. If that gets out, he has to return home right away." I give Rian a pleading look, knowing it's unfair of me to ask her for this when she's already been so great about Adrian staying here.

He puts his arm around me. "I'm not ready to leave."

"Too bad," Rian says. "Not my problem."

I turn to Adrian and place my hand on his chest. "Give me a few minutes with the girls."

He nods.

I motion with my head for the girls to follow me into my bedroom.

They follow, but Rian turns around midway to my door. "And the princess wants tea with non-dairy milk. Good luck."

Adrian says nothing, but the pain on his face is clear. He wishes things were different. Unfortunately, we're stuck with a princess who's going to have a much harder time adjusting to normal life than Adrian did.

I shut the door and Blanca sits on the edge of my bed, Rian in the chair.

"I hear what goes on in that bed," Rian says.

Blanca rushes to her feet and looks around for another place to sit. She opts for the carpet.

"I wash my sheets," I say, rolling my eyes.

"You didn't this morning and you two were extra loud last night."

I suspect Rian's sour mood has something to do with Dylan admiring the princess, not just Adrian's omission, but I'm not calling her out on it. "Okay, I need to fill you guys in on what's going on."

They listen intently as I tell the story Adrian told me at breakfast. They're both kindhearted people, so I assume they'll understand and go along with my plan, but once I finish, they still look skeptical.

"So can she stay, Rian?" I ask.

Blanca looks at Rian and Rian at Blanca. Are they so close that they can have a conversation without any words?

"I'm worried you're going to do all this, bend over backward for this guy you barely know. I mean, he was just straight with you because his arranged bride showed up unannounced. He had no choice. And when he has to return to his 'royal duties'"—Rian puts royal duties in quotation marks—"he's going to drop you."

I suck in a breath and steel myself, turning to Blanca. "And you?"

Blanca is more subtle, shrugging. "Honestly?"

"Always," I say.

"I fear you're willing to go along with this because in some twisted way, you *want* him to break your heart."

I drop my head and stare at her. I wanted honesty, not some Psych 101 bullshit.

"You're hanging out with Ethan too much," I say. "Living with him has made you psychoanalyze everyone."

She holds up her hand. "You tend to go out with unavailable men, whether it's emotionally, physically, whatever. I'm not saying you enjoy being hurt. I just think you keep your guard up so when it blows up you can say, 'See, I knew it.'"

"Don't hold back," I say.

She stands and moves the comforter over the bare sheet before she sits down. "I don't want to be mean about it. That's not my intention." She places her hand on my leg. "Remember our junior year in high school when you dated that senior from Nichols High who had a football scholarship to UCLA? You dated him the entire summer, saying the two of you would be long distance, that he promised you. And what happened a week after school started? He called and said it wasn't working out."

"He was busy with classes."

I'd forgotten about Kevin. He did end up going to the NFL. I'm sure that needed his attention more than a girl back home in Brooklyn.

"Everyone around you knew it would never last. And then there's Ethan. He was hiding his past from you, and from what he tells me, you weren't forthcoming with him about yours either. You had to know that was going to be a major issue. Ethan told me he thought you'd accepted and healed about the loss of your mom." Her eyes widen, silently implying that she knows I'm not.

"And then there was that guy before Ethan who was, like, thirty years older than you," Rian chimes in. "Remember him? He ended up reconciling with his wife."

I throw my hands in the air and stand. "Jeez, you two make me feel great about myself. Thanks so much."

"All we're saying is that you try to protect yourself by dating men who are either physically or emotionally unavailable. Maybe it's subconscious and you don't know you're doing it. But I think you do it so you never have to be all in." Blanca squeezes my knee.

I think of all the men I've dated over the years, right down to my TA in college. Blanca and Rian might be on to something… but with Adrian, it's different. He saw me at my most vulnerable at my dad's house, and he was the one who picked me up. He stayed.

I fix my gaze on them. They're sharing a look with one another again. "I understand what you're saying and maybe that was my MO before, but it's not with Adrian. He's different."

Blanca blows out a breath.

"I'm asking you as my closest friends to support me. I stepped aside so you could date Ethan." I look at Blanca, then Rian. "And I've kept your secret love for Dylan to myself for years. All I'm asking for is a month. Please."

They're silent for a moment and I hold my breath, afraid to make a sound.

Blanca nods. "You're right. You were a great friend to me. I do hope I'm wrong about Adrian fitting into the trend from your past. I'll support you no matter what and I won't make waves while he's here."

"Thank you." My gaze shifts to Rian, who now has her knees pulled to her chest.

She lets her head fall back and looks at the ceiling. "Fine, but the princess needs to figure out that this is not her palace."

"I'll talk to her," I say. They stand, and we share a three-way hug. "Thank you, girls. I heart you so much."

"We heart you, and that's why we're worried. We don't want to see you hurt," Rian says.

"I know. Thank you for being so concerned about me."

"Always," they say in unison.

WE FILE out of my bedroom to find Adrian sitting in the chair across from Adelaide, leaning forward. "They aren't here to serve you. If you want to stay here and live a life without privilege, you need to become self-sufficient."

She nods. "I just asked for tea. She's a thin girl, I figured she had non-dairy milk."

He releases an exasperated sigh. "Do you really not do any of this yourself at home?"

She shakes her head. "No."

"Hey, guys." I break up the conversation.

Blanca hovers by the front door, and I sit on the arm of the chair. Adrian runs his hand along my back and hip. Rian sits in the chair opposite us.

I say, "You can stay, Adelaide, but like Adrian was telling you, we're not here to serve you. We all have jobs already."

"Yes, okay, but will you help me?"

Adrian blows out a breath. It's his annoyed one. "Sure. Why don't we go to the store today and get you settled?"

Adelaide smiles. "I'd like that. I have my belongings at a small hotel by the train station."

"We'll go pick them up," I say.

Adrian stands. "But we have to shower and get ready first. You'll be sleeping in that second room. I'll move my stuff out of there for you."

"Where will you sleep?" Adelaide asks.

"With Sierra."

She nods. "Of course. Okay." Her perfectly shaped legs that seemed glued together turn to Rian. "Thank you, and I'm sorry for this morning."

I turn to Adrian and smile like "See, she's a quick learner." Adrian rolls his eyes.

"Thank you for the apology," Rian politely says.

I'm happy that we're all getting along. Or at least trying to.

"Great. Now it's time for Sierra and me to get ready for the day." He takes my hand and heads to the bathroom.

"You shower together here?" Adelaide asks.

"Water conservation," Adrian answers and I laugh, slapping him on the chest.

"Oh." She looks horrified.

"He's kidding. You're going to have to figure out our brand of humor if you live here. Especially with the guys across the hall," Rian says. "Come on, I'll give you a proper introduction. Which will get you out of here before the moans and loud fuckery noises start from those two."

Rian stands and Blanca opens the door, all three of them filing out.

"Now let's see how dirty you are." Adrian backs me up into the bathroom.

I don't object as he strips my T-shirt off and pulls my pants down to my ankles. "You really think this is going to work out?"

He strips himself down and turns on the water. "All I really care about is you and me. Everything else is just noise."

He steps into the shower and takes my hand as I step over the tub wall and join him. He pulls me into his body as the warm water rains down between us.

"You can't live in a bubble," I say.

"Sure, I can. At least for right now I can. Now forget all that's out there and allow me to thank you properly for being so understanding." He falls to his knees, setting one of my feet on the edge of the tub wall, spreading me wider for him.

Between the warm water freeing the tension knotting inside me and his tongue teasing my clit, I forget all that's waiting for us outside of the small bathroom.

Blanca and Rian are so wrong. Prince Adrian doesn't want a princess. He wants a Wonder Woman.

CHAPTER TWENTY-FIVE

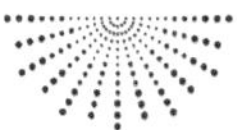

Sierra

Princess Adelaide adjusts well to change. Better than I thought she would anyway. After our shopping trip—where she bought her non-dairy milk and tea, along with egg whites and all the other foods she said she likes—she seemed to settle in okay with the group. It's still obvious she's treating this sabbatical from her life like some kind of fun experiment, but whatever.

I'm not going to lie, leaving her and Adrian alone in the apartment this morning was hard for me, because of that stupid little voice in my head. But another voice in my head tells me that if I don't show up at work, Kay will be the one to get Georgia's anchor position.

"Hey, Mick," I say, walking into the station.

"Did you hear the news?"

I stop and he hands me a few messages.

"That Kay is marrying Jack?" I ask, not looking up from my notes.

"No. She has to get pregnant before he marries her."

We both laugh.

"Some princess is missing," he says.

My hands pause mid flip between my messages and I glance up to see if he's testing me in some way. "What do you mean?"

"Yeah, it's all over those gossip blogs you got me addicted to. I figured you would've already seen. First that prince you love so much and now a princess. Do you think someone is picking off royalty?" He puts his chin in his palm and looks at me, waiting for an answer.

I swallow the lump that's blocking my airway. "I'm sure they just needed a breather or something. They'll turn up."

He nudges my arm. "You should do a story about it. I mean, you already know so much about them. That prince guy used to post, like, every day, and it's been an entire month with nothing."

"I have no idea who this princess is." I hide my crossed fingers behind my back because he's going to be so pissed if he ever finds out the truth.

"Hey, you two," Jack says with an outstretched hand, looking for his own messages. He smiles at me. "How's that story about the prince going?"

"I think the art department is still working on the copy," I lie for the second time in minutes.

Mick looks between Jack and me.

"Did you find the hook? Something that will intrigue our viewers?" He's going through all his messages and doesn't bother to look at me.

My stomach knots and twists. Only about a million things, and if I didn't care for the man, I would've blown up the entire thing and maybe been on my way to being the next

Barbara Walters. I laugh quietly, which makes Jack peek up at me. "Not yet, no."

Mick clears his throat and I glare at him, shaking my head adamantly so he doesn't tell Jack what he just told me.

"I was just telling Sierra that there's a prince *and* a princess missing now."

Jack puts down his messages and looks to me for more answers. "Is he talking about the same prince you were going to get an interview with?"

"You had an interview with him?" Mick asks.

I'm the worst work BFF for never telling him about any of this.

"Sierra won that date with Prince Adrian something or other," Jack says.

"Adrian Marx." Mick clears that up so there's no confusion. He glances at me with hurt in his eyes. If Adrian had never moved in, I would've told Mick. "He's the one who's missing."

Jack's interest is piqued. Just great.

"There's your story. Be that beat reporter I know you are and dig him up." Jack pats me on the shoulder and heads down the hall.

My forehead falls into my hands.

"Why the frown? This is great." Mick pats my head.

"Ugh." I walk away from him, not sure how I'm going to get away with this now that things are different between Adrian and me.

"Are we going to Hilda's today? You missed out last time. It's chicken pot pie soup day," he hollers after me, but I have no energy to give him an answer.

When I slide into my desk, I boot up my computer and type in the royalty gossip blogs I used to visit almost daily, and there it is. A picture of Prince Adrian and Princess Adelaide with the word missing in big block letters.

I scan the article that says there's no word from the two families but that they've been seen together in the Virgin Islands and London over the past week. I shake my head as I read theory after theory, some of them making it seem like they're Romeo and Juliet and ran away together and others that believe they aren't even together.

How ridiculous that a group of people obsessed with them are the ones starting all this crap. Luckily it's only on the blogs, so I should be able to squash any interest on Jack's part. Tell him there's nothing to pursue. The last thing I need is for their pictures to be plastered on the news while they're both walking around Cliffton Heights.

I WALK INTO THE APARTMENT, fully prepared to tell Adelaide she might have to leave because people are looking for her, and Rian grabs my arm and pulls me back into the hallway.

"We have a problem," she says.

"Tell me there isn't another prince or princess—or king or queen—in there."

She shakes her head. "Worse."

Taking my hand, she opens the door and drags me back into the apartment. The television is playing *The Bachelor*, Adelaide is sprawled on the couch wearing a flannel night-gown that Rian convinced her was in style when we went shopping, and fast food and Styrofoam containers cover the coffee table.

"She found Grubhub," Rian says. "And she's watched all my recordings."

Adelaide hears her and smiles. "Oh, hey, Sierra. I ordered this food and they delivered it right to the door. It's just like home, but the food is so much better! I can see why Adrian likes this regular people stuff."

I pick up the brown bag with the Scrumptuals logo on it. "I thought sugar was bad for your skin?"

She doesn't bother sitting up. "I thought about that after the milkshake I tried, but then I figured, why do I need good skin? The man I'm arranged to marry loves someone else. My parents will make me live with them until they find another suitor, so I'm going to eat whatever I want until I leave here."

She's wrong about Adrian loving me but I don't want to argue with her.

"And how are you paying for it?" I ask.

"My parents."

Interesting that she doesn't get cut off like Adrian. Then again, Adrian hasn't really had a shortage of money.

"Dinner is on me," she says, fast-forwarding through the commercials.

Rian looks at me. "What do you plan on doing when everything comes out?"

Adelaide pauses the television as though I'm interrupting her valuable time when it's clear she's been lying there all day. "It will be Adrian who bears the weight of that decision. I'll be the devastated fiancée he didn't want. At least that's how the press will spin it."

Rian sits in the chair opposite me. "Did you want to marry him?"

Adelaide glances at her then looks at the ceiling. "I don't know. It's what I'm supposed to do. I've known for a long time that he was to be my husband. I did worry that I wasn't as adventurous as him. He was always posting pictures of traveling, whereas I stay home."

"How could you marry someone you don't love?" Rian asks.

Adelaide seems to consider her question. "That's how I grew up. I don't know any different."

I mentally make a note to ask Adrian if he was accepting of the arranged marriage until his dad cheated on his mom. Is that what changed for him?

"I will say, seeing the guys here…" She waves her hand in front of her face. "This bachelor guy is gorgeous. We don't have quite the selection you do."

"Well, because we're not looking for a prince," I say.

"Aren't you though? I thought all women over here were looking for one, loved the fairy tale of it all." She picks up a fry from one of the discarded containers on the table.

"It's more figurative. We want our men to be a prince, but they don't actually hold a title." Leave it to Rian to explain it for her.

"I guess that makes sense. There aren't that many princes." A hollow laugh leaves her mouth. "Adrian comes from the best bloodline, so I'm not sure what will happen now."

How can I feel guilty that this woman doesn't get to marry Adrian? My claws should be out, but a part of me feels bad for her.

"Can't you tell your parents you don't want to marry a prince? That you want to meet your own man?" Rian asks.

Adelaide shakes her head. "No, his family has to complement our family. Both families have to get something in the exchange. Royal weddings are about duty and building bridges, not love and passion. Well, unless you're British apparently."

"So what happens if Adrian doesn't marry you?" I ask.

"His country will hate him because they'll look at it as though they're not important enough for him to follow in the footsteps of his family."

"That's absurd," Rian says.

Adelaide shows no emotion. "It's the way it is." She turns

to me. "It's going to be a very hard road for him. There will be backlash… for you both."

I lean back in the chair and try to ignore that pinprick in my heart that says things probably won't end up how I want.

Dylan walks through the door.

Rian blows out a breath, smacks her hands on her thighs, and stands. "Look at your princess now."

"What?" Dylan looks confused. How does that man have an IQ of one hundred forty? He can't even tell Rian has been pining over him for years.

"She found out about Grubhub," I say.

Dylan sits where Rian was and props his feet up on the table. "There's also Uber Eats and DoorDash and—"

"There's more?" Adelaide's eyes widen and she pulls out her phone, searching. "Oh, this place has sushi!"

"Thanks," I deadpan.

Dylan shrugs. "Can you find a bakery? Rian hasn't baked in the past couple of days," Dylan asks Adelaide.

"We have another problem," I say, ignoring Dylan. "All people are talking about on the royal blogs is how you're missing. My boss wants me to dig into the story."

Rian pretends to be doing something on her computer, but her eyes find mine. This puts me in a terrible situation. She knows that.

"What?" Adelaide sits up a bit and looks at me as though she has no idea what I'm talking about.

"The blogs. The people who are obsessed with royalty?" Surely she's heard of these blogs. I mean, movie stars know all about the blogs even if they don't read them.

"Like Sierra was," Dylan chimes in.

"Okay, you can leave whenever you want." I point at the door.

He chuckles, not moving an inch.

"I found a bakery," Adelaide says as though we weren't in the middle of a conversation.

"Great. Order me a chocolate cake. I'll pay you back," Dylan says.

Adelaide waves at him, then her thumbs move across her screen. "My treat."

"Ugh," Rian says.

"Trouble over there?" Dylan asks.

Rian picks up her computer and heads to her room.

"What's her problem? Can't solve her own math problem?" He laughs.

Adelaide laughs too, although I'm sure she doesn't understand what she's laughing at. Aggravation hits me hard and I stand, not wanting to be in the same room as either of them.

"You're leaving too?" Dylan asks.

"You need glasses," I say, heading to my room.

"I have twenty-twenty vision," he says, sounding offended.

I deny myself the urge to smack the back of his head. Instead, I slam my door. A minute later, my phone rings with a text message.

Rian: *The princess needs to go.*
Me: *I know. Believe me, I know.*

CHAPTER TWENTY-SIX

Adrian

Adelaide has been a pain in the ass for the past few weeks, so the remainder of my time with Sierra hasn't been as stress free as I wanted. Instead, Sierra is upset because Rian is upset because of Dylan's new fascination with Adelaide, who seems oblivious to anything that doesn't have to do with her and what she wants.

My phone rings on the way home from the Bagel Place. Seeing Felicia's name, I slide my thumb to answer.

"Hey, sis," I answer.

"Did you know that Princess Adelaide is in the same town as you?"

I freeze in the middle of the sidewalk. A man grumbles and moves around me. "Why do you think that?"

"Because someone snapped a picture of her in a tattoo parlor and posted it on one of those royal blogs. Do you never check these things? I've been following them to make sure they didn't track you down and throwing them tips to lead them away from your trail. Why didn't you tell me Princess Adelaide found you?"

"First, tell me why Declan thought it was okay to tell her."

"He did?"

"How else did you think she found me?" I step under a store awning, so all the pedestrians don't have to keep walking around me. "Oh, and I'm not marrying her."

All I get in response is dead silence for a few beats.

"It's time, Adrian. It's time for you to come home."

"I have another week."

"I'm sorry. Everyone is going to find you when they find her, so you might as well come home before they flood that small town. I'm sending Jean and I guess Clyde too. I'll fire Declan. You get to New York as soon as possible. They'll meet you at the same hotel you stayed at before."

Anger fumes inside me as if someone poured gasoline on already smoking embers. I don't even care that Declan is being fired and he's been my bodyguard since I was sixteen. Because of him, I've had to spend the last few weeks dealing with Adelaide's bullshit and now my time is being cut short.

More than that, I now have to tell Sierra that I have to return home early and I'm leaving tonight. I stop at the corner and try to call her. She doesn't answer, which means she's probably in a meeting or on a developing story. Pocketing my phone, I head to the apartment to have a word with Adelaide.

Adelaide's name being chanted can be heard a block away. When I peek around the corner, sure enough, there's a group of girls outside Ink Envy.

Fucking hell.

I slip into the apartment building and into the elevator without being noticed since their sole attention is on Dylan's tattoo parlor. My phone rings the minute I step into the empty apartment, and I glance out the window to watch the scene below. There aren't too many girls there yet, but enough that it's annoying. I've seen it firsthand how out of control these situations can get.

"Sierra," I say into my phone.

"Hey. I saw. I've been searching the blogs for two weeks. I could kill Dylan."

"He didn't take the picture," I say, sticking up for the man who's been on Sierra and Rian's hit list since Adelaide showed up.

"He probably took her there to show off. What does he see in her?"

"Listen, my sister called."

She stops ranting. "Oh."

"She's sending Jean and a bodyguard to pick me up in New York tomorrow. I'm assuming Adelaide will be coming with me."

More silence.

"I have to go. I have to be in Sandsal when this all comes out."

"Of course," she says.

"So you'll come?"

"What?" Her voice is shaky and unsure.

"Come with me. I'll introduce you to my parents and we'll figure out how we're going to handle this." I close my eyes, hoping like hell that she'll agree.

"I have to work."

"Can you take vacation?"

"I don't know," she just about whispers.

My eyes open. I have to understand that she has obligations here. I can't expect her to uproot her life on a moment's notice. She's happy here.

"Okay. Can you come home now? I want to see you before I leave."

"I have a staff meeting. I'm sorry. But you're coming back, right?"

I hate the pain I hear in her voice. I hate even more that there's nothing I can do to make it go away. "I don't know when."

"Maybe I can get to the city tonight."

Finally she's sounding more like the Sierra I know. "Perfect. The same hotel as before. Same name—Athos Dumas. I'll tell them I'm expecting you."

"Okay. I'll come right after my staff meeting. I should go."

"Sierra?" I say.

"Yeah?"

"Please make sure you come."

"Yeah, for sure. I just have a few things to do at the office. You go and get out of Cliffton Heights so you're safe. I'm going to be late for the meeting. I'll see you tonight."

The line dies before I can say goodbye, and I stare at my phone because I fear it's the last time I'll talk to Sierra. Especially if I get on that plane tomorrow morning.

The apartment door opens, Adelaide dressed in leather pants and a sweatshirt that's pulled up over her head.

"What the hell?" I ask.

Dylan raises his arm to stop me from saying more because when the hood comes off, I see that Adelaide's eyes are red-rimmed from crying.

I don't give a shit.

"Pack your crap," I say. "We're leaving in a half hour to go into the city. My assistant and bodyguard will escort us back home."

I storm into Sierra's room and pull my suitcases out from the closet, shoving all my clothes in as fast as I can. Coming out of the bedroom to get my toiletries, I spot Dylan sitting on the couch.

"I'm sorry, man," he says.

"It's fine. It just sucks that Sierra has to work so she can't come with me."

His face shows no emotion, as though he expected that to happen.

"I only had a week left anyway. Time to stop living someone else's life."

"And Sierra said she couldn't go?" he asks.

I swallow the dryness that's coated my throat since I got off the phone with her. "That's what she said."

"That's bullshit." He shakes his head. "I know she has shit to deal with about her mom, but you two were doing great."

I shrug and disappear into the bathroom. She's the one woman who doesn't want me to be a prince. How crazy is that? Especially since she won a date with me *because* I was a prince.

When my suitcases are by the front door, Dylan shakes my hand and hugs Adelaide. "I'm going to go distract the masses. Take the back exit into the alley. Hopefully we see you again." Dylan only really says it to me, shaking my hand another time. "Keep your hood up," he instructs Adelaide.

We all take the elevator to the first floor and Dylan points to where we need to go. I hate sneaking out with no goodbye to the people who changed my life forever.

When we're halfway to the train station, Adelaide says, "I'm sorry."

"It's fine."

"What about Sierra? Is she coming?"

I shake my head.

"Oh. I'm sorry. But you know it would've never worked out anyway. Maybe it's better this way."

I stop and lean in so I'm inches from her face. "You have no idea what you're talking about, so shut it. Maybe you want to call for your own assistant and bodyguard?"

"I didn't mean that what you two had wasn't real."

"Stop saying had. We still have it," I mumble as we reach at the train station.

"I'm sure it was real. You two were cute together, but she's not princess material. She would never fit in."

"I'm not looking for a princess, but if I were, Sierra would make a great princess. She's caring and compassionate and she did a lot for you, so I suggest you fall off your high horse."

She rolls her eyes. "I was merely suggesting—"

I raise my hand. "I don't need your suggestions. You fucked this up for me and I'm still pissed off, so I'd advise you to keep quiet until we're back in our own countries. And in case I wasn't clear, I'm not marrying you. No matter what."

"I don't want to marry you."

"Good."

She huffs.

Lucky for me, the train comes. I'm still somewhat of a gentleman and let Adelaide board first. The conductor is more than willing to help her with all her bags.

As we pull away from the station and I watch the Cliffton Heights sign pass by the window, I close my eyes, not wanting to say goodbye.

CHAPTER TWENTY-SEVEN

Sierra

"Maybe I should take the story, Jack," Kay says after I tell them that the princess has already been found and she's probably halfway home by now. "I mean, how good of a job was she doing? The princess was found in Cliffton Heights, in her *friend's* tattoo parlor."

All eyes shift to me. Between the fact Adrian is on his way to New York City without me and now this, I'm done. Add on the fact that I've been avoiding my dad since he's been back from his trip and I want to go home and bury my head under my covers and cry.

The buzzer on the phone rings and Jack presses the button. "Hey, Mick."

"There's a Dylan Phillips here to see Sierra."

Jack's eyes find me across the table.

"I'm sorry," I say. "Tell him I'm in a meeting."

Mick sighs. "Yeah, I tried that. He's not accepting that answer."

There's muffled noise and sounds of a struggle for a few seconds.

"Give it to me," Dylan's strained voice says. "Sierra, get your ass out here. We need to talk now!"

"Dylan, go home," I call.

More muffled noise, but I hear Dylan asking Mick where the conference room is, to which Mick says he's cute and all but he's not giving up that info.

"I'm not going home. You are not going to throw this away. You're happy. For the first time since I've known you, you're really happy. Do not pull this bullshit now. Own your feelings, take the risk, show him how much you care."

"Who is this guy? Dalai Lama?" Kay asks.

I narrow my eyes at her for being so ridiculous right now.

Jack holds up his hands. "She's in a meeting and doesn't want to talk."

But the conference room door opens and in walks Dylan, stalking toward me. "Let's go. You're going to be happy whether you want to or not."

He comes over and grabs my upper arm. I try to pull out of his grasp, but he keeps grabbing it back.

"Why is this any of your business?" I argue.

"Because I'm your friend and I love you." He pulls me toward the door but stops before exiting. "Sierra will be taking at least a week's vacation. She apologizes for the short notice and all, but she's going to go chase down the love of her life."

Then we're out before I can say anything.

"He's not the love of my life and I'm going to be fired after this stunt of yours," I say.

"You can report the news in Sandsal if you have to. Surely

after he figures out how to fix this arranged marriage thing, he can figure out a way to let women have jobs."

"Women have jobs over there." I pull my arm from his grasp. "I have to grab my purse."

"Fine."

He waits like a bodyguard outside my cubicle while I grab my stuff. I even take my personal items because let's face it, I'm probably going to get a call later tonight that says I'm fired.

We walk out of the station and into a waiting taxi.

"Rian packed your bags. You're on the next train into the city." Dylan leans forward and instructs the driver to go to the train station.

"Dylan," I sigh.

He turns in my direction and grabs my hand. "You have to jump this time. You have to. I wish I could do it for you, but this is all you. He's going to catch you. I'm sure of it."

The tears I've been holding back since Adrian's call well up in my eyes. Am I that transparent? "But what if—"

We pull up to the train station as he says, "No negativity."

"But when we get there… Adelaide said people will hate him and me too. And it's his family. How can he possibly choose me over his family?"

He wipes one of my tears with the pad of his thumb. "You're enough."

I release a ragged breath. The vehicle comes to a stop, and when I look out the window, I see the station.

Dylan gets out of the taxi and takes my luggage from the driver. "Your passport is in the first pocket. Now go get your boy."

I take my luggage, not feeling nearly as confident as Dylan about how this will all turn out.

"Go, and if he doesn't catch you, I will."

I smile. I have the best friends in the whole wide world.

The train whistle sounds, and we both look to see it pulling into the station.

I step forward and kiss his cheek. "Thanks, Dylan."

"No problem."

I run up the steps with my luggage hitting every step. The conductor takes it from my hands, and I wave to Dylan at the curb. My stomach fills with a light, fluttering feeling. Am I really going to put myself out there?

I guess I am.

I've never been more terrified in my entire life.

LUGGING a suitcase along the streets of New York City sucks. It's tipped on its side more than a few times. But when a bellhop takes my luggage and I walk into the same lobby I did weeks prior, I'm more excited than I am worried.

I tell the lady at the desk I'm here to see Athos Dumas and show her my license.

"Our bellhop will show you up." She raises her hand.

The bellhop who has my suitcase leads me to the same elevator the John Cena lookalike used before. We end up in the same long hallway on the walk to his room. The bellhop knocks on the door. The door opens and I hold my breath. But it's Jean on the other side.

"Miss Sanders?" he asks.

"Yes. Is Adrian in?"

"You do mean Prince Adrian, I assume?" There's a coolness coming off him that wasn't there the night of our date.

"Yes."

"Hold on." Instead of asking me in, he shuts the door.

I'm once again doubting my decision to be here.

I smile at the bellhop and put my hand in my purse. "I can just pay you."

"I have to make sure you get in," he mumbles, his smile filled with doubt about whether that will actually happen.

"Right." I rock back on my heels, thankful I'm at least wearing my work clothes.

It feels as if a decade passes while I debate whether anyone is actually going to come to the door. The bellhop and I exchange another set of smiles.

"He knew I was coming."

The bellhop nods.

Then I hear movement behind the door. Thank God. The door springs open, and Adrian is there, wearing sweatpants and a T-shirt, looking all kinds of yummy.

"You came?" He steps through the doorway, picking me up and swinging me into the foyer.

Ha, bellhop. Told you.

"I came."

He lowers me to the floor and his hands hold my face. "Thank you." His lips capture mine.

The sound of someone clearing their throat interrupts us. "In private, sir," Jean says, handing money to the bellhop and taking my bag.

Adrian's hands slide down my body, grabbing my ass to pick me up, and I wrap my legs around his waist. "I must show you the bedroom now. You didn't get a full tour last time."

"Great idea."

We laugh all the way to his bedroom. He deposits me on the bed, and I slide up as he crawls over me, his lips unable to stop kissing me.

"I didn't think you'd show up."

"Dylan convinced me," I say.

"What did he say?" He kisses my lips then my jaw and my neck, his fingers making quick work of my blouse.

"Exactly what I needed to hear."

He peeks up at me. "He's a smart man. I'll have to thank him."

"Let's not go too far."

He laughs, unbuttoning my slacks. "Oh, we're going all the way tonight."

"That's not what I meant. I was talking about Dylan."

He climbs up my body, grabbing the back of his T-shirt and pulling it off his body. "I don't want to talk about Dylan anymore."

Adrian's lips capture mine and his tongue slides into my mouth.

How can I have missed the weight of his body when I just had him last night?

His hands skim across my skin and he finishes undressing me, his gaze soaking me in as if he thought he'd lost me.

I help him pull down his sweatpants and his dick pops out, eager to greet me. "Nice. No boxers, huh?"

"I wanted to be prepared if you showed up." He smiles, and I grab his face, pulling it down to mine.

For the rest of the night, there's not a lot of talk, though we do make a lot of noise.

CHAPTER TWENTY-EIGHT

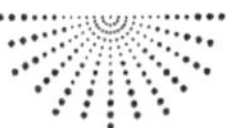

Sierra

Princess Adelaide's bodyguard was at the airport to escort her back home on her own flight. I wasn't sad to see her go. The flight to Europe was long and though we didn't join the mile high club, the private plane was definitely a perk.

This country is exactly as I expected. Almost like the fairy tales my mom would read me as a little girl. Rolling green hills, an overabundance of flower beds, and a big giant mansion in the middle of nowhere. We drive through the gold gates with a big M in a cursive script in the middle and Adrian squeezes my hand.

I feel like I know now what Cinderella must have been feeling when she went to the palace for the dance. Inadequate. I'm a nobody and here I am, interjecting myself into their lives.

Seconds after the car pulls to a stop, the door on my side opens and a man's shocked face appears. He rears back for a moment but quickly regains his composure and offers me his hand to step down from the black SUV.

"Ma'am." He slightly bows.

"Thank you."

"Ned, this is Sierra Sanders," Adrian says, approaching another man to get our luggage.

"Please, sir, allow us," he says.

Adrian laughs and clamps him on the shoulder. "Sorry, I've been in the States too long." Then he hugs Ned, who looks as if he's not used to receiving physical affection from Adrian—ever.

Adrian grabs my hand, leading me up the steps to the giant front doors. Doors so tall you wonder how the hinges hold it up.

The minute we walk in, a willowy brunette wearing a conservative dress and flats runs down the stairs, takes Adrian by the arm, and leads us into a study on the right. "You didn't tell me you were bringing her." Her eyes meet mine.

"Felicia, this is Sierra. Sierra, this is my older sister." Adrian's all smiles, but from Felicia's reaction, this doesn't feel like the time to be happy.

Felicia smiles at me. "Hello. Nice to meet you."

Were they all taught to be overly polite?

She turns her attention back to her brother. "Adrian."

"I don't care. I told you I'm not marrying Adelaide."

"Princess Adelaide," she corrects. "You need to talk to Mom and Dad."

My stomach clenches when I think about meeting the king and queen.

The study door opens and a boy who resembles Adrian

runs right into his arms. Adrian picks him up in giant bear hug. The boy's eyes are squeezed shut as though he's afraid to open them for fear he's dreaming.

"Rowan," Adrian says, and I hear the relief in his voice.

"I missed you so much," the little boy says.

Adrian lowers him back to the floor and the boy looks at me quizzically. "Who is she?"

"Rowan, manners," Felicia scolds.

"Sorry. Who is your friend, Adrian?"

"Better," Felicia says.

"This is Sierra Sanders." Adrian puts his arm around my waist, and I catch Felicia's slight eye roll.

Rowan steps up to hug me, but Felicia puts her hand on his chest. Rowan blows out his breath and nods. Then he does a sort of half bow. "Nice to meet you, Miss Sanders."

"Get up, Rowan. What the hell are you making him do?" Adrian asks his sister.

"Training him to be a king," she says blankly.

A chill washes across the room, and Adrian's arm drops from my waist. "Hey, Ro, go show Sierra your room so I can talk to Felicia for a second."

"Okay." Rowan steps up and turns like a trained honor guard, holding out his arm for me.

"God, look what you've done to him," Adrian says.

I slide my arm through his, but once we exit the study, Rowan drops the act and grabs my hand. "Come on."

We walk up the winding staircase, and when we hit the top, he freezes, throwing his body against the wall. He signals for me to do the same, so I play along. At least I thought we were playing until I hear yelling.

"You cannot blame him. You know he never wanted this life," a woman says.

Rowan puts his finger to his lips.

"You're the one who allowed him to go there and stay for two months. Of course he found a common girl he wants to marry."

"Don't you pin this on me. Maybe if you weren't screwing someone on your desk, he wouldn't have fled the country!"

"Here we go again. I apologized for that. I never wanted Felicia to find me. I didn't purposely leave the door open," the man says.

"You've never been good at being discreet."

"Sorry I don't have a trainer who only wants me for one thing, like you."

Rowan does a somersault past a door as if he's a member of the SWAT team and I almost laugh until I hear footsteps and I freeze.

"Don't you try to put me down. At least my guy can keep his mouth shut—unlike the women you choose, who think they'll replace me."

"I'm done. You figure this out. Just get her out of here before things get more complicated. He *needs* to marry Princess Adelaide." The man who sounds a lot like Adrian walks out and comes face-to-face with the woman he wants out.

He stands there for a moment, his eyes scouring me with a look of disgust. I want to wither under his assessment, but I somehow stay standing.

"Dad, this is Sierra, Adrian's friend." Rowan comes back as if he never heard his parents fighting.

His dad ruffles his hair. "I know. I saw them arrive. Where is your brother?"

"He's with Felicia in the study," Rowan says.

His dad walks down the hallway without even a hello or a handshake. I guess I know where I stand with him.

"Hello, Sierra," a sweeter voice says from behind me.

I turn to find an older version of Felicia.

Rowan hugs her around the hips. "Mommy."

She pats his back, her eyes solely on me. "What are you doing with Sierra, Rowan?"

"Adrian said for me to show her my room."

She bends to his level. "That's nice. How about you go work on your German lessons so I can have a quick word with Sierra? Then I'll send her down."

"*Ja, Mutter.*"

She smiles at her son. "Rowan?"

"Yes?"

"Good job." She ruffles his hair like his dad did, and he runs down the hall. The queen stands and holds out her arm, motioning to the room she came from. "Come in, please."

I enter the room expecting it to be a bedroom, but it's a sitting area with floor-to-ceiling bookcases filled tightly with books.

"Please have a seat," she says, shutting the door.

"Thank you."

"Tea or something to drink?" she asks.

"No, I'm good, thank you."

She sits in the chair across from me, crossing her ankles and leaning her legs in one direction. Exactly like Princess Adelaide did until she figured out the luxury of a couch, DVR, and delivery food service.

"So you're the woman he's chosen," she asks, as though she expects me to answer. "You're very pretty."

"Thank you." I yank at the hem of my dress Rian packed for me. Even though it hits me at the knees, it suddenly feels too short.

"I can see what he sees in you."

I nod.

"I'm sorry you heard the king and me fighting."

"It's okay."

"Do your parents fight?" she asks, which I find to be a weird question.

"My mother passed when I was ten."

A look of sadness falls over her perfectly painted-on face. "I'm sorry."

"Thank you."

I want to throw up at how polite this conversation is. I want to lean back, cross my legs, and tell her that I understand that she doesn't like me, but her son does so, how does she plan on handling it? But I won't do that because it would embarrass Adrian and I need to make sure this goes as smoothly as possible.

"How did she pass?"

"In the Iraq War."

Her hand covers her heart. "Oh, she was a soldier?"

I nod.

"I see. Well, maybe you didn't see it growing up, but sometimes parents fight. It doesn't mean anything." There's a sort of cool politeness rolling off her now.

I should tell her that her son told me everything and she can stop the charade. Right now, I'm wondering if I should tell him that she cheated as well.

A knock sounds on the door and I'm thankful for any interruption.

"Come in," she says, never glancing over her shoulder to see who it is.

"Mother, it's me." Felicia enters the room, her phone in hand. "Dad is with Adrian in the study and he'd like you to join them. I'll escort Sierra to her quarters. Which room would you like her to be settled in?"

The queen stands. "Have her in the east wing. We wouldn't want any sneaking around at night. You two might have been sleeping together where you're from, but that's unacceptable behavior here." Her eyes are ice cold now, any pretense of politeness gone.

I have to clamp my mouth shut from making a crack about the only sneaking around here is being done by her and her husband.

"Perfect," I say with whatever smile I can muster. Felicia waits for me to walk out of the room, but I stop before exiting. "It was a pleasure to meet you." I'm unsure of what to call her.

"I wish I could say the same," she says, and it's like a knife to the heart.

Felicia escorts me down the hall. "I'll have Ned bring your bag to your room. In the meantime, you have your own quarters—a television room, bathroom, and bedroom. The pool is down one level, the fitness room attached to that." As Felicia continues, I feel like I'm being greeted by a hotel staff member.

She walks me to a huge room with twelve-foot ceilings covered in ornate molding, the floor-to-ceiling windows covered with long, heavy drapes. There's a seating area in front of a fireplace, as well as a four-poster bed.

"It's beautiful," I say.

Felicia walks by me and opens a door. "Your private bathroom is in here."

"Thank you." I stand in the middle of the room, not wanting to touch anything because it all looks so perfect.

"I'm sure Adrian will find his way to you at some point." She heads for the door.

"Felicia?" I say, and she turns around, tucking a stray chestnut strand that escaped her ponytail behind her ear. "Tell me the truth. Does everyone here hate me?"

Her shoulders slump and she shuts the door before closing the distance between us. "Adrian put you in a tough position when he decided to bring you here. There's a lot going on in our family at the moment, and the fact that he picked now to fall in love isn't ideal."

I touch her arm to reassure her. "He's not in love."

She looks at me for a moment. "Guess we'll see."

She walks out of the room, and when the big door shuts, my heart free falls to my stomach.

What have I gotten myself into?

CHAPTER TWENTY-NINE

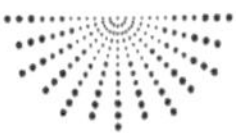

Adrian

*B*ang.

My dad's fist lands on the table. "This is it. We gave you what you wanted. Why must you always push our buttons?"

I cross my arms and widen my stance. "Because I don't want this life. I've been clear for years about that. I don't want to marry a woman I don't love. I don't want a marriage like you and Mom."

My mom enters the room without a knock or announcement. She moves across the room with the grace of a queen, her warm hands on my cheeks as I bend down to kiss hers.

"Adrian," she says, love laced in the letters of my name.

"Mother," I say.

"Good to have you home." Her eyes close briefly and she inhales like she's a dog that needs to smell her offspring.

"Thank you."

My dad stares at my mom, and she nods. When I was younger, I thought they were so in love they could communicate without words, but I was clearly wrong.

"I put her in the east wing," my mom tells him.

"She'll be moving to the west wing with me," I inform them.

"No, she won't." My father's fingers wrap around the edge of the table, his knuckles turning white.

"It's not up for discussion."

Neither of them say anything.

"Are you getting a divorce?" I ask.

They exchange a look. "Yes," they say in unison.

"So I'm to be King?" A sour taste coats my mouth.

"You will be once we go public," my dad says.

"Actually, not until I marry."

"Correct," my mother says. "But you cannot marry Sierra."

I cock my head at her. It's not like I've even mentioned marrying Sierra, but it pisses me off nonetheless that she's trying to tell me who I can and cannot spend my life with. "Why would that be?"

"Darling, she's not ready or groomed to be Queen. Plus, she's not from Sandsal or a country that even has a monarchy. She's from the States. I'm not sure she could do the job that's required." She sits in a chair, patting the one next to her. "Come and sit. Let's talk about this. She's a beautiful girl, but she's not queen material."

I don't sit, and I don't remove my arms from their crossed position. "You don't even know her."

"I know her type. I saw her film bits on that local television show after Felicia told me she was the one who won the contest. We thought she'd be good because she'd give you some good publicity, not overhaul your life."

I hold up my hand. "Please stop. I like Sierra a lot."

"Like is not love, darling," she says as if I'm a five-year-old who couldn't possibly understand.

I laugh. "Oh, did you have to love someone to rule this country? I wasn't aware of that." I look between my parents, my accusation clear.

My mom scowls and my dad shakes his head.

"This is why we suggested Princess Adelaide," Mom says. "Your father and I put a lot of thought into that arrangement. She's beautiful and smart and does so much with children."

"I don't love her." I don't add that I can barely tolerate her.

My father rounds the desk. "Exactly, so then you'll have a clear head to rule. How exactly will you make decisions when people are scrutinizing you for not following rules this family has set out for centuries?"

"You seemed to be able to when you were sleeping with someone on your desk."

My father's nostrils flare and I want to laugh. Stop casting stones when they can ricochet off me and back on to you.

"He's impossible," he says to my mother as if I'm no longer there.

"Now, I want to show her the grounds. Excuse me."

My hand is on the doorknob when my mother speaks. "Just so you know, the press has already caught wind of your little friend. You might want to have a look."

I say nothing and walk through the door, shutting it behind me. Pulling out my phone, I type in a search for my name, and the first article that pops up has a picture of us stepping off the plane. Sierra's red hair blows over her face and I'm looking at her as though she's my everything. And she is.

The headline reads, "Prince Adrian brings home more than souvenirs."

I scan the article while making my way to the east wing. The article isn't exactly nice to Sierra, but it's not horrible either. It's clear she's disliked though because she means change and everyone in this country hates change. My parents are so worried about the public coffers closing if we face enough disapproval to abolish the monarchy, but I say good riddance. It would take some getting used to, but I'd manage.

Stuffing my phone into my pocket, I knock on the door of her guest room. Just hearing her feet on the marble floor makes my heart thump. She opens the door and my arms swallow her up as I kick the door shut.

"I'm sorry," I say, then my lips land on hers.

"It's lonely here."

"Don't worry, Daddy's here." My fingers fumble with the zipper on her dress and she giggles as we fall to the bed.

"Yeah, no Daddy stuff," she says, her hands running down the back of my neck.

"Okay." I laugh.

She presses her hand to my chest and slides away from me. "So what happened with your parents?"

"I don't want to talk about it." I dive down for another kiss, but she dodges me. "Sierrrrraaaa," I whine like Rowan would.

"Your mother and father were both kind of cold to me. They don't like me."

I tuck a strand of her hair behind her ear. "They're old-school. They want me to do what they want me to do. It's nothing against you personally."

She slides up the bed and I want to start kicking and screaming. "What if they never warm up to me? I'm sure they blame me for you not marrying Adelaide."

"No, they blame me. They've known for a long time it's not what I wanted." I crawl on my hands and knees to get near her again, but she rolls to the side and off the bed.

"Adrian, this is serious."

My head falls back to the mattress and I fling my arm over my eyes. "They'll get over it. They always do."

When I crashed the Alfa Romeo at sixteen, they bought me a new one. After the prom when I flew everyone to our house in the Alps and threw a party everyone still talks about, they forgave me. I've done a lot of crap they've had to forgive me for, falling for someone who doesn't have an aristocratic bloodline can be added to the list.

"I know you think that because they've never disowned you after all your stupid stunts, but this is different. This is your country. This is your family obligation." She sits on the edge of the bed.

I roll toward her and put my head in her lap. She runs her short nails over the back of my scalp, and my eyes drift closed.

"I can tell they're not happy about me being here," she whispers.

Truth is, I know that, and I wasn't surprised when my family ambushed me in the study. "I'll handle it."

"I want *us* to handle it."

I turn and look up at her. Her fingers run down my now beard.

"I'm worried, Adrian. I don't fit in here and they know it." She's being vulnerable, which shows me how scared she is.

I sit up and take her in my arms, laying us down on the bed together. "Hey, I'm not going anywhere, okay? This isn't something I'm going to wake up feeling different about."

She nods, but there's a slight hesitation.

"Now where's your bag? You're coming to my quarters."

"No, I'm not."

"Yes, you are."

"Your mom already thinks I'm some hussy. I'm not going to sleep in your bed under your parents' roof. It's completely disrespectful."

"Need I remind you what we did under your dad's roof?" I let my hand trail down and take a firm grip of one of her ass cheeks.

She smacks me in the chest.

I chuckle, holding up my hand. "Okay. Okay. You can stay here, and I'll sneak down during the night."

A soft knock lands on the door. I know that knock well.

Sierra slides out of my hold and sits up on the bed, adjusting her dress and her hair.

"Come in," I call.

Rowan opens the door, runs in, and jumps on the bed.

"What's up, little man?" I ask.

"Mom told me to tell Sierra that dinner is at seven."

"Thanks."

"Want to play *Dance Party*?" he asks Sierra.

"Not now," I say.

"Sure," Sierra says at the same time.

Rowan takes her hand. "Let's go to the media room. Are you coming, Adrian?"

Sierra smiles at me over her shoulder.

"Yeah, I'm coming," I say.

Rowan talks to Sierra the entire way to the media room.

Once they start dancing, it's the first time since we arrived that the tension Sierra's carrying lifts and she's back to being the woman I love. My mind trips over the word.

Sierra does a dance and Rowan totally schools her on the moves. She picks him up and swings him around, and he laughs when she tosses him on the couch.

Yeah, Felicia might be right. I do love her.

CHAPTER THIRTY

Sierra

Dinner with the Marx family is formal. There's no eating around the television like my dad and I used to do, which I assumed when Adrian told me to wear a dress. Too bad Rian only packed me the dresses I wear on interviews and for funerals. I get her reasoning, but they make me feel uncomfortable and less like myself.

After winding through the formal living room because I got lost, I step into the dining room. Adrian's mom is there, inspecting the place settings, straightening forks and knives.

"Are you enjoying your arrangements?" she asks, never looking at me.

"They're very nice. Thank you for having me."

"We didn't have much choice, did we?" She moves a goblet an inch to the right.

"I'm sorry if you feel as though you were ambushed. I wasn't aware Adrian didn't tell you to expect me."

"Thank you for that, Sierra."

"There you are. I went to grab you." Adrian comes in, his arms stretching across my stomach and his mouth attaching to my neck.

I don't reciprocate and catch his mother watching her son maul me in front of her.

"Don't," I whisper.

But Adrian doesn't listen because he doesn't care what his parents think. He goes to the table and switches a few name tags around. "I'll be sitting next to Sierra, Mother."

"Oh, I had no idea how Ned arranged them. I haven't gotten there yet," she lies. I saw her straighten two name tags before she said anything to me.

Adrian slides a chair out for me. "Come, babe."

Felicia and Rowan join us, and Felicia says, "Now, Rowan, slide out my chair like Adrian is for Sierra."

"What are you doing to him?" Adrian asks, shaking his head.

"He has to learn what a king does since you're going to abandon your post," Felicia responds, sitting graciously. Her chest hits the table when Rowan isn't strong enough to push in the chair.

"He's not going to be king," Adrian says, sitting next to me.

"Really? Then who is?" Felicia takes the napkin out of the holder and lays it in her lap. "Not you. You're running from those responsibilities."

"Come on, you two. Let's have a nice dinner. Adrian is finally back, and we have Sierra here," the queen says.

Adrian squeezes my hand under the table as though we're making progress.

"Did you know I handpicked you? Did Adrian tell you that?" Felicia says across the table from me.

Rowan gets in his chair and makes a triangle out of his name tag.

"Right here, bud."

Adrian puts his fingers up like a goalpost and Rowan shoots the triangle across the table. It goes through and Adrian cheers for him. They switch duties and Adrian points the triangle piece of paper at Rowan, who has his fingers up as a goalpost.

"I wasn't aware," I answer Felicia, smiling at Adrian and his brother.

"I did it because you were a reporter. I have one question for you." She looks around. Thankfully, the queen has left to go to the kitchen.

"What?"

"Felicia, let it rest," Adrian says, but he continues to play with Rowan.

"I like her, Felicia," Rowan says, and he shoots me a smile that reveals he's still losing some of his teeth.

"Are you doing all this because you want to get some scoop on our family? Maybe for a raise or a promotion or something?"

"Felicia," Adrian says, his voice one of warning.

I squeeze his hand. "I was actually asked to dig up information on Adrian. I was told that the interview he promised me would need a hook." I glance around the immediate area. "He's informed me of some of the problems here, and I didn't for one second consider using it for my own gain. I'm not in this for professional reasons, but I don't expect you to believe me."

Felicia glances at Adrian, who puts his arm around the back of my chair. "Okay. That's all I needed to know."

"I wouldn't do that to someone."

Adrian squeezes my shoulder and leans close, his game with Rowan over. "She knows. We know."

He kisses my neck right under my ear, and I want to push him away, tell him not to show me any physical affection. But at the same time, his touch makes me believe what he told me earlier, that he's not going to wake up one day and change his mind about what he wants.

The king and queen enter the dining room together, not holding hands or wearing a smile. But the king follows the queen to her seat, slides out her chair, and tucks it back in after she sits. Then he takes his seat at the other end of the table.

A server comes round and pours wine for all the adults and what I assume is juice for Rowan. No one says much, not even Rowan, who hasn't shut up anytime I've been around him.

"We'll be going into town tomorrow," Adrian says, bringing a spoonful of soup to his mouth.

"The press will spot you. Take Clyde with you," his mom says, never looking up from her bowl.

"I'm going to drive us myself. I don't need Clyde," Adrian says.

His dad puts down his spoon and wipes his face. "With Sierra tagging along, you cannot handle all that attention without Clyde. For her safety, and your own, you should take security with you."

Adrian shrugs. "We'll see. Maybe he can follow me."

"What are you doing in town?" Felicia asks.

"I'm just taking her to see some of Sandsal."

"A country you're so ashamed of?" the king asks.

"I could use some new clothes," I add, trying my best to participate in the conversation. "My friend packed for me and some of her choices..."

"I was going to have someone come to the house to fit you for a few outfits. We have a gala this weekend, and you're going to accompany me to a charity event next week."

His mom cuts up her meat as if she's mastered an etiquette class.

"Oh, that's not necessary."

His mom pauses mid-cut and glances at me. I try to ignore how unnerved that makes me. She's watching me the same way she did when Adrian entered the room and kissed my neck. As though she's surprised.

"Be careful. You know how the press is when you've been gone a long time," the king says to Adrian, who doesn't bother to respond.

I've sat through many uncomfortable dinners—ones where my dad barely talked, the one where I had to meet Fae and she kept telling me how much she enjoyed spending time with my father, the first dinner with Ethan and Blanca as a couple, their hands disappearing under the table. But no dinner has ever been as uncomfortable as this one.

"THIS IS THE SMALL DOWNTOWN AREA." Adrian points at the cobblestone road that leads to what appears to be a small town where buildings are built on top of buildings. It's quaint and reminds me of something you'd see on a postcard. "I would've liked to drive you myself, but my father is right. Your safety is my first concern."

Clyde opens up my door and I step out, the sun shining on us.

Adrian follows and his hand finds mine. "I have a chocolate shop I want to show you first."

He walks as though he's on a mission, and I struggle to keep up. A few people point and whisper, but they're smiling. It's what I imagine being with a celebrity walking down Hollywood Boulevard in LA must feel like, but Adrian seems oblivious to it.

He opens the door of the shop and the sweet aroma of chocolate fills my nostrils.

"I love it already." I walk through the tables filled with chocolate-coated everything from Rice Krispies Treats to raisins.

There's a small cafe attached to the shop, where Adrian disappears while I take an offered sample from the man behind the counter.

"Thank you," I say before biting into caramel gooeyness. "It's delicious."

He smiles and bows.

Adrian comes over and hands me a drink. "Latte."

The man bows again, offering him chocolate. Adrian takes one, bowing his head slightly in appreciation. Once he finishes chewing, he sips his drink.

"Did you like it?" Adrian asks me.

I nod enthusiastically. "Yes."

"We'll take a pound," he says to the man.

A few minutes later, we leave the chocolate shop and Adrian hands the bag to Clyde, who I think might be John Cena 2.0's brother. The resemblance is uncanny.

"You said you wanted some clothes? "Adrian asks, his hand on the small of my back.

A man steps in front of us and takes our picture, sliding out of the way as we walk by. Adrian's unfazed and keeps walking while my heart beats a hard rhythm.

"Where do those pictures get published?" I whisper.

"Newspapers, magazines. Similar to the States."

"Oh, so, like, Sandsal knows who I am?"

He chuckles and it draws more attention to us. "They've known about you since we walked off the plane. You really haven't been checking your blogs or news since we got here, have you?"

"No." I don't tell him it's because I'm worried about what they will say.

"Sierra," one of the photographers calls, "what did you do to convince Prince Adrian to go rogue?"

Snap.

Adrian shields me and we duck into the closest store. "I'm sorry. This is part of it."

"Hello, how can I help you?" a woman standing behind the counter asks.

"We're looking, or *she's* looking, for a few things," Adrian says.

A few reporters go to the window, and another woman who works there shuts all the blinds to block their view.

"Thank you," I say, my hand covering my heart. I thought I'd be prepared for the scrutiny of the press, but I'm not there yet.

"Of course. We understand how hard it must be to date a prince." The woman has a kind smile. I need that after being in Adrian's house and being treated as though I'm on top of the FBI's Most Wanted list. "What can I show you?"

I peruse the store. It has a few things that are my style. I was worried I'd never be able to dress how I want here.

After taking all the clothes I pulled off the racks, the woman says, "The fitting rooms are in the back."

Adrian's phone rings. "This won't take long," he says before kissing my neck.

I follow the woman to the back of the store, and she opens a fitting room for me. Thankfully, it's identical to the ones back home. I need some familiarity right now. After putting on a dress, I step out to the three-way mirror and inspect how I look from different angles.

The woman who shut the blinds rests her shoulder on the wall, watching me. "It was made for you."

I smile, needing the sucking up she's probably doing because of who I'm here with. "I do love it."

"You'll need a hat," she says, disappearing.

While I'm in the fitting room, I realize I took the wrong size of the next item I want to try on, so I put my pants and blouse back on and head out to the sales floor. The two women are folding sweaters with their backs to me.

"How does anyone think that Prince Adrian would marry her? She's not even close to a princess level beauty. She's so plain."

The other one laughs. "You know how he likes his women."

"Yes—without attachments."

"Exactly. She's temporary."

"But he did bring her all the way back from America."

"I'll bet she's gone in a week. He loves to piss off his parents. That's all she's here for."

I circle on my heels and head back to the fitting room, my stomach suddenly not feeling well. As I sit in the fitting room, I pull out my phone and read the articles talking about me and Adrian. The skepticism, their ridicule of me, and the judgment that all points to one shared opinion—I'm not good enough to be with Adrian and I will never be a princess.

"Hey, babe, you done?" Adrian knocks on the door.

I clear my throat, wiping any tears from my eyes. "Yeah." I open the door and grab my purse.

"You didn't like anything?" he asks. "I bet your ass looked amazing in that dress."

"Nothing fit the way I'd like."

"Then on to the next store." He grabs my hand.

The woman stops us right before we leave. "I thought that dress was meant for you. You're not going to buy it?"

"No, it was really too *plain*," I say and her smile falls.

Too bad I sort of agree with her. Adrian shines as bright as the sun, and I'm not sure I'm good enough to stand in his shadow. If I continue feeling this way, how can I possibly stand at his side? Somewhere inside me is the self-esteem I need. I just need to dig it out.

CHAPTER THIRTY-ONE

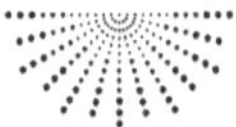

Sierra

After telling Adrian he cannot sneak into my room, I suffer through another night alone in the palace. Three days have passed. After the shopping excursion, I told Adrian I didn't want to go outside.

The queen hasn't stopped watching me as if I'm a science experiment. The king is never around and Adrian acts as though there's nothing wrong. He keeps telling me he'll handle it, but his agenda seems more focused on getting in my pants than fixing the fact that his family hates me.

"Good morning," Adrian says, his lips finding my neck and his hands sliding down my back, grabbing my ass.

We might be alone in the breakfast room right now, but his mom is somewhere nearby, so I circle out of his hold to find my seat. The one that faces the courtyard so at least I can admire the beautiful view during the awkward and forced conversation that's bound to happen over breakfast.

He glances around and sits next to me, taking my hand. My gut twists because Adrian only seems to do that when he's worried whatever he has to tell me will make me want to leave. "The announcement is being made in a few days about my parents' divorce."

I clench his hand. "I'm sorry."

He shrugs. "They're telling Rowan now, but I'm sure he's not going to be surprised."

Felicia walks in and takes her seat across from me, a server popping up out of nowhere and pouring her a cup of coffee. "Rowan wants you two to take him to school instead of Mom."

"Okay," Adrian says.

I slide my hand from his with a frown then thank the server after he pours my coffee. Adrian huffs. He's growing frustrated with me, but I'm not sure what he expects. Should I skip around the house and sing over the fact that his entire country and family seem to hate me?

Rowan comes in, his eyes full of sadness, his shoulders slumped.

"Stand up straight, Rowan," Felicia says.

"Give him a break," Adrian says.

"He has to learn sooner or later, and it seems like it's going to have to be sooner." She gives her brother a pointed glare.

"Piss off. Get off my damn back with that shit. He's a kid, he can't rule." Adrian drops his napkin in his lap.

I focus on Rowan, who slides into his chair and neatly takes his napkin, unfolding it and placing it in his lap, replicating his older brother's actions.

"Who shall rule then?" Felicia asks. "You won't. I can't. Dad will be dethroned after the announcement. We can't all live in the delusional bubble you find yourself trapped in. There are issues to be dealt with."

"I've never promised anything to this family. I've been clear for years that I don't want to rule. I don't want an arranged marriage. Now that I've met Sierra, I'm surer than I've ever been. She's what I want, and if no one can accept that, then fuck them."

I release a breath when Felicia's narrowed eyes cut to me.

"Fuck them? You've known her for two months. That's enough to throw away everything this family has built for centuries?"

"Easy for you to say. You have no pressure on your shoulders."

Rowan sips his orange juice, but the fun-loving kid I've seen over the last few days has vanished.

"You think I wouldn't rule if our country didn't have ancient rules of succession? I'd do it and I'd be proud to serve my country, but my hands are tied."

"That's convenient. You can say whatever you want because it can't happen anyway. You can't speak on what you would or wouldn't do if there's absolutely no chance it could happen."

Felicia grunts and her jaw clenches.

"Stop it, you two." The queen enters the dining room, her eyes rimmed with pink. "I can hear you all the way to the foyer."

"It's his fault," Felicia says. "The boy you let do whatever he wants thinks he can walk away from his responsibilities."

"Your mother said to stop." The King's deep voice sounds before he strolls in and takes a seat at the head of the table. As he places his napkin in his lap, his gaze lands on Adrian. "Your brother has requested you take him to school."

"I know." Adrian buries his head in his plate.

"I suggest Sierra stays here."

"Why?" Rowan whines. "I wanted to introduce her to my teacher." His eyes cut to me, and I offer him a small smile.

"She's coming." Adrian's tone makes it sound as if it's final, but for once, I wish he'd listen to his dad.

"When the announcement is made, things are going to get more intense."

Another boulder lands on top of the already existing boulder in my stomach.

More intense? How could things become worse?

"It's fine. I'll stay behind." I nod and look at Rowan. "Next time." I wink, and he smiles.

Adrian shakes his head. Then the usual silence that fills the Marx's table commences as we all start our day.

AFTER BREAKFAST, I excuse myself to go to my room. Adrian quickly follows and stops me.

"This is never going to work if you cower to them," he says.

This is the first time I've seen an ounce of concern on his face over what we're facing.

"I'm not cowering. I'm just not feeling up to public scrutiny at the moment."

He tilts his head.

"You live with blinders on," I say. "Do you not read the headlines of the newspapers? Do you not see what they're saying?"

He steps back, his fingers running through his hair. He has and thought maybe I didn't, I'm guessing. So we're going to live in denial? Or he's going to hide things from me for this to work out?

"It's only been three days. It's not a Band-Aid we can just rip off."

I walk down the hall, knowing his family is probably hoping this disagreement will turn into a fight and he'll break things off with me. "Three days of me feeling pretty shitty about myself. They don't want me here."

He takes my hand and stops me in the hallway, positioning my back so it's against the wall, where he cages me in. "I do."

He's so beautiful. So gorgeous. "I'm not sure I see where your optimism is coming from."

"Trust me. That's all I ask."

I nod, and he smiles before dipping down and kissing me.

"I'm ready," a small voice interrupts us.

I turn my face and wipe my mouth as Adrian laughs and faces his brother.

"Rowan, you're like a skilled spy, you're so quiet." He kisses my cheek. "I'll be back."

I nod, and our hands slowly part.

"Promise me you'll come next time," Rowan says.

I fake a smile. "Definitely."

He nods, and Adrian gives me that stomach-flipping wink of his before he talks to his brother about *Fortnite* while they walk down the hall.

As I watch them turn a corner, wishing I was going with them, the queen walks past the hallway and stops to look at me. Was she watching Adrian and me?

"Sierra, darling, the king and I would like to have a word with you." She's dressed in a suit, her hair styled to perfection and her makeup flawless. She doesn't look like a woman who's about to announce her divorce to an entire country.

"Okay," I say and follow her.

She called me darling. The same term of endearment she uses with her children. Maybe Adrian's right and it just took a few days for them to realize I wasn't going anywhere.

"I do love this dress." She examines me as our heels click on the marble hallway. "Did you buy it on the shopping trip in town the other day?"

"No, I had this already. I ended up not buying anything."

She frowns. "Maybe next time."

She knocks once on the study door and opens the door without being told it's okay to do so.

"Please come in." The king stands from his chair, waving us in. "Sorry about the fight with Felicia and Adrian. They're so close in age and they just don't see eye to eye. They shouldn't behave like that in front of guests." He gestures to another chair. "Coffee or tea?"

A servant comes in and places down a tray with three coffee mugs, milk, and sugar.

"No, thank you."

The queen sits in the chair next to her husband so that they're across from me. All that niceness I thought I felt from the queen disappears. They've ambushed me.

The king takes his time pouring tea for the queen and handing it to her before he pours himself a coffee. Every second that clicks by, my heartbeat speeds up.

He sips his coffee and puts the cup on the table between the two of them. "How do you think this turns out?"

I scrunch my forehead. "I'm sorry?"

"You and Adrian, how do you see this ending? The two of you marrying? He rules here if he's allowed? You do understand that in that case, you can't work. You'd have obligations and no time for silly bits about water irrigation system and the city pie-eating contest."

My jaw tics. He's watched my segments and feels as though I'm beneath him.

"From what I understand, Adrian doesn't want to rule," I say in an even voice.

"Yes, but he has no choice. Do you think he's going to allow Rowan to rule at his age?"

The queen puts her hand on her husband's arm and leans forward. "As you must know, Adrian cares for Rowan a great deal. He'd jump in front of a bus for him. When the news about the divorce hits, if Adrian abdicates, Rowan will be named king."

"But he wouldn't be married." I shift in my seat.

"No, he would have to wed at eighteen," the king says.

"Adrian won't let that happen." The queen smirks. "So Adrian will rule, and if you two marry, you'll be queen. If that can even happen. We'll have to see how the public takes to you first. They generally wouldn't like someone so…ordinary."

Her words are like a flick of a sharp knife slicing through me without warning.

"If you think the past few days have been difficult, what do you think will happen when they hear you're their next queen?"

I have no answer for the King.

"All we want is for you to think about this, Sierra," the queen says. "Can the two of you have a future when you've only been in each other's lives for such a short time? Should he really throw away his family and his obligation to a country that has honored him his entire life for a girl he met through a 'Win a Date' contest? The news about that is already hitting the newspapers, and everyone thinks this is all very convenient."

I never thought about that. Of course his family believes I don't truly care for their son.

"If you feel for him like you say, shouldn't you do what's right for him?" the king asks. "The two of you have had a whirlwind affair, but now it's time to come down to Earth."

Their words whirl in my head. I know they're trying to manipulate me, trying to make me think there's no hope that Adrian and I can make this relationship work. I know that, but some of what they say makes sense.

"I know you believe you might love him, but if you truly

love him, you'll do the right thing and step out of the way," the king says.

The queen sips her tea, her eyes diverting away from me.

"You want me to just leave him?" I ask, forcing them to tell me point blank.

"We're looking out for you too." The queen pulls out a tablet and puts it on the table in front of us. My mom's face on the screen has me picking it up and staring at it, slack-jawed. "The press can be so cruel."

The picture shows my mom in Iraq, surrounded by five men. All have their guns strapped to their bodies and are dressed in camouflage. The headline reads, "Does this look like the bloodline of a queen? We say no."

The iPad drops from my hands, landing with a clatter on the coffee table. My mind spins.

"There's a car outside. You can take our private jet back to New York if that's what you would like?" The King's gaze locks with my watery one.

I stand and walk out the door, shutting it behind me. Ned is there with my suitcase and purse and coat. They knew what I would do. They dug deep enough into my wounds to know what would send me scurrying away.

I need to save myself, so I walk through the door and down to the waiting car, saying goodbye to Sandsal forever.

CHAPTER THIRTY-TWO

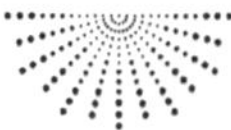

Adrian

After Rowan takes me around his school and introduces me to his teacher for the year, I head back to the palace to finish my conversation with Sierra.

As the cameras flash through the windows of my car and reporters scream, asking if Sierra is already out of the picture, my phone rings. The last thing I want right now is to deal with Felicia, but I slide my thumb over to answer because maybe Sierra's right and I'm not being proactive enough to fix this problem.

"Don't worry, the soon-to-be king was well-mannered and polite when I dropped him off."

"Adrian," she says.

I haven't heard that tone since she had to call me at college and tell me my dog died. Not even when she told me she found a half-naked woman on my dad's desk.

I sit up straighter in the backseat. "What?"

"I swear I didn't know. I know I've been giving you hell—"

My adrenaline goes into overdrive and I feel my blood pressure spike. "What is it?"

"Mom and Dad. They talked to Sierra while you were gone, and she left."

"Like, left the grounds for fresh air?"

"She's at the airport boarding our jet. She's going home."

All the air leaves my lungs. "What the hell did they say to her?"

She's silent for a moment. "If you want this to work, you need to look at what's being said in the press. There's a new article. It talks about her mom."

I pull my phone from my ear and hang up to scan the worst of the headlines, and sure enough, one features a picture of her mom in Iraq, standing in the middle of a group of guys, a couple with their arms around her. Although it's clear to anyone with a brain that the picture is one of comradery, the press has twisted it to imply that her mom couldn't possibly give birth to someone deserving of the title of queen.

"Those assholes!" I throw my phone across the seat. "Clyde, go to the airport."

"I'm sorry, sir, I've been instructed to take you to the palace only."

"Fuck the palace."

We pull up at the palace while I'm still arguing with Clyde to turn around and head to the airport.

I climb out and rush to the driver's side. "Give me the keys."

Maybe we shouldn't have fired Declan. He probably would've driven me to the airport.

"Come inside, Adrian," my dad says from the front door.

"Fuck off," I say.

He distracted me, and now Clyde has gotten far enough away that I can't get the keys from him without taking him to the ground.

I run into the house and up the stairs to my room, my father following me. "She's gone, son, and it's for the best."

Opening the drawers in my room, I scramble to find the keys to my motorcycle. I haven't ridden it since I laid it down on the pavement last year, but it's my only option at this point. My father has likely instructed the staff to keep me from all the vehicles.

Once I find the keys, I run back down the stairs. Felicia and my mom are standing in the foyer with my dad.

"How could you?" I say to my mother.

My dad puts his hand on my chest. "She's gone. The plane has taken off."

"Then I'll get on another. How could you do this to me? What kind of parents are you?" I remove my dad's hand from my chest. "You made your bed. I'm out of your life." I run to the door.

"Do you really think you're going to survive on an hourly wage at a bagel shop?" my father asks.

My feet skid to a stop and I turn around. "I'd rather do that than be tied to you."

"The shine will wear off your situation eventually. You'll never last," my father says.

"You're a son of a bitch, you know that?" I step forward. "It amazes me that you can even act the way you do after what you did to Mom. How low must you be to have an affair in your own home? You tell the people how noble of a ruler you are, how honest and caring, but you cheat on your wife and you force your son into a life he doesn't want. You ruin his future with the one woman he loves. You're no king. You're weak. You try to keep everyone around you down."

My dad's hand clenches, and I don't have enough time to duck before he punches me in the face. I falter back.

"*Stop!*" my mom yells. "Just stop." A tear falls down her cheek. "I can't take this anymore. This house is so angry."

Felicia's back is against the wall, and for the first time, I realize what she's been dealing with by staying here. How strong she is for seeing it through and wanting what's best for us all.

"Your father and I have an arrangement," Mom says. I swear she's looking at me as though she's asking me to forgive her. I've never seen that look on her face before.

"What kind of arrangement?" I ask, holding my face where my father's fist landed.

"Don't, Lucy," he says.

More tears fall from my mom's eyes and she throws her arms to the side. "It's over, David. It's over."

I look at Felicia as she bites her lip. Whatever my mom has to say, Felicia knows.

"Let's go in the study," Felicia says.

We all follow her, my dad shutting the door.

"What arrangement?" I ask again.

"Your father and I had an arranged marriage, as you know. We tried to find love between us, but it wasn't there, so we agreed that it was okay to see others as long as we were both discreet."

I fall into one of the chairs. All this time I've felt sorry for my mom and she wasn't even surprised. Embarrassed maybe, but not surprised. She's been having her own affairs over the years.

"We don't expect you to understand, but it's how a lot of couples in our position get by. When Felicia found your dad, we talked and figured it wouldn't be the end of the world if we got divorced. You're twenty-nine now, more than old enough to take over. Your father was nineteen when Granddad died." She places her hand on my knee.

"Why would you want me to live that way? The same way you two did? Why wouldn't you change it?"

My mom looks at my dad as he sits in the chair across from me. "It's the way it is. We looked hard at a lot of princesses, and we truly believed there was potential for you and Adelaide to fall in love. Your mother and I were thrown together without a lot of research or background because of the rush after my dad died."

Felicia sits on the chair next to me, not seeming at all surprised by anything they're saying.

"Then you went to New York City and found Sierra." My mom lowers her head.

I snap out of the trance my parents' admissions have put me in. *Sierra.* I need to get to her. I stand, and my mom's hand falls off my knee.

"Darling, it's an easier road if you marry Princess Adelaide. Even if you choose not to rule, Sierra will always struggle to fit in here. Don't you see that?"

I stand behind the chair, gripping the back of it, willing my mother to really hear my next words. "I love her, Mom. I *love* her."

My mom looks at my dad, resigned, and turns back to me. "Then go get her."

"But, son?" My dad stops me before I can leave. "We still have the issue of you becoming king. Your mother and I are still divorcing."

I look at Felicia, who has sat quietly as she was taught by my mother. "You have a queen, Dad, you don't need a king. Abolish the male succession rule and allow Felicia to rule. It's time. There's no reason a woman shouldn't inherit the throne."

My dad's head whips in Felicia's direction. "You'd want to rule?"

"Really?" my mom asks.

Felicia nods and gives me a sweet smile. "I love Sandsal and I love what we do. I have my business degree and master's in business." She continues to list her qualifications. More qualifications than I hold.

I walk out of the study, gripping my motorcycle keys.

"Adrian," my mom says, coming after me.

I stop at the door, circling to face her.

"I'm sorry. For everything. I was being selfish. When you arrived, Sierra overheard your father and I talking about our indiscretions. I feared she'd out us, so I tried to get her out before she told you or Felicia. I thought I was doing what was best for you, but I don't want you to have the same life I did. I have no idea what it feels like to love someone but watching the two of you these past few days has made me yearn for it. I never had a lot of examples of love in my life."

I lean forward and kiss her cheek.

"Go get her and bring her back here so we can welcome her the right way." She squeezes my hand. "I love you, son."

"I love you." I hug my mother. Her soft cries tell me she means what she's saying. "I gotta go."

She pulls back from our embrace. "Yes." She wipes her eyes. "Go."

I run out of the house and into the garage to race to the airport.

I ARRIVE in New York in the middle of the night and pay a taxi driver extra to get me to Cliffton Heights. The city is dark and desolate as I barrel into the Rooftop Apartments, the ding of the elevator sounding like a fire alarm ripping through the dead quiet.

I tiptoe through the darkness to Sierra's bedroom door. It creaks open, and I see her in bed, curled on her left side like always. After slipping off my shoes, I crawl into bed and slide my arm around her body, pulling her back into me.

She swings an elbow and nails me in the stomach. I cough and wheeze for breath as she screams, turning around to nail me in the groin. I try to get out of the bed, but the sheet trips me up and I fall on my ass. The door swings open and the light turns on, practically blinding me while I roll around on the floor in pain.

"Are you okay?" Rian asks, looking at the woman before finding me on the floor. "Adrian?"

Once my nuts don't feel like they're in my throat I look at the woman I was in bed with. A woman who isn't Sierra. She's the exact opposite of Sierra, in fact. Dark hair pulled up in a bun, dark skin peeking out from under her tattoos.

"You know this guy?" She points at me.

Rian comes to help me up. "Yeah, he's my roommate's boyfriend. What are you doing here?"

A whimpering sound comes from the other room.

"Is that Sierra?" I move to go to the third bedroom.

"If you like your balls, you won't go near that door," the woman says.

I look at Rian as she says, "That's not Sierra. This is Frankie. She works at Ink Envy. Her daughter is in the other room. They needed somewhere to stay."

"Where's Sierra?"

Rian looks at me and shakes her head as if she's clearing it. "I thought she was with you in Sandsal?"

I run my hand through my hair. "Where the hell is she then?"

My dad said the plane landed, that she refused a car and took a taxi. If she didn't come here, where did she go?

"Adrian?" Rian asks. "What's going on?"

I run out of the room and bang on Ethan and Blanca's door.

Ethan opens the door, naked. "What the hell?"

Blanca laughs and throws him a pair of pants. Her laughter stops when she sees me in the doorway. "Adrian?"

"Is she here?" I ask.

"Who? Sierra?" she asks.

Ethan looks at Blanca. "Why would she be here?"

"He just showed up here frantic, looking for her." Rian appears out of nowhere.

I leave them and pound on the guys' apartment door.

"OMG, you're engaged!" Rian screams from behind me. I turn and see her hugging Blanca.

Great for them. I don't really give a shit right now.

Knox comes from the stairs in his police uniform with Leilani at his side. "Why are you all in danger of having a noise violation?"

"Can you let me know if Sierra is in your apartment?"

He looks down the hall to where Rian is still hugging Ethan and Blanca. Once Knox opens his apartment door, I barrel past him and flick on the lights. Opening the first bedroom door, I turn the light switch to find Dylan alone in bed. Then to Seth's room. He's also alone in bed.

"What the hell? I feel like when I was in college and my fraternity kidnapped me in the middle of the night." Seth gets up as Dylan comes out of his room.

"Sierra ran. She left Sandsal and now she's not here." My ass falls onto their couch. "Where would she have gone?" My head falls into my hands.

There's no way I lost her already. I won't allow it. I can't live without her.

CHAPTER THIRTY-THREE

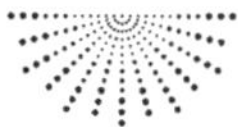

Sierra

A hand nudges my arm and I roll over, almost falling off the bed.

"Whoa, sweetie," my dad says. "Don't fall off." He laughs. I sometimes forget he laughs now. "To what do I owe this visit?"

I sit up in my bed, rubbing my eyes. "Sorry."

He sits at the bottom of my bed, a coffee in his hands. "This is your home. You never have to be sorry for coming. I just wish I didn't find out by finding your suitcase downstairs when I woke up." He smiles at me.

"Where's Fae?"

"I asked her if she could give us some space this morning, so she went to the coffee shop."

"I'm sorry."

He laughs again, handing me the cup of coffee. "Stop apologizing. Do you want some breakfast?"

"Sure."

He pats my leg that's under the comforter. "Okay, I'll go start it. Come on down. You've been dodging me, and we have a lot to talk about. But first I want to know why you're sneaking home in the middle of the night."

He leaves me in my room, closing the door. I see that my suitcase is now in the corner of my room. He's so put together now, it's hard to reconcile with the mess he was for so many years.

Getting dressed, I look at my dead phone. I was too lazy to search for a charger last night, but since only Adrian would be calling, I keep it off and go downstairs.

I smell the bacon halfway down the stairs. A memory flashes through my mind of coming down on Monday mornings after my mom returned from her weekend duties. I always had to go to sleep before she came home, so on Mondays, I'd find her and Dad talking about the weekend, laughing about something someone did or something that happened. My dad would always be touching her and kissing her and vice versa. As though two days was too long for them to be apart.

My dad handled the bacon, saying my mom was too impatient and always burned it. His method of slow cooking it to perfection was the right way, according to him. My mom always made her fluffy pancakes because she said that my dad would mix the batter too long and make them too flat. She'd smother my plate in butter and syrup. Those Mondays were like a holiday.

"There you are," my dad says, turning from the bacon and pouring me more coffee. "Give the bacon another three minutes."

He puts a plate of pancakes on the table next to the butter and syrup, and my nose tickles. He turns his attention back to the bacon and I wipe the one lone tear that falls.

"I called you on your birthday. Fae and I wanted to take you to dinner." He never turns around.

I fork a pancake, finding them dry and hard. I guess some things don't change. "I'm sorry. I've been busy."

He nods. "I called and texted you a few times after that as well."

I sigh. "Yeah, sorry about that."

"I know things with Fae must be hard for you, but she's a part of my life. Do you think maybe you could try a little bit?"

He sets the bacon to dry on a paper towel next to the oven and turns off the burner.

"I've been trying."

He smiles at me over his shoulder. "Try a tad harder?"

I nod, sipping my coffee. I really should. I now know what it feels like when the family you're trying to win over doesn't welcome you with open arms.

He brings over the plate of bacon and sets it on the table before starting on the eggs. His reasoning is that you can only concentrate on one thing at a time. If he does the eggs and bacon together, one of them won't turn out well.

"I saw you were home while I was gone and took the boxes." He eyes me as he cracks an egg.

I knew I'd gotten my journalistic investigation skills from my dad, so it shouldn't surprise me he knows everything. But he also believes in space, whereas my mom hated giving anyone space. When they got into a fight, she'd want to settle it right then and there, while my dad would say later.

"Yeah, I came by. I was surprised to find the house for sale."

"If you'd answer my calls, you would've known."

"And what about all the repainting and pictures being stuffed in the basement?"

He stops cracking an egg when he hears the bitterness in my voice. "The realtor thought it would be best."

"Not Fae?"

He gives me the stern dad look. The one I got when I talked back to my grandparents or didn't say please and thank you to servers at restaurants. "Fae understands your mom is a part of my life. And you as well."

I push away my plate. "Really? Because it seems to me you want to erase us from your shiny new life."

He turns away from the burner and sits in the chair next to me. "Why would you think that?"

I pretend not to see the hurt in his eyes. "Look around, Dad, there's no sign of our lives here anymore."

He sighs. What possible response could he have? "You mean there's no sign of your mother. Because if you look around, you'll see pictures of your graduation, your baby picture, when you learned to ride your bike."

"And not one of Mom? Where's the one where she's holding me right after I was born?" It's in the storage locker of my apartment, that's where it is.

"You might not understand this, but I can't move on with Fae while living in the past. It isn't fair to her to live here with all your mom's things. To wake up and stare at her picture. It's the reason we're selling the house."

"Fae made you do it?" Even I admit I sound like a pissed off teenager.

"No. I made the decision because I have to move on with my life. It doesn't mean I love your mom any less. I think of her every day, but she's not coming back. It's been eighteen years, sweetie." His hand covers mine. "I know right after your mother died, the depression I was in was hard for you. I wish I could go back and fight harder to have pulled myself out of it sooner. But I can't. I also know you resent me for it, and you should. But now you're grown and have your own life in Cliffton Heights. I've finally gotten myself healthy. We both need to move on."

I attempt to blink away the tears that keep building. "Why now? Why are you able to move on?"

He takes a moment to think about it. My dad, always the debater in his head. "I don't have an answer. One morning I woke up and reality hit. How mad your mom would be that I just gave up. She was such a fighter, you know. And I was being a coward, too afraid to put myself out there. Afraid that I'll get hurt again. But that's life, sweetie. Sometimes it hurts." His extra-long stare says he knows more about why I'm here than I do. "I'm sorry. I should have fought harder for our life after your mom died. It's a regret I feel every day."

"Really?"

"Yes. What you must have thought. You practically lost both of us."

I had no idea he felt that way or even realized what a toll it took on me. Fresh tears fall down my cheeks and he pulls me into his arms, hugging me as I sob into his chest. "I think I screwed up, Dad."

"Why are you home?" he whispers.

I shrug.

"Come on. Let me help you out on this one."

The smoke alarm goes off and we have no choice but to let go of one another. I grab the broom as my dad turns off the burner, taking the frying pan of eggs and putting it in the sink. He opens a window and a cold breeze floats in.

After we get the smoke mostly cleared out, we sit down at the table.

"At least we have bacon," he says, shaking his head at the brick pancakes. "Your mom would kick my ass if she saw these sad excuses for pancakes."

I laugh as we hold up pieces of bacon to knock together

before we each take a bite. He's right, I need to try harder. To put aside the past and look to the future.

He listens as I tell him everything that happened with Adrian and my experience in Sandsal. He knew about the picture of Mom because it turns out Fae likes to stalk blog sites too. Great. She hid it from my dad until the picture came out yesterday and felt I needed a little family to stick up for my mother.

"So she's been commenting on the mean posts about you. She might be just as hated as you are in Sandsal." My dad laughs, and a warmness I never wanted to feel for Fae hits my heart.

"Thanks," I say, meaning a whole lot more than just him feeding me.

My dad smiles. His large hand, which bears more wrinkles than I remember, clamps down on my forearm. "It's been too long. Maybe I'll get the pancakes down one day."

"Nah." I pick up one and bite it. "I kind of like that you make dry ones."

He picks up one and bites it after me. "Me too."

Silence falls between us as though we're both thinking of my mom. The woman who left us with huge holes in our hearts that are just now starting to mend.

"So what are you going to do?" he asks.

I shrug.

"You're not a runner. That's never been you."

I stare into my coffee cup. "All I do is run. I purposely pick men who have a slim chance of ever being long term."

He leans back. "You know things happen in people's lives that shape and form them into the adults they become. But sometimes you gotta put yourself out there. You're a Sanders. You come from a military family. We fight for what we believe in. I think after your mom died, we both lost that fight. We succumbed to the grief, and because she died fighting for our country, I think we started to shy away from fighting for what we want. You've fought for everything you've gotten in this life. Now you need to be a fighter when it comes to your heart."

He stops talking. When I don't say anything, he picks back up. "It's still in you. Dig it up, and if you love this guy, fight for him. Don't wait for him to show up on some white horse and save you like the prince he is. Show him you're a warrior and a fighter and that he doesn't need to protect you from his people. That you'll stand by his side with your shoulders squared and your head held high. I guarantee it's why he fell in love with you in the first place."

I consider my dad's words as he stands and disappears from the room. Maybe he's giving me time to figure out what I should do.

But he returns a few minutes later and hands me a letter. "I should've given this to you a long time ago, but by the time you were old enough, I didn't want it to set you back. I was wrong to hang on to it. Just think of it as another fuck-up on my part." He squeezes my shoulder and leaves the room again.

The letter is worn as though it's been read a million times, the folds creased to the point that the paper will soon rip. I suck in a breath when I recognize my mom's handwriting.

CHAPTER THIRTY-FOUR

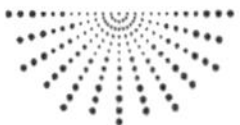

Sierra

I smooth out the letter and read.

Greg,

I don't have to explain this letter. You've probably already written your own to me while you were deployed. We've talked endless nights about what we want to happen should something happen to one of us over here. I'm going to keep this brief because you and I are lucky enough to have discussed so much face-to-face. We both know the dangers here, whereas husbands and wives who aren't both enlisted don't know how high the possibility of something happening really is.

I know we've been in a disagreement about this, but should the unthinkable happen to me, I want you to find a wife for you and a mother for Sierra. She needs a woman in her life to guide her through womanhood. She doesn't have to call her Mom or anything crazy like that though. ;)

In all seriousness, honey, nothing will bring me back, so you need to move on with your life. Sierra is too young not to have a mother to nurture her. I know you'll do a great job. You're a wonderful father, the way you always tell her she can be whatever she wants in this world as long as she's not afraid to work hard. If you won't do it for yourself, do it for Sierra and me.

And one more thing, I know you love the military, but please don't reenlist should something happen to me. As much as I want you to be where I am, Sierra is the priority and the chances are too great if you come back over here she'll end up as an orphan. We both know we don't want to give our parents the chance to screw her up. ;)

Here's hoping you never see this letter, but I'm not naive enough to think you won't. I love you so much, Greg. You have given me a life most women dream of. I'm the luckiest wife in this world to be able to call you my husband. Keep our little girl safe. Kiss her, hug her, joke with her, tell her she's beautiful every day. Even when she goes through those awkward puberty years. :) And clean your gun when that first boy shows to pick her up. I would have done the same thing.

Love you always and I'll be waiting for you (I hope I'm waiting a long time),

Abby

I refold the letter and put it back inside the envelope.

Leaving the kitchen, I find my dad in the family room, his chin in his palm as he stares at nothing.

When he hears me, he turns and stands. A tear slips from his eye. "I couldn't do it. I'm sorry."

I have no idea who went to who first, but we hug and cry and my dad apologizes over and over again for never living out my mother's wishes. I mumble that it's okay. And it is. He was doing the best he could. All things considered, he didn't screw me up too much. Everyone has their issues.

He's right though—I need to fight. Those newspapers have no idea who my mom is, how wonderful she was, or what she stood for. And they definitely underestimated me.

"I love him," I say.

My dad draws back, his hands on my forearms. He smiles with true happiness. "Then let's get you on a plane."

I nod, sniffle, and dry the tears with my hands.

"I'll grab my keys and phone." He heads to the kitchen.

I run upstairs, zip up my suitcase, and pull it down the stairs.

"Ready?" he asks.

I nod. "Ready."

I ignore the anxiety racing through my veins. I can do this. Adrian is worth it.

My dad opens the door and freezes.

I bump into his back. "Dad?"

"Sweetie, I'm not sure you need to go to the airport." He backs up.

Adrian stands on the other side of the screen door. Blanca and Rian stand at the end of the sidewalk. Dylan, Seth, and Ethan jogging down the sidewalk from a cab parked along the curb.

My dad snaps out of his surprise faster than me and he opens the screen door. "Please come in."

"Thank you, sir."

"Greg. No sir." My dad pats Adrian's back and steps out. "Blanca Mancini, how are you?" He descends the steps, giving us space.

Adrian shuts the door, backing me into the room. My suitcase falls on its side from the wheels not rolling on the carpet. Our eyes stay locked.

"You ran," he says.

"I was running back."

The tips of his lips shift up for a moment but then return to straight lines. "I handled it all wrong, I'm sorry. But things are fine now. My parents—"

I place my finger on his lips. "I'll deal. I'm fine. I can handle all of it. The press, your parents, Felicia, the country."

"You will?"

I nod.

"Why?"

"Why are you here?" I change the subject.

"I asked you first," he says, a smirk playing on his lips.

"I was going to sweep you off your feet," I say.

He chuckles. "Role reversal. Too bad I beat you to it."

I tilt my head. "How do you figure?"

"I'm standing in your family's home to win you back."

"I'm no princess," I say. "I don't need saving."

His head falls back and his hands land on my hips. "You think I don't know that? I thought I was clear from day one. I was never looking for a princess."

He bends to kiss me, but I put my hand over his mouth. "Adrian, I'm not going to stand quietly by your side. I can't allow them to talk about my family and me like they have been."

"Why do you think I picked Wonder Woman for you? She's not a princess, but she does wear a tiara."

I wrap my arms around his neck, throwing myself at him, and he catches me.

"I love you, Sierra," he whispers in my ear.

I lean back so I can see him. "I love you. Cheesy hands and all."

EPILOGUE

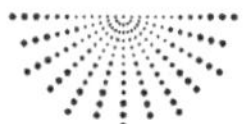

Three months later…

Sierra

I sit in my chair with four chairs to my left. There are three cameras on set, all from different angles. Although it's been three months since everything went down in Sandsal, my nerves still get the better of me when I know I'll be seeing Adrian's family.

"Ready?" Jack asks in my ear.

I nod, straightening my notecards.

The cameraman counts me down, and I face camera two.

"Good evening, Cliffton Heights. We have a few special guests with us tonight. As some of you might be aware, the country of Sandsal just passed a new law permitting women to lead their monarchy. There was talk of removing the requirement for the ruler to be married, but that idea was put on hold for the time being. I'm going to be speaking with

King David Marx and Queen Lucy Marx about what they're doing to bring their monarchy into this century."

I stand as they come and join me on set. They've both apologized to me, and I have forgiven them, though I won't be planning any family vacations with them just yet.

After I bow to both of them, the king kisses my cheek.

"Good to see you both. Please have a seat."

They do, and I still envy the ease with which Adrian's mom can sit with her legs perfectly aligned and tucked.

"The Sandsal monarchy has undergone quite a change. Tell us, what made you want to make this change in the first place? I'm sure these traditions have been in place for centuries."

The king clears his throat, looking a bit uncomfortable. I think they only agreed to this interview to appease me, but that's okay. I've also agreed to do things to appease them.

"At first, we weren't all on board with the change," the king says. "Our son, Prince Adrian, came to us because he didn't want to take part in an arranged marriage. Nor did he want to rule. If he didn't accept the throne, it would have gone to his much younger brother, Rowan, who would have had to marry as soon as he turned eighteen. But Prince Adrian suggested our daughter, Felicia, was the one meant to reign."

"This change stems from your decision to divorce, correct?"

The queen straightens her back. "Yes. Although we are committed to our family, we will be divorcing once Felicia marries next month."

"And is her marriage arranged?"

"No. She's free to marry whomever she chooses."

I nod and straighten my cards. "This seems like the perfect time to bring Felicia out."

Felicia strides out, and we kiss each other on both cheeks.

I really need lessons on how to sit like them. She smiles at her parents, her dark hair in curls that make her look so much younger.

"Felicia, tell us, how did you find a husband in only three months? That's not a lot of time to fall in love with someone," I say.

"I've heard of people falling in love in less time," she says, and I blush after the king and the queen look at me. "But no, I'd been seeing someone. At the time I was keeping it private."

"I imagine it's hard to find a partner on your own when you're a member of the royal family?" I ask the leading question even though I already know her fiancé is Clyde, the security guard she sent to retrieve Adrian when Princess Adelaide got herself outed. But we decided to keep his identity hidden for now.

"It can be, yes. But sometimes love is close to home. My fiancé worked as my security. He's a decorated soldier for our country and a noble man who understands the responsibility our family has."

She's already so practiced, I can't imagine anyone but her becoming the queen.

"Well, I wish you both good luck and best wishes."

She nods and smiles.

"Now the man who spurred the change in the small country of Sandsal, Prince Adrian Marx."

The three guests stand and slide over so that Adrian can sit right next to me. That wasn't planned and it throws me off at first. I recover and stand to shake his hand, but instead he captures me in a hug and kisses my cheek. Felicia and the queen laugh.

Adrian sits down. "You look beautiful today, Sierra," he says as though he's going to conduct the interview.

"You look handsome as always," I can't stop myself from

saying. "So what spurred you to request this change to the succession rules?"

Please do not say me. He refused to role-play this scenario beforehand, telling me he wanted to talk off the cuff. The man does not like restrictions.

"I came to America and I met a woman."

I nod and clear my throat to compose myself. "And you just decided you no longer wanted to rule?"

He chuckles, leaning back with his ankle resting on his opposite knee. He's so relaxed and at ease, it scares me. "I never wanted to rule. I've been clear about that for years. But this woman changed everything. She magnified the reasons I didn't want to be king someday."

"She must be great," I say with a chuckle.

"She's amazing."

"So you've decided to take yourself out of line to rule should something happen to your sister?" It's a terrible thought, but one that people in his position has to think about.

He smiles, his fingers straightening the hem of his slacks. "Once my brother, Rowan, is old enough, I will take myself out of line. He's not ready to rule just yet." He leans over and turns to Felicia. "So no skydiving or anything dangerous until Rowan's twenty-five."

The whole panel laughs, as does our camera crew. I swear, this man. Oh, how I love him.

I ask, "So what's on the horizon for you all?"

The king takes the queen's hand. "A whole new life, right?"

She smiles at him and nods. They look so happy, you'd never think they're getting a divorce.

"Planning my wedding," Felicia says with a bright smile.

My eyes linger on Adrian. He's supposed to say a new

adventure, but the bigger his smirk becomes and the longer he takes to answer, the more my stomach knots.

He drops his leg and puts his hand in his pocket, retrieving a key hanging from a ribbon. "A new place. I love my girlfriend's friends, but we need some privacy."

I barely compose myself. Biting my lip still doesn't make my smile wane. "Wonderful news."

"I think so. Who doesn't want to be naked twenty-four-seven?"

As quickly as he made me blush like he did that first night, I'm shaking my head. I guess we'll be cutting that out.

"Thank you all for joining us tonight." I swivel my chair toward camera two. "Have a great night, Cliffton Heights."

The cameraman gives me the countdown.

The second I get the all-clear, I smack Adrian's arm. "Seriously?"

"What? Wait until you see the apartment. We have our own rooftop." His arm swings behind me and pulls me into him. The man has no qualms about PDA. "Say yes?"

I draw back. "Yes."

"Great! And the whole naked twenty-four-seven thing?"

I giggle. "Your parents are right there."

"So?"

I pat his bicep. "You do know my dad is going to hear you say that in the interview?"

"Your dad loves me."

He's not lying.

"We have to meet him and Fae for dinner tonight. Do you think our parents are going to get along?"

We say a quick goodbye and head down the hallway of the studio.

"No, things don't go that smoothly with us," he says.

I chuckle. "True enough."

He picks me up in one swoop and swings me around. "You were great during that interview, just so you know."

"Thanks." I smile, thankful for all I have.

Georgia retired and I turned down the promotion because I'll be traveling back and forth between Sandsal and Cliffton Heights. Plus, I think Jack was right. Maybe I was born to be exactly where I already was.

THE NEXT DAY

BECAUSE ADRIAN CANNOT WAIT EVEN one day, we have a truck outside the Rooftop Apartments, and he's recruited all the guys to help us move our stuff.

"I can't believe this is it," Rian says. "I'm all by myself."

"Adrian paid my share for the rest of the year, so we only need to find you one roommate. You could leave after the lease is up if you wanted."

She looks across the hall. "I love it here."

"I'm only across the street. The rooftops are the same height," I say, but I know it's still different.

Knox walks in and sits on the couch. We both look at him like 'do you not realize we're in the middle of a conversation?'

"So I have a guy who needs a place to live," he says.

Rian's face scrunches. "A guy?"

"He'll barely be around. He travels and does these shows."

"What does he do?" I ask.

"Fuck, Seth, lift your end," Ethan yells.

"Hey, big guy who works out like five times a day, get your ass off the couch and help," Seth says.

Knox flips him off. "He's a tattoo artist."

"Does Dylan know him?" Rian asks.

Knox nods. "Yeah, but they don't run in the same circle. He's kind of the 'no one will tie me down' type. 'Life is meant to be lived' type of guy. He's from back home, but he mentioned to me he really needed a place to hunker down for a few months. Find himself and figure out what his next move is."

"You just said he wouldn't be around a lot," I say, crossing my arms.

"Believe me, he'll sign the lease and I guarantee you, it'll give him a rash to be in one spot. He'll be back on the road after a month tops."

Rian's hands knot together. "I don't know. I have to share a bathroom with him."

"Listen, it was only a fast fix. If you don't want—"

Dylan walks in with a girl, and Rian rolls her eyes.

"Moving already?" Dylan asks.

"Just getting home?" I ask, glaring bullets at the girl. Although it's not her fault.

"Tell him yes," Rian says without looking at Dylan. "He can move in whenever he wants."

"Awesome. I'll let him know." Knox stands and clasps Dylan's shoulder. "Jax is going to move in here with Rian. Great news, right?"

"What?" Dylan whips in Rian's direction. "With you?"

He leaves the girl and follows Knox to their apartment.

The girl with more piercings than I can count waves to us. "Hey."

I force a smile because it's truly not her fault she's in the middle of this.

We hear Dylan and Knox yelling at one another across the hall.

"What is going on?" Blanca asks, coming into the apartment. "Who's arguing? It sounds like they might kill one another."

"I don't know. Dylan is going ballistic after he found out some guy Knox knows is gonna move in here," I say.

"Hi, I'm Blanca." She puts her hand out in front of the girl.

"Hi." She never offers her name.

Blanca backs up and mouths, "Who is she?" at us.

Dylan breezes past us and into my bedroom with a duffle bag swung over his shoulder.

"You're being unrealistic," Knox says, following him.

"I'm not leaving that douche alone with Rian in an apartment."

Blanca smiles and I smile, both of us looking at Rian.

Could someone be a little jealous?

Adrian walks into the apartment and lifts his shirt to wipe some sweat off his forehead. Damn, it's like picking between cake or a brownie for dessert. I want to take my man and go christen our new place, but at the same time, I want to stick around here. Because whatever happens in this apartment when this Jax guy arrives will be epic.

The End

COCKAMAMIE UNICORN RAMBLINGS

For those you who read our ramblings with each book, you know that we try to write new tropes. Although, I'm sure you've figured out some of our favs. Enemies-to-lovers anyone?!?

Royalty was one we'd yet to conquer so we thought, why not? We knew we wanted to do 'a win a date with a celebrity or prince' kind of storyline but we needed the prince to be in Cliffton Heights since that's where all our peeps are. This time we had our act together before her book and were able to tease out Sierra's love for Prince Adrian Marx on social media and gossip blogs in My Bestie's Ex. It's nice to be on top of it for once!

We weren't surprised with some of the responses to Sierra after My Bestie's Ex, but we do hope as you learned more about her life story you saw why she reacted the way she did. And that's the great thing about character arcs... they always change and learn something by the end! :P

This story wasn't meant to be so heavy with emotion. We like our stories to be lighter, but just as we try for new tropes in stories, we try for new backstories in our characters.

Rayne says she's never cried this much while writing a Piper Rayne book. Maybe it hit home because she went off a lot of her own personal experience. A fact about Rayne, her first husband was in the National Guard. His unit was called to go to Iraq in 2003, about the same time as Sierra's mom. Preparing in the seven days they had to get their lives situated before he would leave is something she'll never forget. All the scary unknowns and heartfelt talks about what ifs that they discussed on their way to federal offices to assign Power of Attorneys and other paperwork. The trauma of it all was hard and they didn't even have children. Even though their marriage ultimately didn't make it, she's happy to say he returned home safely from his tour.

We promise The Rival Roomies won't be as emotional! Just lots of fun! But of course we're going to make Dylan work for it! ;)

SUPER HUGE THANKS to our team who if not for them, we'd never be able to finish these books!

Danielle Sanchez and the entire Wildfire Marketing Solutions!

Cassie from Joy Editing for line edits.

Ellie from My Brother's Editor for line edits.

Shawna from Behind the Writer for proofreading.

Hang Le for the cover and branding for the entire series.

Wander Aguiar Photography for the great picture of our Sierra and Prince Adrian.

Bloggers who consistently carve out time to read, review and/or promote us.

Piper Rayne Unicorns who shout from the rooftops about our new releases and love our characters like we do.

Readers who took a chance on our book with so many choices out there.

Up next? Our favorite baker, Rian and the tatted-up man she drools over, Dylan. Oh yeah and a sidekick roommate named Jax. There's a lot you don't know about these three. Like is Dylan really that blind to Rian's feelings? Does he have feelings of his own for her? All things that make us go hmm…. ;)

XO,
Piper & Rayne

Sexy Beast

Hollywood Hearts

Mister Mom

Animal Attraction

Domestic Bliss

Bedroom Games

Cold as Ice

On Thin Ice

Break the Ice

Box Set

Charity Case

Manic Monday

Afternoon Delight

Happy Hour

Blue Collar Brothers

Flirting with Fire

Crushing on the Cop

Engaged to the EMT

White Collar Brothers

Sexy Filthy Boss

Dirty Flirty Enemy

Wild Steamy Hook-up